Terminal to Terminus

Vivvy Anne Le Fey

ISBN:
ISBN-13: 978-1493778775

ISBN-10:1493778773

In February 2012 I was diagnosed with stage 4 stomach cancer and given only a few months to live.
My life changed pretty rapidly, and I was forced to retire on ill health from a job I loved where I had worked as a despatcher for the first emergency service for 20 years.
I was offered chemotherapy treatment as palliative care, which we all hoped would prolong my life and it did.
After 21 weeks of treatment I decided I wasn't going to sit around and wait for 'it' to happen and decided to take a holiday and travel to Europe. Unable to fly, I opted for a Leger coach holiday travelling to Italy for 16 days.
Despite a setback in October 2013 when I required further treatment, my holidays with Leger have been and still are ongoing. As well as travelling to various locations in England, Scotland, Wales and Ireland under my own steam, I have been fortunate to travel to numerous countries throughout Europe.
This book contains details of my exploits whilst on holiday both at home and abroad.
Originally this started out as a daily text message to a friend, later escalating to my status updates on Facebook . I understand these postings became very popular with my friends who looked forward to reading my account of my outrageous behaviour and hilarious, mischievous adventures.
Some of the words I have used don't exist and the grammar in places may be poor. This is intentional and anyone questioning this would be told 'it is my authentic voice. So butt out!'

DEDICATION

Remembering with great fondness Robin Hillier and Diane Abbot-Obrien - RIP dear friends

This book is dedicated to all of my friends and family.

"Wherever you go, go with all your heart." - Confucius

Mary

God we go back a long way, don't we?

It makes me feel old when I think back to those days at New Bridewell. I have so many fond memories of brilliant nights out, where T3 entertained the troops that were on night shift after a night out at McCluskys. Singing up to the third floor windows and doing our Spice Girls dance.

I'm surprised we didn't all turn into raving alcoholics. Lol. You will be glad to know I am still perfecting and honing my drinking skills to this day.

I just want to say how grateful I am for all the support you have given me over the months.

You have been a lovely friend and I am sure it's because I have people like you in my life that I have stayed so well for so long.

I so enjoyed meeting up with you and am looking forward to the next time.

This book is a diary of my travels and consists mainly of all of the funny stories relating to the people that I have met while on my 'coachcations' and 'carcations'.

Basically it's what I placed on FB and what a lot of people suggested I make into a book. Well I did it, and this book is specifically dedicated to you. I hope you enjoy reading it. xx

1

ITALY – IN SEARCH OF GEORGE!

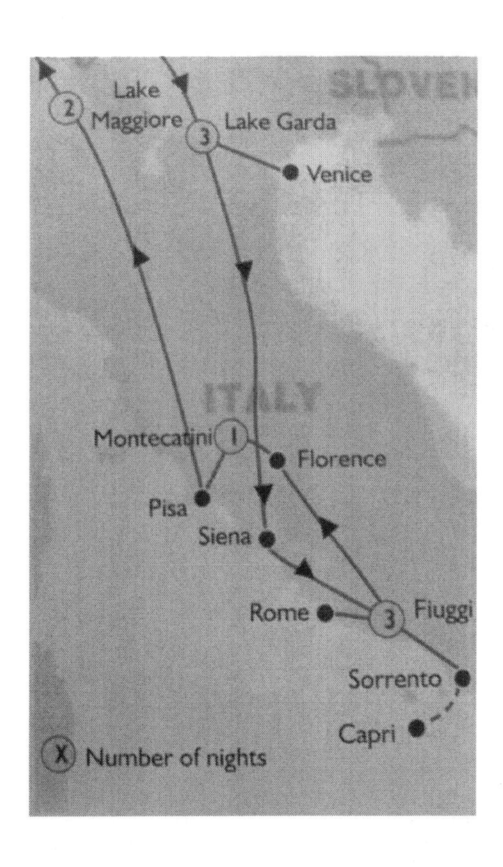

17/09/12 How long am I going for?

Off in search of George.
At Dover, with a load of bed hair pensioners. I am the youngest here.
Get me to a bottle of gin. George where are you?
En route to Reims.
06:30 start 2moro off to Lake Garda for 3 day stay, loads of trips planned.

18/09/12 Strasbourg for lunch.
Heading off to Switzerland.
Should be at Lake Garda in 30 mins.

19/09/12 Breakfast at Lake Garda early morning.

Sirmione for lunch.

Lunch for one. Mission accomplished and lost my entourage. Lol...

Next book title 'In search of George but I found Shrek's Dad'. Lol..
In Limone with my entourage who have asked if they could join me again. Lol.

20/09/12 Well it was inevitable I suppose. Three days into the trip and I'm in the shite. For the record:
I did not force anyone to overdo the local delicacy Limoncella, can't help it if the pensioners are unable to hold their drink. I'm up at 0545 and ready to head off to Venice. Am I late for brekky? No. I rest my case m'lud. Ram it!

Venice.

Now working as an escort, photographer and tour guide to the elderly and bewildered. I have gone from 6 to a group of 18. Ruining any chance of pulling anything but a muscle. Lol.

21/09/12 Sienna in the sun.

22/09/12 Off to Sorrento and Capri with the infirm and bewildered. My name today is Duchess which is better than yesterday's Pepe le Pew; who the frick is he?

Mount Vesuvius — at Sienna.

Bay of Naples.

My mate Jim.

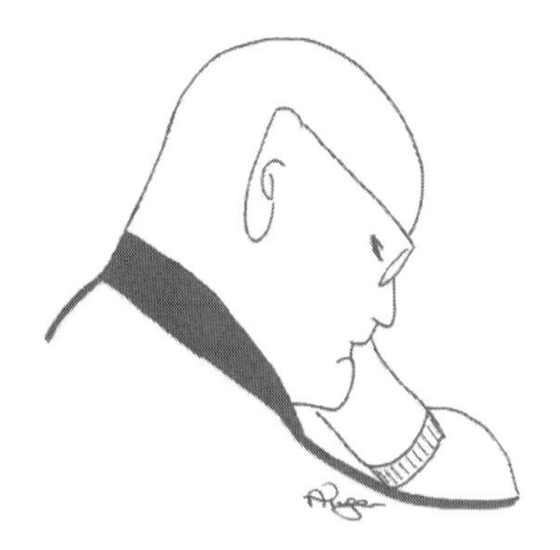

Someone effing get me away from Jim. He is driving me to drink. Moans about his heart and diabetes but carries a prop. A walking stick which affords him special privileges. Un effing believable. I am now off of pensioner patrol. The alternative euthanasia or a pillow. Lol.

23/09/12 Rome today.

Obviously a follower of fashion.

I cried. What an emotional place.

And cried again.

Finally the duffers have realised that the elderly and infirm cannot do all of these trips. I have recruited 3 extra carers having been left to deal with a woman who fell on the moving pavement escalator. Press the button did not register with the bewildered... female saved and all well. Jim continues to cause problems but the lads have given him a good talking to. Florence tomorrow. Undergoing a drinking session tonight having been led astray by trainees. Heavily into Limoncella and fast becoming hardened drinkers. Lol.

Just been told off for laughing too.

I am in the twilight zone; the pensioners are falling faster than skittles. The bar has run out of Limoncella and it's my fault. How so?

24/09/12 Florence.

At Monticatini. Heard today that Jim, the 78 year old pain in the butt, has taken a shine to me. In his dreams. Lmfao.

25/09/12 Off to Pisa.

Free from Jim, he chose McDonald's over the tower!

Hell bent! in Florence, Toscana, Italy.

26/9/12 Everyone dropping like flies. 2 in hospital. 6 in bed, not together! 2 have flown home. Despite his moaning Jim still going strong. Hoping to lose him on Lake Maggiore.

Off to Stresa and a boat cruise. Jim in tow. Stressed in Stresa then.

27/09/12 Managed to lose Jim yesterday, who promptly told everyone I abandoned him. They thought it hysterical. I have never met someone so insecure and attention seeking. His latest is pretending we are a couple "darling could you come over here please we need to talk". HELLO. So as you can imagine the only word for it was the one beginning with F and ending with Off. Heading to Paris now.

Jim — in Pisa, Toscana, Italy.

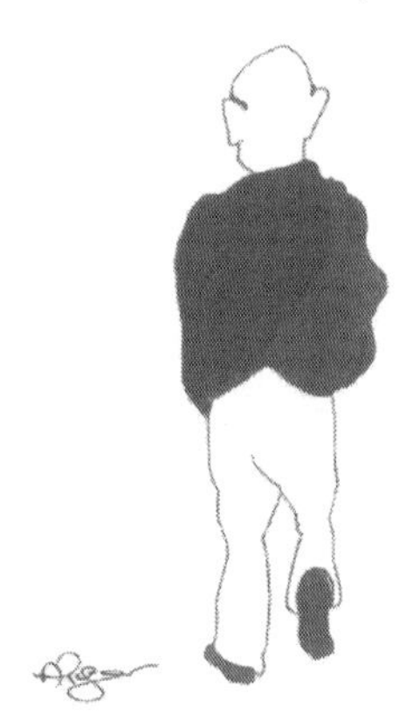

The Swiss Alps.

Swiss Alps - he's awake and angry cos I left him on the coach. Lmfao.

28/09/12 The sound of Jim's stick and the sight of him removing half eaten cheese from his lower palette will haunt me forever. Yukhowvile Lol.

04/10/12 For the info of the concerned few; and to ensure clarity of info being spread around, I returned from Italy without George and very unwell. Currently I am in bed and for those of my friends who are speculating about a second wedding on the horizon; I am alone and at a different end of the country, far away from Jim. I have no voice and a very bad chest infection. Nothing to worry about, the whole coach of peeps caught it. I am taking antibiotics and each day I feel that much better. I am far too unwell, Adabank, to be thinking about spreading chocolate; even though I have to say my current temperature would make it that much more pliable. I have my iPad for company and require no visitors thank-you. I believe it was my sister who called me a grumpy cow and that would be a good descriptive, so be warned. Give me a few days and I am sure normal service will resume. After all I have to get fit for my second meet with the big man. Handwritten invite no less. Adabank, if you have time on your hands I suggest you start writing a book!

2

ST IVES

18/11/12 Peace and quiet, the smell of the sea, stunning scenery. Pasties, ice cream, cream teas, crabs. Where am I going? Soooo excited.

19/11/12 The eagle has landed. Uneventful journey, apart from one duffer accelerating every time I tried to overtake him. Came unstuck on the hill just prior to Greatwoodwidger. How was he to know I am the master of the double de-clutch. Tosser.

I just had to smell that smell — at St Ives Beach.

Think this is the sea wall where we used to go crabbing.

Food and a beer — with Vivvy Anne Le Fey at Chy An Albany Hotel.

20/11/12 Another beer after a lovely day. Just resting a while before going to dinner. — with Sarah Russell and Joanne Ridgway at The Sloop Inn.

A perfect day with my surrogate daughters ends with a bud in the bar. Picture the scene. I am in the poshest restaurant in town. Go to the loo. Interrupt a couple shagging... yes, I do not lie. Could only happen to Viv.

21/11/12 Make a wish!
Make two wishes double rainbow!

Look at the rainbow! — with Joanne Ridgway and Sarah Russell at St Ives.

Found the spot the photo was taken in.

Dennis this is for you. Flooding where we are!

What an eventful day. Surfer decides to get naked while stood right next to me. Didn't know which way to turn. Sky rat robs me of my £3:60p ice cream. Injures my nose and sends my specs tumbling to the floor. Where are the police when u need 'em?

The culprit.

22/11/12 Off to the Eden project, on the train sat next to elderly gent who has Tourettes. Keeps saying chocolate, and making monkey and train noises. I'm a celebrity get me outta here. Lol.

Now wrapped up in some emergency on the St Austell line. Train forced to stop! Standby for update... Items on the track due to extreme weather conditions.

Terry Tourettes, the tap dancing train traveller, is keeping the rest of us amused. I may be pulling the emergency cord soon. Why is it I always end up sat next to a person with issues? When I retired I didn't realise I'd be stepping into a world of bemused and bewildered. Lol.

At the Eden Project.

The locals are impressed I know about the ship wreck the Tory Canyon. I was here when it sank! Having a beer with the sailors. God they can drink!!! — at The Lifeboat Inn.

23/11/12 This is where I want to get married — at Minack Theatre.

3

AUSTRIA AND RHINELAND

22/12/12 On my coach, window seat. Grotto behind me. No companion until Folkestone. Stand by update. The end of my world could be nearer than I think. — at Gordano Services M5 Northbound.

Near Seal via Mobile. Christ, the pensioners are getting pissed and we ain't even got to Folkestone yet. Packed lunches and hip flasks. Oh and bad taste jumpers are the order of the day. Only spare seat on the coach is next to me. There is an air of expectancy and tension, will it be another Jim type bloke that dabbles with her or perhaps Charles Bridge?

That's right show off when ordering wine, then let yourself down by ordering fish 'n' chips. Peasants. It was cheap plonk you tit. Lol.

Met some great people. Having a whale of a time already. Love people watching. More domestics than BR on a Friday nite. Just sit back and watch the show. Lol.

At Holiday Inn Brussels Airport – SKOJ.
23/12/12 – 0515am in real money. Nice boutique style overnight stay. No hangover. No strange men found under the duvet. Off to Austria after brekky. 1 metre of snow awaits.
Grünthal, Bayern, Germany Air conditioning on the coach has packed up. It is soo hot, nearly passed out. Someone has just crapped in the non crappy toilet. Only number ones allowed. Guess who was seen walking away and got taken to one side and reminded of the rules. The air was already blue from the stench the male passenger left. It was worserer by the time I'd finished with 'em.

Christ knows how Julie Andrews managed. Having negotiated Everest we are safely in our hotel. The proprietors are called Mumma and Poppa, wear traditional dress and do not speak English or Bristolian. I am on a floor level with the 'chiming every 15 minutes' church bells. But, and there is one... wait for it... I got snow, loads of it. — at Wsv-Brandenberg.

And they allow smoking... not that I'm a smoker. Beam me up Lol.

24/12/12 Snow from my window at 0730 — at Wsv-Brandenberg.

Crying in Strazbourg — at Unipark Nonntal.

Entertainment tonight is Roger in his maroon suit and Pete the coach driver. BMUS...

By the way I'm in Salzburg not Strazbourg; knew it had a z in it. Too much Stella. Lol. BMUS.

Near Leopoldskron, Salzburg, Austria via Mobile. Going on a sleigh ride. If the big man forgets anyone it's because he's with me. ;))) I'm soo excited and I just can't hide it. La la la.

Thought herran meant her toilets. Wrong! Sorry Doc, did not observe the etiquette and looked. Not worth hanging around for!!

I know you are all gonna be shocked but just to say I got married in a small Austrian Church at quarter to midnight. Ideally I would have loved you all to be with me but logistics and all that. My man is wonderful and everything he should be. Thx Hugh Jardon for making me so very happy. I love you.

I do and I did — at Wsv-Brandenberg.

25/12/12 Sleigh ride with Mr J.

Me and Mr J - we got a thang goin' on boo boo ba boo. xx

Fantastic wedding prezzy, off to Dubai.

Don't know why you all think I'm joking.

26/12/12 Skiing or Après Ski? — at HANS the BUTCHER.

Risking life and limb — at Binderholz Bausysteme GmbH.

Sightseeing — at Praha.

28/12/12 Day spent with two Texans and the nuttiest Aussie with Tourette's. Hilarious day. And yes guys its bloody cold.

Off to a monastery to sample beer. Rather sample the monk but hey ho!

Didn't take long; back to looking after the elderly, infirm and bewildered. Quote of the day. RG to Caff: 'Hon what do you want me to do with my gloves?' Caff to RG: 'Whats wrong with your glove?'

Reply: 'Should have taken it off before I wiped my ass!'

Guess that's Texans for you. Nothing for it but to sample the ale — at Strahov Monastery, Prague.

29/12/12 Adagun.

Near Brevnov, Hlavni Mesto Praha, Czech Republic via Mobile. Before we all get bogged down with New Year festivities and also while I am still sober.

Rare occasion! I would like to say thx to all my family, friends and Caff's Champs for supporting me with love and kindness throughout the last ten months. I intend to keep on behaving badly and insist you all keep up the abuse and mental cruelty. Love you all and wish you a really happy, healthy 2013. Now that's said I'm going for a beer. Xx

30/12/12 Going Skiing.

Back safely and preparing to catch the Norovirus off the other coach party who were hospitalised. Hopefully the neat alcohol coursing through my veins will help kill off any noros. Skiing again tomorrow. I'm really good at it... BMUS.

Beer o'clock — at Ramada Hotel Brühl.

31/12/12 Out on the piste again today. Thought this skiing lark would be painful. Could be on a black run before I know it... BMUS.

Near Brühl, Nordrhein-Westfalen, Germany. The Rhine is so high the boats cannot fit under the bridges. Great planning. Lol.. Another beer then me finx.

Near Brühl, Nordrhein-Westfalen, Germany via Mobile.

I'm not gonna make any New Year resolutions. Just continue to be me. Like it or lump it. Have fun guys and gals, stay safe.

4

EASTERN EUROPE

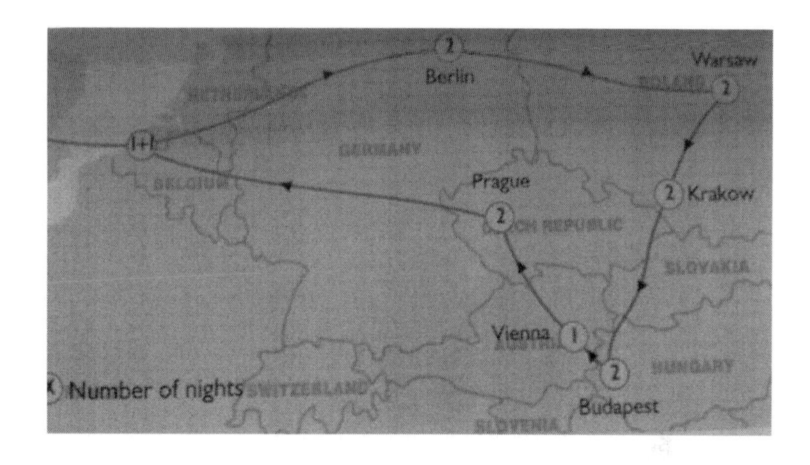

20/04/13 For the duration of this trip and for this trip alone I will be known as Thirza. A name suited to the people I am travelling with will make me feel less out of place. That distinct smell of lily of the valley hit my nasal receptors as I alighted the coach followed by a more overpowering smell. A mixture of old spice and prostrate. The person I am to be paired with has yet to be decided by the gods. I am ever hopeful. A nice bit of military muscle wouldn't be too much to ask and would complement the abundance of Chelsea pensioners and land girls that make up the 32. Hopefully Folkestone will bring a sparkle to my eye. Stand by. I do have to perform a work of art on my face though. Didn't sleep at all last night and have bags under my eyes heavier than my luggage which apparently is overweight x 2. Speak to my ass that has had the same problem for years. Ear plugs in, pointless trying to funk up a coach full of hip replacementees.

Dover - Have been seated next to lone male. An Andy Williams with anorexia lookalike. The seat in front was empty and was where I fully intended, with permission, to move. That was up until Mr Purple Jumper, with wool balls due to bad laundering and not dressed to pull, moved in. First impressions; guy with hair by Jonathan, thinks he is pullable. In his dreams me finx, who will soon be told to shut the eff up, if he don't shut the eff up. What a tosser, walks with his jacket slung over his shoulder with a John Travolta swagger. Piccies to follow over next few days. BMUS.

Ok. So the Andy Williams lookalike is named Roy. Very pleasant. Purple jumper got moved back next to wifey who he said had a large ass and was his reason for moving. I'm now in the seat I wanted on my own. Chatting through the crack in the chair to Roy. Lol...

21/04/13 Well after the driver received a medal DSM VD and bar for having water on board and the merits of buying bottled water from Aldi were drained dry, I left the pensioners to discuss medication and went to bed. This morning at breakfast it was watching to see who could outdo the other with the amount of medication taken. The winner goes to Mrs 'I can't walk far unless there is a food incentive'. Shut the door. Lol.

Kempen, Nordrhein-Westfalen, Germany via Mobile. Watching The Dam Busters.

Mohnesee Dam — at Moehnesee.

East meets West — at Gedenkstätte Marienborn.

21/04/13 Fichtenwalde, Brandenburg, Germany via Mobile. I have decided that Mr Purple Jumper, which I hasten to add he is still wearing, was a former postman or railway worker. He walks with one shoulder lower than the other kinda Quasimodo'ish. We also have Mr Major Combover and Mrs Over Annunciates. Roy, my chaperone, is very pleasant. A cross between Andy Williams and whatshisname who danced with Ginger Rogers. Got most of them drunk at lunch time on peach schnapps and raspberry beer. Lightweights. Heading for Berlin watching German war films. The coach driver thinks that two of the guys are from bomber command I think. Doesn't realise they were trade unionists who bought people over in the '70s from England. I shall enlighten him soon. We think it's funny so letting him carry on. BMUS.

Berlin-Lichtenberg, Berlin, Germany via Mobile. Roy, bless him, thinks he has a harem. Now, I am under no illusions whatsoever and know I am a pretty big bird. But Roy, there is only one of me so that does not constitute a harem. I know I can multi-task and I'm good and hey I can be anything he wants me to be. But a harem? That's pushing it. I'd be worn to a frazzle by Tuesday. Lol. BMUS. Note to hotel management: get rid of full length mirror. I thought there was someone else in the room! I scared myself. New Year's resolution. Turn the lights off...

Remaining in the bar with Vivvy Anne Le Fey.

22/04/13 Harem of 1 survived the night and surprisingly does not have a hangover. Roy attended room 309 at 0745 hours asking if I had a spare teabag.
Fortunately, as if expecting this unannounced visit, I had alighted from my bed early in search of something long, cold and wet. My skin looking fresh and healthy from the cold shower, make up and chignon in place, I answered the door with an air of confidence and a manner in which only Viv could get away with. Request of a builder's brew fulfilled, Viv did what any self respecting single woman would do and ate breakfast with another man. The squadron leader.

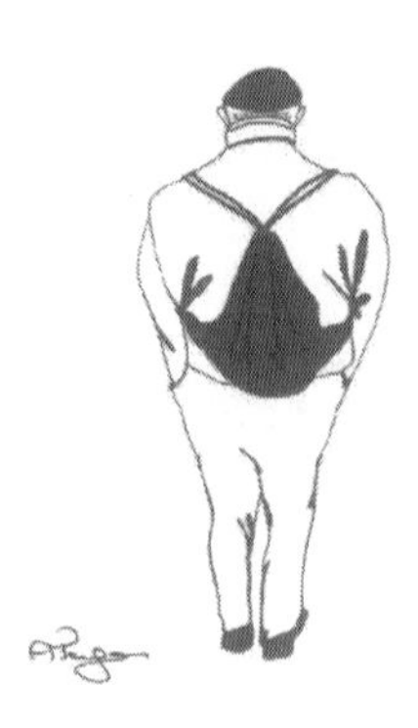

23/04/13 Well, I am most put out. Upon my return to the coach; following a day of sightseeing, avoiding being arrested by the Stazi and scaling walls, I was insulted by the squadron leader. He said, and I quote, "you look knackered!"
Now how the hell he could tell that, when my eyes were concealed behind my CK's I will never know. Earlier that very same day I had performed a work of art in the bathroom of room 309. How very dare he. Giving perhaps more time to his remark than I should do; I concluded that perhaps he was referring to my strange walk, which probably if I am honest resembled that of a nag en route to the knackers yard. Upon reaching the hotel, whilst travelling in elevator one to the third floor, all became clear. I had that unbrushed hair look, the 'get out of bed and don't look at the back' kinda hair which was slicked to my scalp. The perspiration from the heat of the day likely cause. Well Squadron Leader, yesterday I might well have looked as though I ought to be put out to pasture but I certainly will not be putting out. For someone with very little hair I thought him most rude. Flying past me finx.
24/04/13 Ochota, Warszawa, Poland via Mobile.

Sun shining in Warsaw today. Lovely hotel, albeit on the main drag. Thought I had been bitten all up my legs only to discover the reason for the itch is... new hair trying to break through following first waxing of the year. It's tough being single sometimes and bloody hard work. After all, I can't have me pension being the main attraction can I? One thing's for sure, my normally lovely turn of ankle looks as though it's on the turn. Must try and perfect my tired look at the end of day and practice a sleek swag. And I did say swag. Standby for events of day later.

Paul Chandler, book that holiday today. Stop ringing me - I'm busy in the bar.

25/04/13 Well, what a display of bad manners. 2 elderly passengers kicked off at dinner last night. All over Mr Major Combover's wife being allowed fruit salad instead of the Madeira style cake with lemony coulis. Highly entertaining; he sat there, red faced, arms crossed and it necessitated me putting a do not resuscitate sticker on his back. Squadron Leader is sitting with Mrs Over Annunciates who has become all skippity and regressed 75 years into a giggly girl. The cataracts replaced with sparkles. Not pleasant though, when she smiles her top set of falsies drop. Mrs Wrinkled Décolletage has been spoken to and has been asked to stop referring to people using their impediments. "The man with the twitch, the man with the huge stomach". Lol..

Off to pay my respects at Auschwitch.

Szczesliwice, Warszawa, Poland, Warsaw.

Auschwitz no words — at Auschwitz Memorial / Muzeum Auschwitz.

26/04/13

Hard day yesterday. Had a run in with Squadron Leader because he didn't remove his hat whilst in the gas chambers or crematorium at Auschwitz. For ex forces I was horrified and he got a right dressing down and boy did I go full throttle. Disrespectful pompous ass. Arrived at hotel which is fabulous. Played bird songs going up in the lift, which got on your nerves after going up and down for half an hour, no one had the sense to read how to operate the bloody thing. You needed to use your room key to get out. Duhh. Made it through the night without any visits through connecting door which was initially a tad unnerving. I like to see whose coming! The shower/wet room continued with the bird theme which again was a bit weird, cross between a scene from the birds and psycho. The bird noises are supposed to make you feel calm. Don't know about you but I don't particularly want a repetitive dawn chorus while trying to dump thank you very much. Roy fell over and has an injured eye, chin and hand. Mr PJ has pissed off just about everyone on the coach off. Mrs Over Enunciates has become my drinking buddy and is hysterical. Mr Do Not Resuscitate is still sulking and Mr Combover wants to join my gang, having witnessed me put the Squadron Leader in his place rendering him speechless. Jury is still out, may have to get him booked in with hair by Jonathan. Mrs Droopy Décolletage is still out of favour and is creeping, having been given the nod that we are pissed off with her. Coach drivers are fab and love us back seaters. Standby for shenanigans in the Salt Mines. — at Hotel Galaxy, Kraków, Poland.

Krakow my most favourite so far. Ellie Joslin you would love it. — at Cracow, Kraków.

People watching — at Rynek Główny.

Have now left Poland and can breathe a sigh of relief that I didn't end up as a political prisoner. Well, actually a politically incorrect prisoner. Now the fear of my phone being bugged has passed I can tell you the story. We get dropped in the square in Warsaw on Weds. Some important dignitary is visiting a pizza restaurant. This is true; hard to believe I know, but yes, a pizza place. He has an entourage of about 20 police cars, plus 90 thousand grey suits with ear pieces and a van full of masked hooded men wearing sunglasses and holding sub machine guns. Once the dignitary is inside the building the cars, vans, bikes and helicopter move away. We go on walkabouts past the hooded SAS wannabes who are being fed ice cream and pizza through a small opening in the van by the grey suits who were also stuffing their faces. I make a remark that I thought it disgusting and stated in wouldn't happen in the UK, well not on my watch it wouldn't. This was met with a retort from a man nearby "madam it's all under control."! To which I replied "yeah I can see, they've got a great fast track pizza delivery service going on. Hold on Mr Terrorist could you wait a while so I can finish me Margarita?" The ice cream dripping down his chin should have been the giveaway.

I got pulled to one side and instructed to leave the square. Needless to say I will be putting pen to paper upon my return.

Krakow was fab. The visit to the Salt Mines gave new meaning to the expression " Going Down!". After being squashed in a tin can with 8 other peeps, bearing in mind I'm claustrophobic, was not pleasant. 60 metres down a sprightly 70 plus year old expected us to descend a further 100 metres on foot. Jeez I never thought I'd get to the end of the tour. If I ain't got a waist and arse like Marilyn Monroe by the end of this trip I want me money back. In the air lock I tried to push the door open early to see if Mr Combover's hair moved, it didn't. The squadron leader had a run in with the tour guide and told her to learn some manners. Pot calling... Anyway I will be writing to bomber command about his behaviour in Auschwitz without a shadow of doubt. Even if he does have a nice ass. Have had one domestic take place. Bit of a controller who needs to be sorted. He treats his wife like shite. Squadron Leader is deffo making his move. I'm just being my cool calm self and ignoring all advances. He'd never have won a war that's for sure. Too subtle for my liking. Standby for further goings on. If no update alert the embassy.

27/04/13 Kazimierz, Krakow, Poland. Off to Slovakia.

Dunakeszi Pest - Well would you believe it? Mrs Over Annunciates has a toy-boy with her called Dave. He has just moved to Lake Windermere to be near her. Met on a cruise they did. Dave has been banned from singing and I have told him he can only conduct. Reckons he taught Gary Barlow's mum. Hmmmm. Like, what?
The squadron leader has asked me if it is usual for me to leave carnage wherever I go. I told him to fly me and find out. I had been drinking

heavily. Raspberry vodka, cherry vodka, chocolate vodka, vodka vodka, at least I've had two of me five a day. I can report back honestly to Dr Hilman that I am meeting all dietary requirements.

I think I'm being bugged as unable to get voicemail since the Warsaw Pizzagate incident, so may have to be a bit more cryptic.

Stayed up chatting to ScarFace aka Roy until 2300, way past his bed time. Told me he wouldn't get married again. Didn't know I had asked him. Vodka is gonna be my downfall.

New character has come into the mix. Mr Causer of Major Incidents. Small guy with the laugh of a hyena and looks like a cross between the goblin in the Harry Potter films and the naked bulgy eyed thing in Lord of the Rings, the one that keeps saying "my precious". He was loudly relaying a story of another incident that occurred in the ghetto area of Warsaw. Fortunately I was there at the time and able to correct him. Luckily the tables close by were happy with my explanation of the real event that took place and he wasn't arrested for some racial offence. Needless to say he was dragged off to bed by his wife at a great rate of knots.

Mr Purple Jumper has lost his corduroy jacket. He turned the coach inside out trying to find the bloody thing.

Mr Do Not Resuscitate is still sulking and mentions fruitsaladgate at every opportunity.

Mrs Wrinkly Décolletage is wearing more revealing tops and bends over displaying her wares to the Squadron Leader most days. I can't tell what his eyes reveal as he wears sunglasses.

Weather has been so hot I had to buy sandals. Prior to leaving YUK I checked the long term weather forecast and my Manolo Blahniks were suitable foot attire. How wrong was I and the forecast? My sandals are very Romanesque and complement my turn of ankle. Thank God for black nail varnish which covers up my gangrene toenails.

Have saved two elderly fallers today. Mrs Over Annunciates fell down the steps that lead to the side door and loo, she fell backwards and is badly damaged. Vera Duckworth fell down the restaurant steps and has injured knees. It took two chunks of hunk, leather clad, bikers to assist me helping her back to her feet. Something about the smell of leather.

Just driving through the Carpathian Basin awaiting first sight of the Danube.

Beer o'clock — with Vivvy Anne Le Fey at Novotel Budapest Congress.

Pest, Budapest, Hungary. In search of Dracula...

28/04/13 I am sure the Squadron Leader thinks he is a Bruce Willis lookalike. I know they filmed Die Hard 69 here but please, just because he's wearing a pair of trendy Rayburn sunglasses doesn't mean he can strut around shouting out Yippee-Ki-Yay to all and sundry. Anyway, as I remember, it was yippee kayay mother f--ker.

Last night we went in search of Dracula. Didn't have to look far, he's sat two seats in front of me. Every time the coach pulls up quickly his teeth get stuck in the headrest in front of him.

Went to an organ recital and listened to world famous Laslo Ohjackapip playing and singing. Mr Domestic Abuser became an instant aficionado of organ music and spent the whole recital on his knees in prayer, causing me to have an hysterical outburst where I couldn't stop laughing to the point where I snorted loudly and had to leave the auditorium. Bit of déjà vu going on as a similar incident occurred just before Christmas in Chichester where I embarrassed my niece and allegedly upset the rich!

I am being allowed to stay on the Buda side of town despite being called a pest. However for a woman with as many impediments as I have the Pest side would be better as it's flatter. Flatter for the fatter.

Had major majors with Mrs Wrinkly Décolletage. I have never encountered such a rude and vile mouthed woman in my life. I suggested she may like to consider how someone would describe her to another coach user, and that she may want to take another look in the mirror where she would discover that her ass wasn't as small as she thought it was. Said confrontation took place on an ascending lift with numerous Japanese tourists who did what they do best and took pictures. Yours truly sorted the vertically challenged, spiky haired, TK Maxx shopper, who needs to dress more in keeping with her age, with several brilliant sharp of tongue one liners.

Mrs Over Annunciates aka Janet has invited me to use her log cabin on Lake Windermere at any time FOC. 2 beds and a bar, all I have to do is just ring her and she will arrange for me to be collected. Apparently she thinks I'm wonderful for dragging her from the loo pit when she fell yesterday.

I understand back home a campaign has been started to free the Worle one. Should all go Q on the Eastern front please call the embassy soonest and send in SWAT. Ensure they have been fed copious amounts of pizza and ice cream first before deploying.

28/04/13 The Japanese tourists bowed to me this morning when I left the hotel. I really think I'm being followed, loads of grey suited men in the hotel lobby this morning watching my every move. No pizza or ice cream evident though. Could have it concealed in lunch boxes, may even have a mini fridge in their black Marias which are parked just below my balcony. Maybe a rehearsal going on for a milk tray ad I suppose. We'll see later.

Today the way the Squadron Leader is acting it's obvious he thinks he's Liam Neeson playing out a scene from Taken. Jumping around the boat like a crack monkey from deck to deck. He doesn't quite cut it. Picture the scene...

"I don't know you. I don't know what you want. If you are looking for a wife I can tell you, I don't have one. But what I do have, are a very particular set of skills. Skills I've acquired over a very long career. Skills that make me a nightmare for people like you. If you let my great granddaughter go now, that'll be the end of it. I'll not look for you. I'll not pursue you. But If you don't, I'll look for you. I'll find you and I'll bore you to death". Or...

"I have a wish to become a CBeebies operative. I was wondering if you have any tips".

"Yeah, I do. Pick another career".

As far as I' m concerned there's enuff agents around here. Just thought I saw a sub telescope to the side of our boat. I am sure I am under surveillance.

What's more worrying is that Mrs Munchenhausens daughter reckons there's a shortage of pizza places here. Now that is a worry.

Lovely lunch on the Danube but didn't think it very blue. Sat opposite the Squadron Leader who hummed a Strauss waltz all through lunch. Is that romantic?

Bit fed up with this Hungarian Goulash. I know it might be a good idea to get my stomach acclimatised to this type of food in the event I am captured and thrown into Mokotow prison but for goodness sake; breakfast, dinner and tea! If I'm honest I could do with less Gnocchi and a bit more Nookey too.

29/04/13 Töltéstava, Gyor-Moson-Sopron, Hungary.
Well, agent LardAzz has evaded capture for another night and is free to waltz through the streets of Vienna.

I'm definitely being followed and have become aware of more grey suits arriving daily. They have been trying to blend in by pretending they are attending business meetings that are held at the hotel. Well I'm on to them, ain't much that gets past me I can tell you.
I was asked today if I had tried sauerkraut. I haven't. I may have sampled sour trout but I'm happy to report she has been quiet since yesterday's run in.
It appears I'm travelling with a right load of nutters.
The driver of the tour coach advertised his wife for sale on eBay see attached link. http://news.bbc.co.uk/2/hi/uk_news/wales/3109533.stm
Also Munchausen's daughter practices Domancic Bio Energy Therapy, see: http://www.therapybioenergy.com/zdenko_domancic.
If you ask me Demonic would describe it better. It wouldn't have been so bad if she had treated her patients in the privacy of a quiet room instead of the hotel bar. The patrons must have thought we belonged to some weird religious sect. Lots of arm waving, prodding and closing down going on. Poor old Roy was one of the guinea pigs, who then demonstrated how well the therapy had worked by dancing like a

Cossack all over the hotel. What worried me more was that baby munch had built up quite a sweat, had a smile on her face, rosy cheeks and was very out of breath. Enough so that I offered her the use of my puffer. Obviously another name for Tantric sex me finx.

Over the next few days you may notice my updates will have an injection of all things cultured. This will likely be Vienna rubbing off on me. By the way, in case you're wondering, I'm not referring to a bit of Frotage or dry humping.

It would appear the Squadron Leader thinks he's bloody Iron Man today and is dressed all in red. Not at all fetching. He's actually more important than I thought, overheard him talking to Mrs Over Annunciates and he's a judge. Can't say I have ever seen him on the X Factor or Judge Judy.

The elderly and infirm are all going down with various ailments and I'm currently travelling with a coach load of whiners. I'm sure dinner tonight will be a battle to see who is worserer than the other. May have to order a batch of pillows to put them out of their misery or divert the coach to Hotel Dignitas.

The Worle One remains free. BMUS.

Near Heiligenstadt, Wien, Austria via Mobile. Major incident in Shell garage. Mrs 'I can't walk without a food incentive' fell over on the garage forecourt. She was carted off to hospital with injured shoulder and is flying home today by plane. Otherwise she'd be flying round in circles.... Bhum. Bhum.

The coach driver thought I was the best man for the job and decided it would be me that led the throng of pensioners to the cathedral while he sorted out broken shoulder and damaged forecourt paperwork. Like I know the place. Hello. Is my name Moses? Anyway I found a nice bar and pointed them in the right direction.

Lunch was lobster which was positively orgasmic. Have to get my kicks somewhere. Eating nice food is the only oral sex I'm gonna get on this trip.

Went to see the Weiner Royal Orchestra for a concert of music by Mozart and Strauss.

I thought Weiner was a rude word, but obviously not as rude as I thought it was if they've used it to name a world famous orchestra.
Didn't particularly care for Vienna, could have been anywhere really. Smog city with numerous oil refineries. Wasn't able to tell if I was being followed as too many people around and you couldn't see your hand in front of your face.
Mrs Over Annunciates' toy boy David is humming every hit Mozart ever had and it's doing our heads in. Especially when he does a mix up of Magic Flute and Marriage of Figaro. I'm sure he thinks he's DJ Tiesto. God help us if he starts on Strauss.
After visiting the house of Hundertwasser the driver asked if everyone was back on the coach; everyone shouted out yes except for Mr Purple Jumper aka Speedo Pete, who got left behind. The lasting image I will hold is him jumping up and down waving his arms as the coach disappeared over the bridge. I informed Mrs PJ that her husband had been left behind to which she replied "leave him, since he retired he's changed, I can't stand the bastard". So I left him and said nowt. Someone raised the alarm as we got half way to the hotel. Guess who got the blame when Mr PJ told the driver I had waved back at him.
I have been asked to go global 'blog fashion' with my updates. I'm far too busy so have appointed my nephew George to get on with it. Hopefully he will send me the link and give it a suitable title. Apparently we are going global and viral. I think the last virus to achieve that without any effort was a guy called Asian Flu.
Talking of Mr Purple Jumper he owes me a bottle of perfume after dumping in a no dump zone. Number ones only zone. Yukhowvile.
The Worle one is still at large much to the disgust of Mrs Wrinkly Décolletage who hates anyone over a size 12.
Currently out alone with the Squadron Leader, stand by for update. On this occasion if you hear nothing do not alert the embassy. Any spelling mistakes blame it on Chardonnay.

30/04/13 Jetzelsdorf, Niederosterreich, Austria.
What a night. Because the coach had to return to collect Mr Purple Jumper aka Smelly Dumper we only had 90 mins to prepare for the

opera. As I said in my previous post, somehow this was all my fault. Tell me why?
The rooms are the worst by far. I have practically had to rewire mine and have extension leads running from plug to plug. There is no air conditioning and the oscillating fan is a trip hazard especially at 0300 after a few sparkling vinos!
Not having had hair on my recent previous travels I had never used the hair dryers provided in the bathrooms. Now, electric in bathrooms doesn't quite smack of safety where I'm concerned. Balancing on one foot while the other is pushed against the wooden bathroom door in order to earth me, is no mean feat. Well not for a woman with neuropathy and numerous foot related impediments it ain't.
Mrs Over Annunciates wanted me to take a look at her chest today. Apparently she has bites all over it. Now whether its love bites or midge bites I have yet to assess. Having managed to use a lack of time as my excuse I avoided seeing what the chest of an 80 year old looked like. Yukhowvile. What bothered me further was that I found myself wondering if people with false teeth could give a height of passion bite.
Still you never know what that little blue diamond shaped pill can do for the old 'uns. I was quite surprised having checked, I have in fact shifted quite a few from my stash.
I have become a bit of a drug dealer over the last few days. Having an impediment such as mine I have to come away with all manner of medication. Before you start to worry, I have retained sufficient for personal use and at this time I don't believe dealing in Strepsils, Lemsip and Zapain is an offence over here.
There has been no further sightings of the men in grey. However there are a heck of a lot of black cars following the coach and a helicopter overhead. I think the room they have given me is to prepare me for my imminent incarceration at Mokotow prison. Still if they try to arrest me while I'm being seduced by the Squadron Leader I have rigged the room with numerous booby traps. (Not those belonging to Mrs Over Annunciates I hasten to add.)
My nephew George has set up the promised website, he has called it Travels Of A Madwoman! He asked my permission to give his account

on what he thinks is truly happening. I have of course granted him that permission reminding him that there is still time to cut him from my will. Lol.. I can however think of worserer titles. "My life In Lycra." for instance or "A life Without Teeth". Talking about teeth provides me with an ideal segue...
The Squadron Leader. Lovely evening, nice eyes, voice, stocky, and good company. Well up until he smiled that was. He has a gap. A gap where a tooth should be. Now those of you who know me will be aware I have a thing about teeth. I couldn't stop thinking that if I got into a snog with him, would my tongue automatically go straight for the hole? It was like when you are sitting opposite someone with a zit. Read the script.
Roy had number 2 of 4 of the demonic healing sessions that he needs in the ante room at the hotel, better known as the breakfast room. It doesn't quite flow for me. If 4 people have got to help the therapist aka baby munch up off the floor so she can complete her closing down it's all a waste of time if you ask me. She needs to improvise a bit more I think. Do more stuff at ground level.
I asked her how much she charges per session. "Nothing. I get paid with the exchange of energy." Yeah rite love, get a bit more than that if you keep dropping to yer knees in front of men. Dream on. Her answer was actually a very good one, well-rehearsed but seemingly spontaneous. Momentarily it seemed to satisfy the head of the Newcastle branch of the DWP. He did ask her how she managed to afford so many holidays away. (More than me and she's only 48.) "Savings, I have always saved. Saved for a rainy day." With the amount of fucking rain we've had back home she must be near bankrupt. Me finx someone's benefits may be looked into.
The Worle one, soon to become two, (is that a Steps song?) is AWOL and behaving badly. Jury is still out on Squadron Leader. Watch this space.

http://travelsofamadwoman.wordpress.com/about/

01/05/13 Malá Strana, Hlavni Mesto Praha, Czech Republic. Proof I'm being followed.

Near Smíchov, Hlavni Mesto Praha, Czech Republic via Mobile.
Yo. Apologies for slight delay today in posting. I have had a disastrous morning. Hangover that no amount of Anadin or Neurofen will cure. I awoke thinking I had something wrong with my eye, which I was treating with Optrex, only to discover a prescription lens missing from me specs. My hair wouldn't go right and I look like a beatnik. Basically I'm wandering around Prague looking like Noel Gallagher. Attractive!
I had to force my walking boots on and my feet look as though I have elephantitis. Care in the community would not have been turned away today. As for jumping on and off trams and escalators it ought to be an Olympic sport.
I have been managing to avoid the police and have evaded capture. I know exactly what the 7th Earl of Lucan feels like now. I can confirm that I am being followed. I have photographic evidence, see Facebook pics. If I get captured here I'll likely be sent to some Russian Gulag. Up until recently I thought that was a dish local to the area.
I suppose the only consolation in all this is that I do know a few high ranking officers who could post my bail.
I mean I've only been in trouble once before. Vehicle related stuff. Mainly speeding. Like, as if you can in a Renault Clio Sport and non payment of fines. As I said to the judge it's no good sticking a note on your car saying parking fine when it obviously isn't? And the idiots still

use the same system.
Baby Munch ain't talking to me today. 'Fraid I got very drunk last night and held my own biodegradable healing surgery. Had loads of patients who apparently are now all free from pain. Magic! All I did was a bit of hand waving and wailing and the only closing down that took place was when we got kicked out of the bar at 0230. The only help I needed was from the Squadron Leader as he talked me down from the tabletop. I was reminiscing about the tap dancing barmaid at the George 'n' Railway who sang songs by Frankie Sinatree. Could have done with rehearsing a few of the songs beforehand. I don't seem able to reach the high notes like I used to and I could deffo do with a stepladder to reach the bar. Tap dancing in flip flops you just don't get the same effect. I perhaps pushed the envelope a bit too far when I took the piss out of a souvenir she had bought. Tell me who the f--k goes to Vienna and buys rubber ducks? Anyway Mrs Munchausen is trying to comfort baby munch by secreting her biscuits and every now and then gives me the evil eye. I've already been vetted by the devil so am I bothered?
Friends of Mrs Wrinkly Décolletage, that being Mr and Mrs First Class, have apparently had a word with her about her rudeness following my outburst on the Danube. They were interested to hear why I would offer to place my foot in her fat mouth. For the purpose of clarity, what in fact I did say was "I will wait for you to get to the bottom of the steps. I would hate to slip and end up with my foot in your fat mouth". Loads of people overheard what she had said and have told her off for being so rude.
The Squadron Leader managed to stay up last night and a we had a brilliant session. Good when someone lets their hair down. He's quite funny and is very knowledgeable without being condescending. He says I make him laugh.
Today he wanted to see the church where the Heydrich assassination took place. He blamed the fact we couldn't find it on my accent. When I had asked for directions we were sent in the wrong direction. Subtlety is not his strong point.
If I make it back to Blighty, (likely I might, as have survived a major gas explosion and a red army siege) I am going to stay down at a seaside

resort before returning back to base. Don't call the embassy. Standby for further updates.

Protest on Charles Bridge - To Free The Worle One.

02/05/13 near Kist, Bayern, Germany via Mobile. The tram trip was fab. Champagne sing along. Music provided by an accordion. The songs were all way before my time, however a lot of the songs I had learnt as a child at the Christmas parties which were spent singing around the piano at my Nan's house.

The Squadron leader was my chaperone and was in fine voice. He really thought he was Andrea Bocelli although I don't think I have ever heard Andrea's rendition of "Hitlers only got one ball."

Roy had his last domancic bio energy session. It transpires he is as sceptical as others are. Claims it hasn't worked. Regardless he has a permanent smile on his face.

Baby Munch is speaking to me again, having found her sense of humour at the bottom of the tin of biscuits she has just been force fed.

Mrs Over Annunciates has a new do. She even had her make-up done for the tram trip and also bought new shoes. Both her and her toy boy got into trouble for hogging the lounge area on the coach.

Mr PJ the secret dumper did it again. The back of the coach were hysterical. 8 minutes in Trap One wasn't gonna ever result in a number

1. Unless of course he has prostate problems. This is gonna cost the coach company a new bottle of perfume. The drivers reckon he behaves a bit thick thinking he'll get away with it. Wrong. We dropped him right in the shite. Would never have got away with it at Living the Dream!
I have managed to maintain a very high level of bad behaviour and have also been the last to bed the whole holiday.
Lots of police at the hotel last night. My disguise obviously effective as I remain free.
Off into Germany today. Party tonight.
Have discovered the Squadron Leader is not missing any teeth he was just deprived of a brace as a child. Sueable offence nowadays.
Getting closer to Blighty, will keep you posted.
Keep the Worle One Free!
Drunk stuffed and lucky.

03/05/13 Near Zaventem, Brabant, Belgium via Mobile. Unavailable for comment ufn. BMUS.

Oh yes, yes, yes. I got the heaviest suitcase ever award. They said I need to register it as a HGV. Proud moment.

04/05/13 Well what a tiring few days. I have laughed and laughed and laughed.
Once the cultural stuff had been dispensed with, it was time to party. The coach was involved in a pretty big crash and the party started 5 hours late. I am safe and well and suffered no injuries. Nobody bothered to change their clothes and get dressed up and by 2am even I had to

admit defeat. It had been a long day. You will be pleased to know that Viv managed to keep the British end up and lasted until dawn. I am pleased to report the Squadron Leader, although late for breakfast, had a spring in his step and a sparkle in his eye that I hadn't ever noticed before.

Oh yeah whoever the male caller is who persists in ringing me non-stop you ain't funny. So Dave Bitty or Dave Vitty whatever your name is; stop bothering me, I'm busy. Thanks for offering me a free place on another coach trip ha bloody ha. Like I'm gonna get paid to go on holiday for 30 days. Tosser. Anyway just think how many cases I would need to bring with me.

Hugh may have survived a 16 dayer in the hold, plus a gas explosion and a crash but what with nightly performances, 30 days travelling all around Europe is maybe a bit too much to expect of anyone.

I have included several photos of the wonderful people I am spending time with...

5

WEST BAY

30/05/13 Broadchurch.

Off to hear Steve Black and Alan West, apparently famous in Axbridge. I must remember to get a plastic pill box with the days of the week on each section. OMG. On a better note good night with fab entertainment.

31/05 /13 Doing a 'Meryl' on The Cobb.

Well Mr Palmer managed to wear me out, well my ears anyway. STFU Terry. Lol. proud of all the walking I did without my stick.

Rant over, just put a 16 year old waitress in her place. Scared the shite out of her. She will never question anyone who orders a table for one again. Lesson learned, take a man next time. Mr Bridgeman where are you?

01/06/13 Hive Beach to West Bay — with Vivvy Anne Le Fey at Hive Beach.

And well deserved — with Vivvy Anne Le Fey at The West Bay Pub.

My review of West Bay; don't look behind you! Incredibly beautiful, loads of death defying walks. The scenery makes up for the shabby resort and poor service at several of the restaurants. Youngsters that work there, know your manor - it's not all about Broadchurch. Needs a cash injection to rid the place of cheap housing blocks and maybe a designer chef. In need of a lick of paint and a damn good bleaching.

Who's in heaven? — at The West Bay Pub.

02/06/13 Watching a bottom of the cliff real rescue. What a twat.

Drinking my 2nd pint listening to an entertaining domestic. Love it reminders of BR. Apparently it's been the best two weeks of her life... Buy I some chips.

Lush walk - West bay to Eype - managed 5 ½ miles even with me impediment.

This, me being sat at a table on my own, bugs more people than you'd think. Man wearing sunglasses (yes and at this time of night, just ordered show off Champagne for his much older date) is talking about me. Trying to conceal his comments behind the menu. Tosser. Me being me struts over and tells the frontal lobotomy, loudly, "mate if the choice is between you or being on my own, the on my own would win. You have all of the attitude that normally accompanies a man with a small penis". What a W--k--. The landlord pissed himself...

03/06/13 PMSL. Guess who is sat opposite me this morning? Mr Small Penis and his mum. Lol.

04/06/13 Playing dad, date, husband or someone else's. Good game, good game.

6

CROATIA

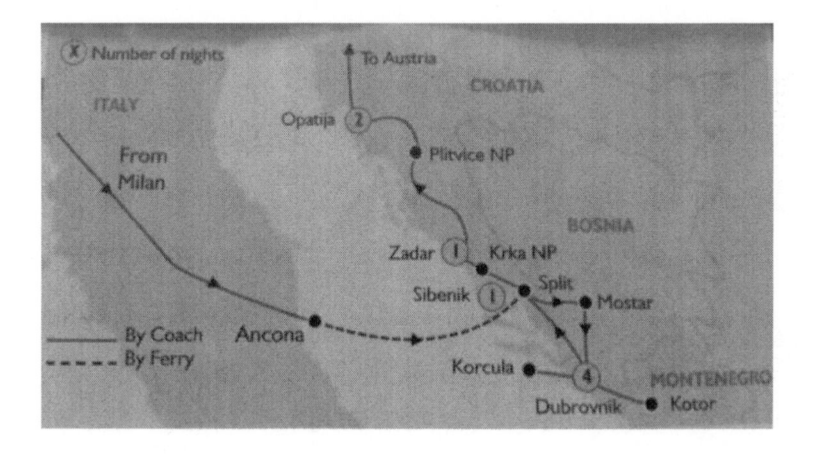

Number of nights
To Austria
CROATIA
ITALY
Opatija 2
From Milan
Plitvice NP
BOSNIA
Zadar 1
Krka NP
Split
Sibenik 1
Mostar
By Coach
By Ferry
Ancona
Korcula
4
MONTENEGRO
Dubrovnik
Kotor

22/06/13 My coach-cation has finally begun. I'm not really sure that it was a good idea to dye my eyebrows two days before I was going away on me hols. I look like one of the candidates off the apprentice. Also I have no skin above my top lip following a waxing incident leaving me with third degree burns. Thank God I did my moustache first. Just think, I could have rendered myself inactive if I had worked me way up instead of down! Anyway after a restless night, I awoke at 0530 and performed a work of art. The final act just prior to leaving my castle in singledom was to apply a squirt of my favourite eau de colon. I probably packed a bit too last minute and there was still room in my case. Despite having a ticky list I'm really worried I may have forgotten something. My stomach was on rinse and spin and fast forward all at once as I stepped into the taxi. I knew I would have to wait until the feeder coach reached Dover before I would know who I had been twinned with. The holiday brochure warned that there would be a lot of walking so I am hoping it will be an eligible bachelor minus Zimmer frame. An ex military chunk of hunk would be nice she says, humming the tune to one day my prince will come. Oooooh I'm so excitative. Standby for updated update from Dover.

Near Cobham.
Well. Do I look as though I work in Starbucks? There I am stood nicely in the queue waiting to be served when I am informed by the person behind me that there are no trays, and that I will have to help her back to the table. I don't think so. My reply was swift of tongue and spiked with a toxic dose of venom.
The anticipation of what's to come is getting too much and I'm so excitative. I just want to know, totty or grotty.
The tour bus has the appropriate number soixante neuf, that has to be a good omen for sure.

Caught up in a ModBall rally. RSPCT — with Vivvy Anne Le Fey at Dover to Calais Ferry.

Near Bellenglise, Picardie, France via Mobile. OK, this ModBall Rally we are caught up in. Not too sure what it is but it involves Porsches, Lamborghinis and other lush cars. The drivers are so hot I needed to put my sunglasses on so they wouldn't see me looking. God I'm in seventh heaven and will most certainly need a change of underwear. Trying desperately not to puke, bit of a swell is an understatement.

My coach buddy I have been twinned with, I have to say, is the worsest by far. He looks like that guy who got eaten by pigs in the Hannibal Lecter film.

The coach drivers I know from my first trip and the Jim saga. They purposely let me sit down next to him so they could see the horror on my face. The coach driver announced out loud that I had left a lasting impression and that's how he could remember me. I am frantically trying to recall if it was in his pillow. Bloody chemo head.

Getting back to Mr Pig Swill he must be at least 197 and has numerous walking aids which he has insisted he put in the overhead compartment, moving all my stuff in the process. Once again I needed to venomate. By the way, if the words I use don't exist they should. I am now in a seat on my own and am being discussed by the narrow minded people sat forward and aft. I may continue this trip as Viv and cause more mayhem than Caff would. Will update you if I manage to successfully kidnap a Porsche driving Modballer.

Wow — at Cathedral of Notre-Dame, Reims.

23/06/13 near Reims, Champagne-Ardenne, France via Mobile. An uneventful night, stopped from progressing because the British Police French side stopped the Modballers en masse from proceeding any further. They are hauled up somewhere further back. Also the bar closed at 2345. A bit of a sleepless night. Thought I had a noisy bird of prey outside my window which was open wide, turns out to be nesting pigeony things. Seem to be going through a 2nd change of life and resemble a sweat ball at the mo. My fellow passengers are taking a while to come out of the closet. So far we have Mrs One Named Peter One Named Paul. She points and uses her hands when she talks, it's an exercise regime in itself avoiding and dodging getting yer eye poked out. If you are too young to know who Peter and Paul were, or are, ask your mum! Mr and Mrs D District are very pleasant and were my drinking buddies last night. Mr Pig Swill is still offloading his walking gadgets which thankfully keeps him away from me. Update so far. Viv is working hard to cause more mayhem. WTS.

Stork nest — at Kork.

Heading down through Switzerland towards the Gotthard Tunnel and then on to Lake Como — at Badi Olten.

Snow! — at San Gotthardo.

Lake Como — at RABAJA' Luxurious Lounge.

24/06/13

Anzano del Parco, Lombardia, Italy via Mobile. I think I may have been adopted. Mr and Mrs D District have taken to making sure they save me a seat at meal times. They are lovely. People are beginning to come out of their shells, bit by bit. All a little slow this trip but we have some right characters. Mr Two Sticks can run if no one is watching and when it rained he would have given Linford Christie a run for his money. Mrs Rock 'n' Roll name speaks for itself, but if Mr iPad plays Elvis once more to get her to dance he's going off the balcony. Mrs Overdressed and Mrs Saggy Back are trying to outdo each other in the fashion department. Both clearly shop at Faux Pas. You don't wear a backless number with side slits that reveal 68 year old skin which has lost its elasticity. She's also a rock 'n' roller! Still, the bridal outfit Mrs Overdressed wore today won first prize.

Mr Waiting To Explode is argumentative and doesn't like women who have a voice.

Mrs Candy Crusher racked up a heck of a score during the thunder and lightning and had to be dragged to safety when it got a bit dangerous, although her husband said to just leave her there. He reckons that's all she does is play Candy Crush and drink. My kinda gal...

Had my first holiday poo this morning. That'll please the oncologist with an early entry now showing in my dump diary. However I did forget the colour chart so I just had to guess. I ticked 'good'. Well I felt good, went down at least one dress size (those of you who know me understand I don't poo away from home with ease!) Anyway no more talking shite. Off somewhere fab today, Viv will keep you posted, involves a boat and a cabin. Anchors aweigh...

Castelferretti, Marche, Italy via Mobile. Crossing the Adriatic from Italy to Split. Considerable storm expected. If you don't hear from me again I was with George when it all went down.

25/06/13 Split. Spot the mistake. Lol.

Near Kucice, Splitsko-Dalmatinska, Croatia.

Near Mostar, Federation of Bosnia and Herzegovina, Bosnia and Herzegovina.

Near Lapad, Dubrovacko-Neretvanska, Croatia. View from hotel.

26/06/13 near Ploce, Dubrovacko-Neretvanska, Croatia via Mobile. Arrived safely at The Argosy Hotel, right on the beach. Food is fab and views spectacular. Didn't realise I was on a shared patio. There I was wandering around fresh from the shower, trying to dry my hair with the patio doors open and only partially clothed. I then expertly applied my make up only to discover I was being observed by the Aunt Sarahs. Christ knows how long they had been watching. I was a tad miffed as they could have picked up some of my trade secrets. After all, looking fabulous is a bloody work of art these days. The only plus side of this patio is that it's easy to sneak people in. Poor Hugh has been traded in for a newer model, Terry Bull.

Today did not pass without incident. WE were late back to the coach and got bollocked. Nothing new there then... (WE being Mr & Mrs D District and Mr Explosive Chemicals and his YES wife.) We would have

been on time if Mr Explosive Chemical hadn't wanted bleedin' separate bills at the restaurant. Anyway he reckons he was overcharged and we are all suffering for it. The fact his wife ate most of my sandwich and Mr D Districts chips didn't matter. After dinner tonight he caused quite a scene. I'd paid my bill and was not gonna get involved. If he had split the bill 5 ways he would have been on a winner, serves him right.
Wandering around Bosnia was a bit scary, bullet scarred buildings and a warning to watch out for deadly nose horn vipers, as well being as being mindful we were in earthquake territory. Like I'm gonna hang around to sound the klaxon or do a Terry Phillips, I think not.
Bit of culture tonight with a pianist and a violinist. Don't think they appreciated my dance moves. Can't please 'em all. Surprised me really. The accordion players at dinner loved me joining in to Alouette and dancing around the restaurant. Bit of nostalgia, first song I learnt at school.
By the way this holiday rates as a ten out of ten, the views are spectacular.

26/06/13 Bar b q. So happy I could cry. Fab time, fabber people. Lovin' it. Me singing c'mon baby light my fire. Lol. . Epic performance. — with Vivvy Anne Le Fey at Old Town In Dubrovnik Croatia.

27/06/13 Near Dubrovnik, Dubrovacko-Neretvanska, Croatia.

Writing this while waiting for the others to return from a cable car ride. Bit too close to God for my liking. I'm sat in the shade on a patio with my third beer.
Well after yesterday's fiasco it was only a matter of time before Mr Explosive Chemical erupted. What was it over? Yesterday's bill and the fact he thought he had been overcharged. We are talking the cost of 1 beer. He said the bill cost him 1000 kuna. Now Viv, being an expert people watcher, saw him hand over 200 not a 1000. When you consider my bill was 69 that was about right for two. (Hugh pays for himself.) He made breakfast a bad place so Viv had to do the do...
Now his wife might be scared of him but I ain't. You can imagine I venomated. Can't even remember what I said but apparently I did it without saying the f word once. Mr and Mrs D District were extremely impressed. He gives men a bad name and he has been left sulking, as I told him he was responsible for his own bill - any miscalculation was between him and the restaurant. Anyway his wife Mrs Meek and Mild is my new BF, she hasn't left my side. I have advised her she needs to seek help if she is being abused which I truly think she is.
Following the annihilation of the tosser... Dressed to stun in my killah daps and matching t shirt, we set off to explore Dubrovnik (Viv does it so well for an old bird.) What a fab place, right up there with Italy in my opinion.
Everyone is starting to open up and I'm with some real characters. Most of them try to outdo one another with holiday destinations visited and

how big a garden they have. Makes a change from the other trips where it was the amount of medication people were prescribed. The Aunt Sarahs are still wanting me in their gang but I am steering clear, preferring mingling among the Geordies who can drink as much as I can. Got mauled by a feral cat and had to have a jab. Before people get worried and start ringing me (mauled was Vivs choice of word mainly to make it sound more dramatic; I have suffered worserer in le jardin, remember I am on holiday and unavailable for comment) I'm fine, it provided the entertainment at the bar b q and I got free beer when I returned from the medic centre. (Obviously didn't realise how much I'm capable of putting away.) My ass is a bit sore and so is my wallet. What with no insurance and all that. Think the hotel might reimburse me anyway. Plus Mr Explosive Chemical got into mega trouble for feeding the cats and is being bullied into paying my bill by most of the coach... Asshole!

Delay in posting photos of Dubrovnik as I didn't register or sync my iPad at home before I left. Too bloody complicated to do it here. Well that's what Hugh said ;-)))))

27/06/13 - Near Perkovic, Sibensko-Kninska, Ston, Croatia.

Korcula — at Korčula, Croatia.

28/06/13 Another fab day — at Montenegro, Kotor Bay.

Doing a Shirley — at Hotel Argosy.

Near Lapad, Dubrovacko-Neretvanska, Croatia via Mobile. Sorry I haven't posted words for a while, been busy sight-seeing and drinking. Got into trouble again yesterday; Granny Chuckle Gums got drunk on 29% proof cherry brandy, we were making up rude songs and lowered the tone at the wine tasting. Granny is 89 and had to be carried up the cellar steps. She lost her teeth somewhere on the coach and we all had to get off so the coach drivers could locate them. I won't need Botox for a while, I laughed so much my cheek muscles ached. Yesterday lunch time Mr and Mrs D District thought I had pulled as the very attractive Venetian waiter kept bringing me different food to try. An offering from a god... Hugh was not amused. Talking of Hugh we are not talking at the mo. Totally embarrassed me this morning by telling everyone he believed he had been in bed with a young teenager until he woke up with a start, thinking he was in the wrong bed, and turned the light on. He thought he had been groping my extremities and had lay,there thinking how pert everything was not realising I was covered in mozzy bites. He said it was liking crossing the Himalayas. (You know me. always like to take my men to new heights!) Well, needless to say he's in my bad books. I work hard at strapping everything in and he totally ruined the illusion I like to create. Mr Chemical Explosion has decided we have all been diddled by the coach driver. Think he may have his exchange rates muddled. Needs to go careful or he could be walking home.

Mrs Saggy Back and her hubby Mr Grecian 2013 (he dyes his hair) are not speaking, he has been drinking and is getting on her nerves. Mrs Overdressed is still wearing white. I'm wondering if she's on her honeymoon.

Mr Two Sticks offered to be my Romeo when I was reciting Bristolian Shakespeare from a balcony, not quite what I had in mind. I managed to decline politely.

I am now the official weather girl and navigator through streets without a map person. Pretty impressive seeing as I'm winging it every time.

Found out Mrs Meek and Mild has been married five times, fair play! Mrs D District says I make her laugh and she's happy when I'm around, even though she has never been in so much trouble. All drink or late back to coach related. So not a tower offence. My maul wounds are drying up nicely and I have not encountered any further aggressive feline behaviour. I must admit staying out of the bushes helps.

Coach has just arrived at hotel so off to the bar.

29/06/13 Split — at Splitska Riva.

Near Spalato, Splitsko-Dalmatinska, Croatia via Mobile. Major majors on the coach today. Mr Explosive Chemical confronted the drivers about the 12 euro discrepancy he believed there was. Basically an overcharge of 25 euros per couple for the trips in his opinion. Held the coach up for ages till it got sorted. He was bang out of order and, as I stated, miscalculated. Duffer. The rest of us were ok, just stayed in the bar for an hour longer.

Mrs Saggy Back asked me if I would remove a mosquito from her bathroom. Her hubby Mr Grecian 2013 was still sparko. Well that or dead. Difficult to tell as he was quite tanned and marble floors are always cold anyway, aren't they? I pointed out that she needed housekeeping, the fact I had been bitten by 99% of the mozzies in Dubrovnik did not make me an expert. Entomology is not one of my strong subjects. Anyway, offender swatted, I returned to sort out Granny Chuckle Gums as she wanted to ask me something. A few days before on the way back from the winery she asked me if she could have the plastic bag my wine was in. I handed it over no probs. She asked if I wanted the bag back. I said no we had already drunk the wine the day before. Oh thank God she said. Where you made me laugh so much I wet myself on the coach and I have been using the bag to sit on because the seat is wet. Everyone up front had been saying they could smell pee and thought one of the feral cats had gotten on board or the toilet needed seeing to. Every time we look at one another we can't stop laughing and I'm the only one who knows her secret. Bless her.

Trogir.

30/06/13 Where the water is so soft or hard, whatever it is here it's causing problems with my hair. I've kinda got a Liam Gallagher look. A bit beat nicky. Not too unlike Rose West actually. I can't use me gel as it attracts wasps, I looked like Medusa earlier. I am now bill sorter, navigator, carer and weather girl. If it rains I will be strung up.
Bit worrying as we are now in bear and wolf country. There are bridges built across the road for them. Sod the humans. Let's hope the guide knows the difference between recent and not so recent poo. I'm too bloody knackered to kick off but have insisted the guide sleep in with me, the Aunt Sarahs and Granny Chuckle Gums. I got us moved away from the big hole in the ground, I was trying to remember why they called The Bear Pit in Bristol, The Bear Pit. Sure it was something to do with bears so I was on it and got us relocated. He hasn't even got a gun! He reckons they will stay away. Does he realise who he is with? We have the biggest fire and enuff wood to take us into next winter. I have sent him out again to gather more with Hugh and also to buy more provisions in case we get attacked and have to dig in. Just call me Davey Crockett.
Had a bit of an embarrassing sitch earlier. Thought this little shop we came across was for dressing up and getting your photo taken. I of course enquired thinking it would be fun. Wrong. It was an extremely, as in mega, expensive dress shop... so no photo of me I'm sorry.

Rupert Murdoch's boat and Sibernek.

Krka — at Krka National Park.

30/06/13 near Zadar, Zagrebacka, Croatia via Mobile - You will all be pleased to know that, despite a sleepless night for both myself and the guide, there were no sightings of wolves or bears other than on the warning signs. Comforting! The guide is not happy, he didn't know all the words to the songs we were singing in order to stay awake through the night. He is not best pleased with me. However I think it was my singing that kept us, the group, safe throughout the night. I will be writing to bear and wolf management upon my return. By the time you had walked up the 90 million steps you'd be too tired to fight off a bear or a wolf. I ought to know I've fought off many a wolf in sheep's clothing. Deffo safety issue here me finx. I mean come on, I'm heading up the rear needing to look down 'cos of divots, Granny Chuckle Gums can't straighten up, Mr Two Sticks has no heels so wouldn't see what's hot on 'em, Mr and Mrs Cataracts says it all, Mrs One Named Peter One Named Paul would just point and say nothing, and the two Dorises from the front of the coach don't have an effing clue what a bear is. Come on, what chance of seeing a bear has my group got?
Oh by the way, and digressing slightly, I have received an email whilst away on my travels. It looks as though my tireless campaign to reinstate the map in the centre of Bristol might now in fact be happening. For all you youngsters this is where everyone use to meet before a night out in Bristol. "On the map". The toilets will not be reinstated for obvious reasons. I could be on the news rather than in it.
Arrived at the Solaris Hotel Ivan. Nice! Well, nice if you want someone watching you go to the toilet. Glass door, large glass door. Then glass door to shower. Meanwhile, back in the bedroom, if you pulled back the modesty curtain there was another glass partition where you become

on full view to room-mates or other watching public in the garden. What the bloody hell is that all about? Hugh is in his element. Sicko perve.
Had a run in with a jumped up motorcycle cop who was gonna fine me for Hawking. Didn't even know what that was . Thank the eff for Google. What had in fact happened; I had taken a swig of water just as someone made me laugh. I choked and the water spurted from my mouth all over his bike. Unwise move Murray. You try explaining that one away. No sense of humour.
Me fellow coachers have said normally by this time in the holiday they have read two books. But 'cos they are having such a laugh haven't yet finished the first. Nothing like a bit of laughter.

01/07/13
Think me bloody head is gonna drop off from either watching where I'm walking or taking pictures. Like a bleedin' nodding dog.
The coach has been bleached today and a cover placed on Granny Chuckle Gum's seat. One of the drivers took me to one side and asked me to try not to make her laugh too much. We are all planning to have a few drinks tonight in Zagreb, well somewhere beginning with z anyway, and Granny is coming too. Might just be a problem there...
Off into bear territory tomorrow for an overnight stay. My nerves are already frazzled. Today in Krka was bad enuff coping with poisonous tree snakes and mating frogs all over the place. I got told not to get too close. Like I court their company. Can't help it if they come to me can I?
This trip is fab but tiring, I will need to sleep for a week when I get home.
We have now added keeper of loose change and finder of toilets to my list of talents. Bloody endless this holiday.
Mr Chemical Explosion has gotten better by the day, he always hangs on until the last minute to get cash out and he is forever asking for toilet money. Yesterday I had to tell him to repay what you owe first, I'm not a charity. His wife Mrs Meek and Mild is great fun but still goes through it when she wants a drink, asking him for money. He hands over the exact amount, using his torch if its dark to do it! No pockets in shrouds folks!

Ought to have heard sockgate this morning when she hadn't laid out short socks and he had to roll down his M&S fairisle things. Did I take the piss or did I take the piss? I don't let Hugh wear socks with his sandals. It's a Brit thing, and as I tell everyone he is a French chef and plastic surgeon (every girl my age's dream) I don't wanna ruin the illusion. He plays the part well. Although the last couple of days he has been overdoing the accent and if he calls me his petite pomme once more I'm gonna chin him.
Watched the sunset last night and listened to the sea organ. Everyone congregates there and even more than usual as Croatia joined the EU yesterday. We all have hangovers and had a great time playing name that tune. Singing songs into our mobiles to see if the song could be recognised. Several of the coachers didn't understand you didn't need to improvise and do the la la la's or the do do do's, the words were all that were necessary. Sin Gin or St J (he's the guy who speaks to me on my iPhone 5 phone) got quite pissed off and failed to get the songs right. He was better with the '70's stuff more so than the '20's. The drunker we got the funnier it got.

Stealth bomber butterfly and Dilly duck at Plitvice National Park.

Bearing my soul! Never been so bloody scared — at Plitvice Lakes National Park.

02/07/13 near Icici, Primorsko-Goranska, Croatia. Wrecked. Totally, hence no update.

A Bora wind closed the motorway but we finally made it through bear, mountain cat, deadly snake and wolf country. It was comforting to know aforementioned creatures were banned from the park between 0700-2300. Well that's what the signs said. The steps out of the park, all six million and one of them, nearly killed me but having a grizzly bearing down on you certainly helps.

Out on a boat trip in Opatija, got totally wrecked. Granny Chuckle Gums and I started at 0930. It went rapidly downhill from there. Somehow we ended up on a nudist beach. We were ordered to get our kit off so beat a hasty retreat. Hugh was game but there was nothing there to keep me occupied. The 20 mins I spent scanning from the secluded cove had been sufficient time for me to arrive at that conclusion. Hugh got 'em all worked up into a frenzy. Funnily enuff he has the same effect on me.

Mrs Off The Shoulder Get Those Moles Checked Out caused a stir. Climbing the steps of the boat in unsuitable clothing, skirt billowing in the wind, hairy legs and lower abdominals on full display. Yuk how vile. Once, up on top deck, sat there with her legs spread and mahoosive breasts out on show not thinking anything of it. We were screaming with laughter. I had been convinced her boob tube was gonna slip down

all week, well it definitely did today.
Off to a Latin American themed night later.

03/07/13 Woke up this morning with my finger rammed in my ear. The bedroom I had spent the night in was the noisiest I have ever slept in. At one point I thought I was on the M5 on a BH Monday. Plus the air conditioning unit sounded like a 747 landing , mix all that with the hangover from hell x 5. Not nice.
Mr Explosive Chemical turned again. Not a surprise. We were all given tickets for free water to accompany dinner. The little scrap of paper had a picture of a bottle on it. When the waiter produced tap water he was not best pleased and asked the waiter to explain how they worked out the costing. The topic took over the conversation until I was asked for my input. Clean out of anti-venom I was unable to bite my tongue. Needless to say I vented. I have to pay for my tap water back home so why not here. Anyway I wound him up further by ordering bottled water and getting it for the extortionate cost of 1 kuna. 10 pee. He was highly embarrassed. Twat.
Was invited for drinks onboard a very large yacht yesterday. The Wet Dream was owned by a wealthy Yank known as DK, I just called him Dick which he found hysterical. He said he loved my accent and my humour and could listen to me all day. Surprised really 'cos the yanks can be a bit dense when it comes to Brit humour (my brothers family excluded.) I was allowed to take my entourage of 10 which included a drink fuelled Granny Chuckle Gums. We had a brill time. Granny said she felt like the queen, which was so lovely. Listening to everyone change the way they spoke was hysterical, all going really posh, Mr and Mrs D District did it so well. Getting off the boat the next morning caused a bit of a problem and I'm a bit unsure as to where my false eyelashes were abandoned. Dicks man servant said he would ensure there was no trace of any additives I'd abandoned. There was a huge cheer as I arrived for breakfast back at the hotel, even Granny Chuckle Gums hot footed it over to find out the score. Yanks six, Brits nine. Can't quite see his yacht parked up in Weston Super Mare harbour somehow! If there is one.
Off to Slovenia today. Dick has my schedule and is hoping to catch up

again in the next day or so. Won't hold my breath. Stand by for update. Despite hangover I am apparently blooming WETFTM.

New meaning to Drunk and Incapable Lol. — at Triassic Park.

Just getting ready to go out on a horse and carriage ride. Off into bear country again with schnapps on board and my drinking partner Granny Chuckle Gums, who incidentally left her teeth in the yacht bathroom. Bit of a reconnaissance mission needed to get those back and a huge detour. Trouble was, the bloody coach drivers have lost Dick's business card with his phone number on. They have assured me they will try and locate it soonest. Other than that I will have to learn ship to shore morse code from W-S-Mare pier.
Currently situated on a precipice 600 million metres up a mountain. Couldn't get any closer to God if I tried. Can't stay down in the valleys. Oh no, every day an Alton Towers death ride. Saw the Chitty Chitty Bang Bang castle and going up to Where Eagles Dared tomorrow or the day after. Also visiting some bloody eagles nest. Thought they were top secret to stop egg burglars. No doubt there will be a rock climbing expedition thrown in just for good measure. My thighs are to die for, just the rest of me that needs a bit of firming up.
My current room has all the added extras that an alcohol dependent lady needs. Chair in shower and bog side hand rails. However nowhere for Dick to dock, not a drop of water in sight. I have two beds in my room and have allowed Hugh the bigger of the two with the balcony

view. I've seen enuff bears to last me a lifetime thx.

05/07/13 near Diegem, Brabant, Belgium.

Knackered or knackered? Woke myself up on the coach with a snort. So loud everyone turned round. Stretched out with my trousers undone and it all hanging out. Not very attractive.
Still in bear country and have a long walk ahead of us. Vertically as predicted.
Coach drivers failed to find Dick's business card and have refused to go through the rubbish they send down the chute (I particularly like that job, sucks all the hairs off your arms, so I use my feet to kick it down. Saves on a leg wax. Also good for keeping in touch with Hugh. I can send him morsels of food.)
Watched a roe deer give birth to a baby (as in baby roe deer) last night, while sat on our balcony.
Can't get a signal up here, too many mountains, we are so high up you'd at least think we be able to pick up a satellite connection.
Mr Two Sticks revealed further impediments while trying to outdo a man from another coach. He has a false eye which he removed and a denture set not dissimilar to Silva which he vilely removed to show us.
Off up to the eagles nest, Christ knows how high up that is.
Wish me luck.

7

WOOLACOMBE

29/07/13 No memory of this place. Yet so many happy memories!

My third of the day.

Just been asked to move from my seat in the sun to allow a large family to sit together. Did it without comment. Need to do something to make my halo slip. — with Vivvy Anne Le Fey.

Wench on a bench!

30/07/13 Near Woolacombe via Mobile. So I'm in Woolacombe. Ensconced in the WB hotel. What I have observated so far...

The hotel dates back to the 18th century. The views and grounds are stunning. There is no Wi Fi unless you are at the back of the hotel balancing on one leg while having a stand up pee. I look like some drunken prozzy touting for business posting this. There is no air conditioning, which in this weather is not good. The menus aren't all that and, having the only two decent restaurants in the whole place, I'm surprised they haven't done more. Once out of the gates, I was

horrified. Woolacombe seems to cater more for the self catering holiday makers. As a child I enjoyed similar so this is not a criticism. I have fond memories. The restaurants, if you can call them that, are not good.
Today I am going in search of a lane, that we used to walk down as kids, from a caravan park to the beach. Very muddy, narrow and involves crossing a field of sheep. The locals think I have made it up. Even asking people of a similar age, they ain't got a clue what I'm talking about. Also there is need to find a decent restaurant. (As you all know I have an acute fear of anorexia.)

31/07/13 Wench on a wet bench. One who came prepared with bin liners. Sun is trying to get through. — with Vivvy Anne Le Fey at Woolacombe Bay Hotel.
Blue skies are still trying to break through. I don't relax normally, but I have bought two books and I'm on the terrace reading and people watching.

01/08/13 Spent yesterday exploring. May have been a bit unwise to use the steps that lead down to the rocks. I would have preferred my knight in shining armour to have been at least 30 years younger. Still fair play to him he got me down onto the beach.
Prior to the rock rescue I had nearly wet myself laughing watching the antics of a 65 year old surfer. Kissing the grass, waving his arms around in a very weird fashion and then kicking his legs out like he had received an electric shock. Kudos to him though he paddled out the furthest and rode the biggest wave, even if he had to wait two hours for it.
I went in search of the path I used as a child to get from holiday park to

beach and failed dismally. Instead I walked to Putsborough Sands, a two and a half mile shoreline walk.
Earlier I had witnessed a strange ritual of people drawing circles in the sand. Not unlike crop circles in the fields. Also saw numerous parties, prior to throwing down their towels, using a bucket 'n' spade to collect what I thought was poo from the sand and throw it onto the rocks. Once down on the beach I realised it was the ridding of jelly fish from the sand, and the circles drawn in the sand a warning to other beach users. There were so many jelly fish scattered and I mean thousands, the ritual of circling ended after several hundred yards and it was down to the beach users to navigate their way through.
I'm not happy. The hotel encourage the jackdaws to use the hotel grounds. They are so noisy, outdoing the seagulls. I'm not able to leave the large window in my room open as there is a fire escape which allows access from above and the ground. The bloody critters sit there nattering like they own the joint. If you shoo them away they don't move. Just give you a crow like look and carry on squawking. They don't shut up! May have to organise a culling holiday.
Loads of characters to tell you about. Will keep you posted.
For instance; the women who lets her toddler run riot in the restaurant, putting his chocolate fingers all over my white linen trousers. And then, argues the toss with the wine waiter about paying corkage on a bottle that has no cork and is a screw cap. They may have a point but Hello.

I have been asked by several people if the mother of the stainer of white linen trousers is still on this planet. She is. The manageress, or manager to be politically correct, of the WBH is not.

I pointed out to said manager: to have a toddler, and I mean about 18 months old, running amok in a packed restaurant is not good. In my day the baby would have been in bed asleep not screaming at the top of his voice running around like a crack monkey having been overdosed on Eeeeeezzzzz.
Also to advertise Wifi when clearly there is not is even worserer. All me bleedin' pirate ships have sunk and I was on a mission winning every battle. Took me months of hard work to get into the top players. Regressing back to childhood so I understood the game was not easy. Candy Crushers would sympathise I'm sure.
Got stung by a bee yesterday and didn't sleep all night wondering if it had died or not (shortage of them and all that.) Google couldn't help 'cos I can only get a connection in certain places and it was far too dark to hang off a cliff or visit some back alley. At the time I was running my hands across the top of some unknown flower/weed on the cliff top very much like the girl used to do on the Nimble Advert and the beesterd stung me. I have had a throbber all night and it weren't Hugh.
Walking to Morthoe today.

02/08/13 - My summing up of my stay at the Woolacombe Bay Hotel. Clean, staff friendly, grounds beautiful, food good. No air conditioning in the rooms. WiFi; although advertised, is only available in certain hotspots. Outside or near the reception desk. The provision of coffee tea etc in the rooms plentiful but out of date by 17 months in some cases. Fire doors shut 1 night in four and impossible to close them without aid when locked open. I appreciate there was the need for air to circulate through the corridors as it was so hot but not good.
The walk to Morthoe was lovely, although I should have taken the cliff path to the lighthouse and not some secluded off the beaten track route. This would have obviously been fine if accompanied and is a beautiful walk. I ended up scaring myself to death when I bumped into a strange man, on this occasion not Hugh. My impediment stops me from running and, although a force to be reckoned with, I was already exhausted and a slippery sweatball who by the time she hit Morthoe was physically unable to fend off any would be attacker. To calm myself

I took pictures of flowers which can be found along the trek back.
I never made it to the lighthouse but arrived back at the hotel safely.

The walk from Woolacombe to Putsborough.

8

LULWORTH COVE

22/08/13 Arrived at my destination. Note to self: remember name of hotel. No service down here if you're on Vodaphone network. Let's hope I don't get into difficulty. Lol.

Well I arrived safely. After a fashion anyway. Pays to know which hotel you are staying in. Also helps to do some research before booking a hotel instead of being swept away by the romance of it all.

My room takes me back to a place in the mid '60s when pink plastic bathroom suites were all the rage. In fact I remember having similar in our family home on Garden Downs Estate. The artwork is '70s style and likely to give me nightmares. Numerous framed clown pictures. Smacks of Chucky. The single bed arrangement has more than pissed off Hugh. The matching pink candlewick bedspreads did it for me! The upside, there is WiFi, it is free, but no signal, my phone says 'No Service'. Apparently its 02 and Orange down here. WTF. How they can justify charging £95 per night is totally beyond me. I may have to turn to drink. The place may be dog friendly but this old dog is gonna have to dig deep to find a sense of humour.

The cove is beautiful and, with dinner pre-booked for 1830 at The Lulworth Cove Inn, life is good.

After the week terribleus I have had, as long as me Fosters is chilled so am I. Tomorrow I am off to Durdle Door in search of crabs 'n' lobster.

23/08/13 -It may be that these postings are arriving days after they are written. I am on the Jurassic coastline. I have been told to climb as high as I can and maybe I will pick up a signal. More chance of contacting people by ship to shore. Do they not know I have an impediment? Climb? Do I look like Steph Davis?

I made it through the night. Underneath that pink candlewick was a comfy bed. The windows open and although being above the busy beer garden and kitchen, I managed to sleep. I am unable to use the light in the bathroom as my ass would be on display to the whole of West Lulworth if I did. The hot water also takes a time to drip through, rendering a hand held shower sat in the bath ('cos of that window) impossible. The kettle works.
As always Viv is enjoying people watching and eavesdropping. Major majors going on up on the cliff top. Over worried dad who wouldn't do anything because he was worried his kids would hurt themselves. Not allowed to go swimming, canoeing or crabbing. What a life. People seem to think I'm some kind of mobile information centre. "Where is the local supermarket, nearest American Embassy (aka Maccy D), toilets etc etc. I could answer the questions but, Hello. Obviously missed my calling.
Having now eaten at the Lulworth Cove Inn and returned the chef's first attempt, and second, I can recommend you avoid at all cost. Vile even though the manager and host went out of their way to try and rectify the problem. The one saving grace, they allow all and sundry to use the loos but ask for a donation to Macmillan. What a good idea.
Had far too much Prosecco to drive to the Embassy so filling up on the desserts.

23/08/13 - Fabulous walk today from Lulworth to Durdle Door and back again. Took the low route to get there, via the coastal path, through the fields and then took the high route for the walk back.
On the way back came across a lady mid 60s who was out of her face. Initially she looked as though she was in some distress, stroke like. Me being the caring soul I am asked if she was ok. In a drunken slur she replied would you be ok if you'd pissed yourself? She then headed off with her wet trousers on full display to the heavily populated beauty spot.
The restaurants are crap, no other word for it. The service is atrocious to the point of disbelief. People were just getting up and walking out.
Have become addicted to Prosecco, my escort prefers I drink from a

wine glass rather than a pint mug. Despite attempts to get us into better accommodation there is nothing available. I'm not prepared to lose money so turning to alcohol is the only option. Being checked daily for flea bites is most off putting.

Apparently this place used to be a flambé restaurant. They changed to pub grub, and bad pub grub, because they claim people don't want fancy food! Be interested to know who or what they flambéed. Can't eat inside because I have watched them wash down the table tops ignoring the edges where the dog slobber drips. Yukhowvile.

I wonder how often they de-flea the place? Hugh has already gone into print to the hotel/inn and also the restaurants but I have made him promise to send the emails on the day we leave fearing reprisals. Those clowns are scary.

24/08/13 Met two fabulous people last night and their lovely non-slobbery dog Mollie. Good conversation but too much to drink. The world is full of lovely interesting people.

24/08/13 - near Swanage, England. - Today my imaginary friend Hugh and I took the slow and dirty from Lulworth to Corfe Castle. Bad experience with three undesirables who were swearing profusely. There were kids on the bus and their dads sat and said nothing, obviously didn't have a backbone between them. It was left to me to advise them that the c and f words weren't an appropriate choice of words to use and to tone it down. Hugh wanted to intervene, he's very protective, but he was just taking too long to get lathered up.
Once at Corfe Castle I decided the £8.50 entry fee was better spent in the pub. On the recommendation of Debra and Gordon, the two people I met last night, I ate in The Greyhound, a hostelry which dates back to 1090. I had lobster salad which was bloody lush, washed down with a pint of the amber nectar.
After a few hours at Corfe we took the steam train to Swanage where we ambled along the front eating ice-cream. All very civil.
Now heading back to Hovel Hideaway to enjoy a few more glasses of Prosecco.
The bus timetables here are way too complicated. Apparently it'll get worserer in September.
Discovered today I had packed four odd shoes/flipper flops, they matched only in colour. Hugh was not amused. He keeps reminding me of the 6 p's like I've got memory capacity left to store that gem. No sign of any Pirates in the cove more's the pity, fancy seeing him walk the

plank.

Below: a selection of snaps. Swanage to Corfe.

25/08/13 Hugh and I have decided to call it a day at Hovel Hideaway and are heading off in search of decent food.
If I had to sum up Lulworth I would say:
Fantastic place for cider drinkers, every conceivable flavour you can think of, great for walkers, stunning coastal paths and views truly beautiful. Entrance fee to Corfe Castle expensive but the kids would love it, so get a National Heritage Discount Card. Beach not as nice as Woolacombe Bay and not much of it, however families were making the most of it. Seems to be a place for kayaking and canoeing. Durdle Door is stunning and is apparently good for swimming. Lots of camp sites around and I would suggest if people come here, 'cos it is beautiful, go self-catering. The food here is of a low standard and expensive and the service is poor too. I will be making an entry on Trip Advisor. Oh, and if you are on Vodaphone network your phone won't work!

9

GREEN SPAIN

30/09/13 via Mobile - After a weekus horribilis and with heart scan booked, blue veiner PIC line implant booked and chemo sesh booked, I am finally at sea. And what a lovely day to set sail into the unknown it is. My travel log begins. I have now decided on a name, that being Terminal to Terminus, very apt I thought.
Once again I am likely the youngest on board the coach. Smacks of Italy minus Son of Shrek. Jim.
95% of the passengers are challenged in one way or another. Tripod walking frames with wheels are the must have accessory and hearing aids the gotta get ear bling.
Have already sorted out one elderly couples domestic. A Hyacinth lookalike with hat, hitting her hubby with the Times because he was breaking the law and refusing to wear his seatbelt. Perish the thought. I never wear one. I have assisted in organising seating and conducting arm rest up and arm rest down training courses.
I am travelling with the same coach drivers who took me to Eastern Europe and they could still remember the antics with the Squadron Leader! And the weight of my suitcase. Erm, no comment. Apparently it's heavier. I don't think so.
It was comforting to get back into travel mode after so long at home. However the sweet sickly smell of incontinence from the person in the seat to the front of me bought back memories of Granny Chuckle Gums, bringing a tear to my eye, and the smell of Saturday night/Sunday morning couldn't be bothered to shower hung in the air like eau d' chien mouille.
Currently in Club Class lounge with Capt Jury Davis (another name to use in my book) drinking champers and eating posh nosh. I lied and said my travelling companion was in the loo so they left me two glasses. Needs must and all that, and me being a victim of alcohol abuse. Anyway Jury said I could have his, he doesn't drink and drive.
Met a former colleague from Taunton who is on the same trip (Carol who retired when we merged, hoping we got on but I can't remember!)
Stand by for more antics from the wild one. The coach has empty seats and this Jury cap'n chap is rather lush.

30/09/13 via Mobile. - En route to Paris and I had to move seats. Wet The Bed in front of me and Vile BO behind me. However, the woman behind me now has not taken an effing breath. Just STFU. If I hear the name Megan, Madison or Billy one more time I am gonna resort to Japanese torture. A choice of two. Grow bamboo shoots up her bum or fill her full of water and then jump on her stomach. Times like this when I wish I could go into man mode. "Oh look ploughing the fields, might be for next years crops." Hardly likely to be for this year you idiot woman. "Think we are pulling into a petrol station." Yes, the Shell sign is the giveaway. BMUS.
Hyacinth and Victor Domestic are still arguing, he is so grumpy and rude.
Dear Lord or Lucifer please let me get old so I can be lairy, opinionated, cantankerous, sarcastic and beat someone with a newspaper when they piss me off and get away with it!

30/09/13 -Aahhhh! — at Le LOFT - PARIS (OFFICIEL.)

01/10/13 near Palaiseau, Ile-de-France, France via Mobile. - If I had to describe my mood today I would liken it to a rabbit with mixie. Not best pleased. What is wrong I hear you say? I have left my skin fixing BB foundation at home. The one that makes you look 20 years younger foundation. Now I know it's only 3rd in line to the throne after me mascara and lippy, but a woman my age needs her slap first thing in the

morning. And I don't mean slapped with a newspaper. Yes that's right I got slapped on the back with the French equivalent of the Times. Swatted like a bluebottle on shit by Victor Domestic. Talk about care in the community. Once he had attracted my attention he said "You gal, get my bag for me will you and bring it to my seat." Does it say swat here for porterage services? No it does not! Victor was advised in my most severe tone (scared meself with my ferocity) that he had just assaulted me and that I wasn't there to meet his demands, which over the past 24hrs have been numerous.
Reminded me of my French teacher Mr James who use to shout "you gal" before making me stand on a chair with me hands on me head.
The coach driver cannot believe the amount of elderly and infirm people he has aboard. Out of 28 people 22 are challenged in one way or another. Although having observated quite a few of them I am sure most of the ailments are manufactured.
Update to follow later when I have recovered from the occurrence which occurred at breakfast earlier. SFU.

01/10/13 near Brive, Limousin, France via Mobile - With lunch out of the way I now feel able to tell you about the goings on earlier this morning.
At breakfast us coachers were segregated from the other guests. Zoned off I think they call it. However through the perspex partition I observated a women of the night administering a hand job to two trunker truckers. Unbelievable I know, but true. At the breccky table in full view of moi, and two of them at the same time. Talk about early risers it was only 0615 FMT. Put me off me scrambled eggs it did. Now I don't know whether she was advertising her services or what, but no one seemed bothered. That was except for me of course. Perhaps she had a special on, two for the price of one. BOGOF. Whatever, I went into shock. I already looked white due to the lack of BB, I went Persil White. I'm not even sure I have properly recovered yet either.
I am interested to know how much she earned for said performance.
The hotel is called BW. I thought that stood for Best Western, obviously not! Talk about one flew over the cuckoo's nest, I'm with 20 of 'em. Smacks of the twilight zone almost as though I have been transported to

planet bewildered and bemused. BMUS.
Mrs STFU turns out to be a residential home owner for the post operative seniors. She's in her 70's easy. Most of the inmates are male and are prostrate patients. Nice!
BTW she still hasn't STFU. This morning's classic line, ' the whole coach is asleep Bert'. No they weren't, I couldn't because she still hadn't STFU! She has given me a business card to look her up. Mmmmm.
There are three women that talk to themselves on board. Mrs In continence has a toy that she talks to and punches. It resembles my chemo buddy's dog's humping toy. Although I have to say, unlike the toy that belongs to my CB's dog, this thing has not been washed in a long while. Yukhowvile.
It sits on the chair shelf in front of her and is called Virgil. F.A.B.
Mrs Cru C Fix has dyed black hair but the fresh out of bed style she chooses to wear, and has opted for, shows the grey coming through; and with her centre parting and flattened crown, a cross is clearly displayed. Is this a sign maybe? Whatever, I have never felt close to God and it's most unnerving. Feel like I'm being vetted.
Mrs Puff, or rather out of puff, chain smokes. As the nicotine withdraws she rocks back and forth and chants.
There seems to be a lot of male stroke victims travelling with us. The advert is obviously doing the trick and having an effect. I am assisting as best I can but draw the line at dribble and fly zipping up. I'm not qualified. Remind me to tell you about the raffle tickets and loogate. I'm trying to make notes to jog my memory.
3rd vino rouge on its way. TTFN. SFU.
I am trying to be nice and failing dismally. My non-existent filter has not reappeared and with a session on Gin and Tonic I am in a state of flux. Do I slit my throat, slash my wrists or jump?
I know I have deep and meaningful conversations with my radiator when I'm at home but no-one knows about that and in the main our conversations are deep, meaningful and most of the time intelligent. Virgil is taking a right battering and Mrs Incontinence is on one. She is now doing a voice pretending Virgil, the stuffed humpy toy, is replying to her questions. I'm trying to think of who it sounds like but whoever

it's annoying.
Mrs STFU is still going on and on and on. She states the obvious. 'Look at all that green.' Yes it's trees and grass. 'High up that is ain't it?' Yes it's the effing Pyranees. 'Bit wet down there.' Yes it's a river!! Help BMUS. Did you know Essex has no cows?

02/10/13 near Andorra, Teruel via Mobile.

Well am I vexed or am I vexed? Ended up sitting next to Mrs BO and Mrs Cru C Fix at dinner last evening. Other option was worserer, but I lumbered Carol with them. Mr and Mrs Spit n' Chew, who told us thirty years back we'd have been calling her Memsaab. Hello!
There are a lot of people here with bad table manners, using a water glass for wine is the tell tale sign that they ain't as posh as they would have you believe.
Mrs Cru C Fix has a floppy arm as a result of radiotherapy, very sad but it happens. She has a most unfortunate manner and; as I pointed out to her, I don't mind helping out but I'm not there to cut her meat, carry her bags or fetch her drinks from the bar. If she needed a carer then she should have bought one with her.
First pain in the arse sorted. Last night I met some very nice people and we sat drinking gin and tonics into the early hours. Cheap as chips here and they just throw the gin over ice, no optic measures here. Bit delicate this morn.
I have decided, after several run-ins, that it's far better to mix alcohol

with prescribed hardcore drugs to help dilute the crocks on the coach.
If you can't beat 'em join 'em.
I asked Mrs Incontinence how Virgil was today. She claims she doesn't know who I am talking about and she denies having a humpy toy. On a mission now to get photographic evidence. Need to identify what the bleeding thing is anyway. I know I have an imaginary friend but this is ridiculous.
Mike the coach driver just laughs as he walks past my seat. He feels my pain.
Yesterday late evening I needed to speak to Mrs STFU, who still hasn't BTW. I was going to subtly tell her to STFU. When I turned to talk to her, I discover she is sitting on her own. Who the eff has she been talking to all trip and who are Bert and Mark? We have been wetting ourselves. Carol and I have the same sick sense of humour, she keeps coming up to me and tapping me on the shoulder to reveal more Sec 132 stuff.
Mrs Knicker E Lastic - who comes out of the toilet tucking her vest into her large pants. We couldn't walk where we were screaming. She also has a beard which attracts and draws my eye.
Off shopping and skiing now. SFFUL. Need BB as a matter of urgency and waterproof mascara.

02/10/13 near Andorra, Teruel. – Us ex Avon and Somersetters are in the kack. Carol has just shut Mrs Cru C Fix's arm in the door. That would be her floppy arm. Carol thought Mrs C had followed through the door and didn't look back. Unfortunately her good arm has lost muscle power due to lifting 25kg cases on and off of the airport travelators. Yeah rite. Course me and Carol are helpless and can do nothing to aid her plight. Mrs C had decided she was gonna spend the stay in Andorra speaking Spanish, obviously not understanding what the hell she was on about we just left her.
I now have BB cream and waterproof mascara. I have also been to church, lit a dozen candles and prayed hard for the quick return of my sanity or should that have been sobriety.
Carol is a bad influence and between us we have nicknames for most of the coach. Her and her hubby have also smelt wet the bed and BO.

Thank the Lord it's not just me. They have also seen Virgil. F.A.B.
I have decided I am still gonna keep my pill and gin intake up.
Have found other sane people on the coach. Hallelujah.
Lots of eye candy to keep me happy. (I wanted to say moist but thought my nephews and nieces would be disgusted so I have refrained. Viv wouldn't have.) Hugh is missing me and threatening to arrive in Barca tomoz. (Barca is short for Barcelona.) Off to lunch if I can sneak past Mrs C C Fix. Thank god for Bear Grylls. SAS approach req. SFFUL.

Mission accomplished. Virgil. Sat on the balcony.

03/10/13 near Andorra, Teruel via Mobile. - It's gonna take a bit more than BB cream today. Hangover mixed with no sleep and the fright of my life. If I have not turned grey by the end of the week I will be flabbergasted. I went to bed at 0300 ish AMT. Must have dozed off, gin induced, only to be woken by voices coming from the passage leading to the loo, shower facility and the entertaining lounge. I nearly pooed the bed. I don't easily scare but had gone to bed naked, not a picture to labour on I admit. Remember I was anticipating Hugh's imminent arrival and had even gone to bed leaving my makeup on. My night attire was in the case in the hallway where said voices were coming from. Taking my collapsible stick from my bag and assembling in the dark, I ripped a sheet from the spare bed tying it tightly around my voluptions. Brandishing said Timpsons stick I headed into the passageway and the unknown voices were louder there. Slowly I slid the sliding door open. Pitch black, apart from a glimmer from the Christmas street lights. I turned to check the room and saw a ghostly image in the full length mirror. I let out an almighty scream before realising it was an image of my good self in the mirror. I swiftly exited the room waving frantically to night security on the security monitors. Eventually someone arrived to offer aid. I couldn't speak and was oblivious to my near naked state. Room 314's door had closed shut and I was stranded until my knight in shining armour arrived. Upon investigation. Transpires. There are 24 light switches in my room and somehow, just somehow, I managed to hit the switch that plays radio channels into the bathroom. No strange men in my room just one very strange woman dressed in Romanesque style clothing brandishing a stick.

Note to self. Stop drinking gin, go to bed earlier preferably sober and wear full nite attire.

The coach drivers have delighted in telling their version of the story detailing an exaggerated chain of events to the whole coach. Har Har...

Just call me Koalemos. Mark and Bert do exist, dad and son. Mark is late 30's and constantly asks his mum, Mrs STFU who is still going on about the bleedin' cows on the mountains, if he is allowed to do things.

Remind me to tell you about bum width restrictions on board the mobile care home AKA Crock Coach. SFFU.

03/10/13 -I tell you what, it's all going on. As the week is progressing the odour on the coach is getting more and more unpleasant. I have needed to invest in air fresheners as I'm not wasting anymore perfume. Mrs Knicker E Lastic, Deaf Dot (the name she gives herself), Mrs BO and Mrs Incontinence are the worsest by far. Gradually people are moving away from them and they will eventually all end up sitting on a table together with the spitters and the whistler.
Now the whistler, whistles as he talks it's hysterical.
Initially I thought it was a duff hearing aid but I'm now of the opinion it's a false teeth impediment.
Carol has had to move tables twice to get away from Spit 'n' Chew who eat with their mouths open. She reckons she's had to change tops twice already today.
Mrs Cru C Fix has upset other guests. She is speaking to everyone in Spanish and or French, but what's funnier is they are replying in English. She told a French guy he needed to improve his accent. I nearly fell down the steps laughing so much.
Virgil hasn't been seen since yesterday lunch. Wonder if he's coming to Barca with us.
This cow fetish Mrs STFU has, I'm wondering if it's the same as the Welsh are about sheep. Although I have to say of the many Welsh friends I have (or had) not one has ever drawn my attention to them grazing in the fields. Maybe it's just an Essex thing. A conundrum.
Now then about RaffleTicketGate. Un-believe-a- ball. At the start of the trip passengers purchase raffle tickets to buy drinks with. Saves messing about with change. Most drinks cost 1-2 tickets and you buy them 20€ at a time. The raffle tickets we are issued with now are very different to the norm. They have a blue edging. This is to stop the devious among us from bringing their own raffle tickets on board. One couple had a book in every colour and were trying to sell the tickets to other coachers for half price. Ingenious I know but they have been outsmarted.
They reckon on other trips they've made a right killing. We, the ex A & S'ers think that might well be a theft of some kind. Also the free bottles of wine put out at dinnertime have been disappearing and at a rate of about 2 bottles a table. The six offenders have been dealt with this

morning. Tight fisted mothers. Wait till I tell you about CoachBogGate and the criminal damager we have amongst us. SFFUL

03/10/13 near Andorra, Teruel.
Hot off the press from Crooks and Crocks Mobile Care Home.

What a tiring day. After arriving in Barca we were given two hours to explore before our guided tour. I only got 20 yards from the top of La Ramblas before I was sucked into Deɘiqual. What a shop. Muchos euros later I set off to check out Gaudi's work. Quite frankly I wish I hadn't bothered. Fortunately the trees, which are in abundance, conceal much of the objet d'art. My God that guy was taking some serious hardcore meds when he thought that one up. What was he on when he built that monstrous monstrosity? I'm telling you if some of the visions I had ever came out of the ground, I'd be sectioned for sure. Likely the reason he threw himself under a tram. Must investigate. It's like an octopuses tentacles that have rigor and leprosy. Vile and it still ain't likely to be

finished until 2026. See I was listening to my tour guide. Talking of stiffs the three at the back of the coach were a bit lively today. Must remember to tell Mike to hide the jump leads. Far too raucous for my liking especially after the night I had.
Spain have certainly had their share of loopers. Salvador Dali, Gawdy Gaudi, Miro, Picasso.
Although out of the four I favour Picasso, my fave painting in the whole wide world being L'Etriente. Don't look it up on Google if you are in work it's a bit racey.
Hugh and I posed for a likeness as a wedding gift to each other earlier this year. We were gonna put hinged flaps over the revealing bits to protect our modesty but as the painting is headless naked torsos and legs only, no-one would ever know it was us.
Oh I have to make a huge apology too. Earlier I told you about Deaf Dot. Faux pas of the day. Well once everyone had regained their composure and stopped laughing it was made apparent that I had in fact misheard what Dot had said. She had been introducing herself and her husband to the table. However at the time said husband was not there. It's ok this is not another imaginary friend, he does exist. What she had in fact said was Seth and Dot and not Deaf Dot! I have apologised to Dot who fortunately for me has a sense of humour and all is well.
I must also apologise for the lack of photos but today the trees got in the way. And up until five mins ago I didn't know how to close down me open apps on this ISSA 007 thingy download and the battery kept dying. It's just a case of press twice and flick up. Should have known that. Duh!
The CoachBogGate incident before I forget. When travelling place to place we stop every 2 and a half hours for the loos and a stretch. Normally it's a pay and pee and costs 50 cents. Well this tight mob won't pay and so when they think we are getting close to stopping there is a mad rush for the loo on board our coach. Now I sit opposite the bear pit down to the loo so while queuing people think they can sit in the spare seat next to me and eat my sweets. Well think again. I am not having those smelly bums on my seat. I'm already running low on Flash wipes and can't be coping with wet the bed. So we have a system. One of the drivers texts me 15 mins before eta at stop off. I assume the

position, plug my headphones in and make like I'm asleep. Works a treat. However you can imagine my horror when this very morn Mike suggested we all move up the coach to plug the gaps. There were only 15 out of the 28 that wanted to go to Barca. It don't take a lot to work out where I would have been sitting and that's without me even telling you. Not a chance.

You have to realise what I am going through. These men are incapable of flicking dick or stopping the drop. There is stainage all down the front of their trousers. Fly zipper area. Boys, don't wear beige trousers if you can't adhere to trap etiquette or droplets, wear tenor pads. I can't stand it. Every time they come out of the loo I have to force myself not to check their nethers. The women are far easier they just walk out pulling up their drawers as they go. It's all so very detasteful.

If this coach gets diverted to Switzerland I would not be surprised.

04/10/13 near Andorra, Teruel. - I have some very devastating news to impart. For those among us that may be easily shocked and distressed, do not read further.

I know you will, you just can't help yourselves can you? Be warned this is gruesome.

It would appear that during the night/early hours security were called to a distressed female in Room 666. You and I know that room is occupied by Mrs Incontinence. I can confirm sometime between 2300 and 0430 someone broke into the room and stole Virgil. F.A.B.

A thorough search was made of the hotel and outer perimeter. Nothing. We were, we being Crooks, Crocks, Caff and Carol, woken early by unexpected alarm calls and frantic door knocking in order that we could

assist in the search. Of course I was the last to see Virgil on the balcony and prime suspect. We are still awaiting CCTV footage to prove I was with Hugh, entertaining in my lounge. After a three hour search we found Virgil in a very bad state of repair. He was in fact binable.
With as much sympathy and decorum as I could muster (which wasn't easy) Virgil was reunited with Mrs Inc. (courtesy of the Sainsbury carrier bag I used for me dirty nicks.)
A vigil will be held for Virgil later today at one or other of the four American Embassies; Maccy D's, Burger King, KFC, or Pizza Hut all of which are situated directly across the road from the hotel. A ticky box form has been provided for people to make their preference.
Any information leading to the detention of the culprit is welcomed.
My theory is Mrs Inc had an invited visitor who, following a row, nicked Virgil upon leaving.
I think it was the Whistler.
Also I would prefer it if Carol stopped telling everyone what a brilliant sewer I am (that's sew er and not sue er.)She may well have won an assortment of my beautifully hand crafted Xmas cards in a Comms raffle but that hardly qualifies me to deal with rabbit innards, especially as we don't know where Virgil has been or what his purpose was before he was abducted do we? There are no amount of Flash wipes that will make me stitch his wounds either.
Everyone has been forced to hand over the sewing kits nicked from the rooms so Mrs Inc can make a start on repairing Virgil later today.
Carol and I have decided to have a whip-round so we can purchase a new toy to tide Mrs Inc over till Virgil is up and hopping again. It's gonna take a while for his ears to dry out me finx.
Pictures have been provided but are not for scaredee cats.

05/10/13 near Andorra, Teruel via Mobile. - I have been a very, very naughty girl.
Mrs Cru C Fix. Picture the scene. A very thin, short haired, version of Olive from Off The Buses. Reckons she's has been chatted up by three men in their 30's on the smoking verandah. One, who has three mistresses, has allegedly written her a note. We asked her what the note said and although being able to speak Spanish she could not answer the question. Soo in my bestest handwriting, on hotel paper, I have written her a love note. For purposes of said note I am Georgio Rodriquez Alexandro the third. I am of course tall, dark and handsome. I have invited her to attend a certain room number for Champagne and canapés later this night. The room number given is that of the coach drivers who thought it very bloody funny to order me pork cheeks at dinner last eve. Basically a ball of wobbly fat. Wrong person to mess with boys. Said note has been translated into Spanish using Google and then checked by the onside barman for discrepancies. SFUL.

05/10/13 near Suances, Cantabria, Spain via Mobile.
God I'm so good at this plotting. Stealth like I'd say. Thank goodness for Bear Grylls, the SAS training has paid off. Unfortunately I needed to involve more people than I had originally wanted to. But I have to say it was necessary. I needed people to go on a recce to find out room numbers for Mrs Cru C Fix and them two bad boyz. They would have gotten suspicious if I'd been caught on their floor.
I used the other sane ones. There are only seven of us in total. Of the seven, three of us have impediments and I was a tad worried the mission would have to be aborted. Anyway after a worrying few hours I am pleased to announce it was game on.
The note was delivered prior to supper by hand, courtesy of the porter. We had a failed attempt earlier when the note wouldn't slide under the door. The well written note, almost poetic when read, invited Mrs C to attend the third floor at 2130 hrs. The Spanish eat later and so under advisement we thought this was the best time to go for. Plus after an 11 hour drive we knew the boyz would be tired and in bed. It was a bit touch and go at times especially when Mrs Stoop offered them a beer

and they accepted. Plan was almost foiled.
With a few delay tactics and Carols quick thinking. Mrs C was told it was good to be late and not to seem over keen.
I have to say Mrs C was done up to the nines. Glittery top and tight fitting skirt. She had only told certain people about the invite and I wasn't one of them so I had to remain quiet. Difficult!
I was wetting myself. Put me in mind of when we crushed up Sennacots and put them in my vile boss's coffee. Long drive to North Devon. We laughed for days.
The Stealthlike Seven couldn't use the lift to follow her up to the third floor so I had to give myself a head start. Climbing 6 flights of stairs when you can't stop laughing, are drunk and dying to use the loo is not a good combination. John and Derek had decent cameras and were hoping to try and catch the event on camera. All systems go.
Talking of Thunderbirds. Virgil is in the hold of the coach laying in a state. Vernon is settling in nicely. But as you can see from earlier photos he has already suffered a broken leg at the hands of Mrs Incontinence.

06/10/13 via Mobile. - Major majors. Halsey and Bennett up for an award without doubt. Saved a life. SFU.

06/10/13 near Comillas, Cantabria, Spain via Mobile. - Will update you regarding the Stealth Sevens antics later.
Suffice it to say mission ??????? You will have to wait.
Major incident at Hotel Suances and reasons not to take the piss are listed below.
Awaiting our welcome drink in the salon most of us are in the bar.

Unbeknown to Halsey and Bennett, Duff Dave has slid off his seat onto the floor. We then witness Mrs Cru C Fix asking him a series of questions that even I wouldn't know the answer to! It transpires he has type two diabetes (sounds familiar.) I have sweets in my bag and bomb over to help, with Halsey hot on me heels, before he dies from verbal interrogation.

Now Duff Dave had not endeared himself to many of us. He had a bad habit of taking his false teeth out, spitting on them and polishing them with his finger. This occurred at the dinner table and was repulsive. He was also very unkind to his wife Mrs Knicker E Lastic.

This couple are perhaps not the full ticket and I asked Mrs K if she had a pricky tester kit or some glucose tablets for him. I wasn't surprised it was a negative to both questions. Anyway he seemed to recover slightly and with coach drivers alerted he was helped into the salon with the hotel manager skipping alongside, fanning him with a menu. Hysterical. It gets worserer.

Mrs Cru C Fix, Incontinence and Big Bertha (she's scarier than I am) were all having their photo taken by Mike the coach driver. Halsey and I are doing rude things behind them, like you do. The waitress is handing out hors d'oeuvres and sangria and we see Duff Dave list to the side. Halsey remarks should he be that colour and I tell you it was corpse like. In one swift movement I nick Halsey's orange juice and bomb over. I'm convinced he has had a stroke but manage to get him to drink juice just in case he's gone hypo. An ambulance is called and the skippity manager is back improvising with the menu again. Obviously after a good work report. Duff Dave gradually starts to converse but looks very poorly. 2 paramedics arrive and are of the belief he has had a stroke. Halsey and I are commended for our quick thinking, see that bloody advert works you know, and Duff Dave with wife and 2 drivers is carted off to hospital in Santander. It gets worserer.

Mrs K and the two drivers return from hospital. Duff Dave is in the cardiac wing being monitored.

Halsey spots Mrs Cru C Fix sat with the Mrs K writing down sentences in Spanish so she can ring the hospital to find out how Duff Dave is. Although Mrs Cru C Fix can allegedly speak the lingo she is not happy to call on behalf of Mrs K as she won't be able to see the lips of the person she is speaking to and they would speak far too fast. Now one would assume if you ask a question in Spanish you will get a reply in Spanish. Mrs K can hardly string a sentence together. Halsey to the rescue, dispenses with the question sheet makes a phone call to the hospital and puts a smile back on Mrs K's face. Duff Dave has had a good night. In fact Mrs K is so happy she is leaving; NO, correction, abandoning her hubby in a strange country in what is primarily a Spanish speaking hospital while she comes on the day trip and guess who's left sorting the insurance. Halsey delegated and that would be Moi.

06/10/13 near Suances, Cantabria, Spain via Mobile. - What a day I've had. Managed a bit of sightseeing in between the dramas, of which there were many.
Last night's little jolly was the funniest thing I think I have ever witnessed. I had to change me nicks and have had to resort to me puffers to help me breathe.
At approx 2145 last eve dug in at a well thought out OP concealed on the fire exit staircase, which I have to say couldn't have been better placed as in almost opposite the targets room. Four of the seven stealthers watched through the wired glass window as the principal approached. The others had followed up in the lift armed with cameras. I had to gag myself to stop laughing which almost became a bit of a DIY Dignatas, 'cos I rammed too much blouse material into me gob (I was wearing a floaty number, one that Hugh favours. Provocative but not slutty mutty.)
Anyway, as I was saying, Mrs Cru C Fix, the principal, approaches the target's room with her top glistening in the hallway lights and reeking of eau de toilet. She checks the room number on the note and taps on the door. Nothing. She taps again. Nothing. Harder this time with the palm of her good hand. Nothing. So then she decides to use the protective plastic casing she wears on her floppy arm. She hit the door so hard I thought it was gonna cave in. By this time I am helpless, we are beyond help. The door is answered by both drivers who think some disaster has occurred. Mrs C shows the boyz the note. They can't read Spanish so

haven't gotta clue what it says. They were absolutely fuming, the air was blue. We beat a hasty retreat and made for the bar, I have never run so fast in my life. Mrs C is convinced Georgio Rodriguez Alexandro wrote down the wrong room number. She does not believe it was a wind up. Despite her 72 years men still hit on her and this type of thing is a normal occurrence. She always gets love notes!

Anyway today she has been stressed, apparently it was the Duff Dave incident and an altercation between our coach driver and a Range Rover driver that is the cause. She claimed she went to the beach to empty her head and clear her brain. Why it took two hours I will never know.

The coach drivers are convinced I was responsible for them being awoken from their slumbers. Don't know why. Har har.

Duff Dave was released from hospital late this afternoon. The diagnosis; a hypoglycaemic attack and a transient episode. The amount of alcohol he has consumed he'll be readmitted if he's not careful. His wife Mrs Knicker E Lastic was so delighted to see him she left her teeth in the hotel room and was unable to eat her meal. The other crocks on the coach call them Roy and Hayley Cropper off of Corrie.

Big Bertha caused a row at dinner. She has to have black pepper on everything. There is only one pot of pepper in the whole restaurant, which is disguised in a salt cellar.

Carol also likes pepper, goes in search of said pot and an argument takes place about how Carol knew that she (she being Bertha) had the pepper. Hello, it's pepper. Soo, I've nicked the bloody stuff. Lifted it en route out of the restaurant. Carol does know. Bertha doesnt! Har har.

07/10/13 via Mobile. - Mrs Cru C Fix has been reading out the love note to all and sundry. The contents however are not what I writted. It's definitely my disguised handwriting but I most certainly didn't write what she is telling everyone. The stealth seven are still managing to act the innocent and, despite the knowing looks from the two drivers, we are still undiscovered. When she asked reception what room Mr Alexandro was staying in Manuel, the Spanish born porter who doesn't understand a word of Spanish, told her he had left. Please don't tell me there was actually a Mr Alexandro in the house. Phew, close call.

Carol is convinced the reason for everyone dropping like flies is because I asked if we could pre book 21 places at the famous graveyard we visited. Mmmmm debateable.
It is evident that there are a high number of people on board who have issues of the mind. Sometimes there is just no helping them. I buy some glucose sweets for Duff Dave in the event he is taken ill again and I entrust said packet to his wife Mrs Knicker E Lastic. After all Halsey and I don't wanna be performing first aid all holiday do we? Prior to boarding the coach today I check to see if she has the emergency supply. '"No I ate them when I hadn't had anything to eat" Aaarrrgggghhhh!
Today's thought: Donde esta la pimienta? (Where is the pepper?)

Off to Picos De Europa BASE jumping and white water rafting!

07/10/13 Near Suances, Cantabria, Spain via Mobile. -Wot no pepper?

08/10/13
Santander today.

08/10/13
Where we sat all those years ago. Elaine Elliott-Reynolds

08/10/13 via Mobile.
Apparently I am gonna be prosecuted for assault. Bring it on Pepper Pig with the fat lip! I think you'll find there were no witnesses.

08/10/13 Near Suances, Cantabria, Spain via Mobile.

Okay, for the record, I am always on my best behaviour. I have young nieces and nephews that are of an impressionable age and bad behaviour would be most unacceptable. This holiday one friend has called me outrageous, well that might well be true but I prefer mischievous. Over the last few days Big Bertha and Mrs Cru C Fix have been winding everyone up trying to outdo each other, a bit of a fight for supremacy hence all the practical jokes. Today Big Bertha aka Pepper Pig as she is now known, and not named by me I hasten to add, verbally attacked the coach driver. She wanted him to drive the coach 50 metres up a slope like the French driver did for his passengers. Apparently she has a bad knee. The way she spoke to him was totally unacceptable. Extremely abrasive and in a vile and aggressive manner. I was shocked and in response merely stated that is was a pity her disability did not affect her tongue. She is one of those who speaks loudly, boasts about her life and believes she is better than anyone else. We play grenades on the coach and pretend to throw them on to her and Mrs C's seats. Even 88 year old Dot has had enuff. Well she came at me like a wild woman from a country yet to be discovered!

Boyz you would have been proud of me. I did not move a muscle, after all I'm used to being charged at by elephants so that stood me in good stead. She was right in my face demanding to know what I meant (not a wise move Murray) so I imparted the information she required. I then walked the 50 yards down the ramp to where my chariot awaited with 26 others in tow dying to know what had occurred.
On the coach to Santander a story is being told about a woman who on a previous trip had upset the drivers. Everyday at breakfast this woman would be the last to leave the breakfast room and this was so she could load a bag up with food unseen. One particular morning, after taking more abuse than they should, they merely pointed out to the operator of ticky sheet at the door (one who ticks off room numbers) that it may be an idea to check said woman's bag. Which was done by the manager. Now I knew this was a subtle warning to Pepper Pig because, like the drivers, I too had observated the theft of food on a grand scale. So again I merely shouted out they should check the bag of the woman sat in

front of Dot (that being Pepper Pig) and they would get a bit of a shock. Well it went rapidly downhill from there and she followed me into the cathedral for another attempt at one of her venomous attacks (I carry anti-venom in case I bite my tongue so covered there.) Anyway, I managed to deflect her spit from my designer outfit and moved away to enjoy an al fresco lunch with a spot of people watching. A little while later several Gardi men, damn good lookers too, joined me on the terrace upping my street cred if I'm honest. I managed to make them feel welcome, and I think relaxed, using one of my many seduction techniques. She had told them I needed removing from the square and that I didn't wear a seat belt on the coach. To cut a long story short no one in the cathedral had witnessed the alleged fracas she claimed occurred and as you don't need to wear seat belts sat outside a café (yet) all is well and the Worle One remains free and without criminal record. She is lucky she didn't end up in the sealed crypt. I have taken to the gin bottle which is currently being provided FOC by my fellow coach travellers. All's well. Later we are going on a pepper pot hunt. I've hidden it somewhere in the hotel. Bottle for the winner. Something to keep our spirits up!

08/10/13

Who did it? Ms Scarlet or Col Mustard?

09/10/13

Off to San Sebastian today, will update later as need full charge to take photos.

09/10/13
Emotional day today. Old memories mixed with the new! — at Saint Sebastien, Espagne.

09/10/13 Near Ciboure, Aquitaine, France via Mobile.
Halsey has purchased a bloody tape measure. Apparently if you travel on a coach holiday your arse cannot be any bigger than 17.71 cm but I think that should be inches. Don't you? She wants me to pose in a group photo with Mike the driver measuring me ass.

Now I know my derrière ain't small but it's not the biggest on board. I mean if you take a look at Pepper Pig's one slap and you could ride the ripples. And I have to say mine does carry a warning. 'Operator will need both hands' !

Anyway Hugh loves me the way I am and after a few sessions of chemo I'll be back down to a size 12 in next to no time.

No one found the pepper pot. I left a note inside so anyone finding it will think it's a geocache or more likely someone's ashes.

Mrs Cru C Fix has a migraine and is looking for sympathy, will let you know if we locate her!

Duff Dave fell over in the shower and broke the toilet seat. He also has pins and needles in his arm. Worrying.

Pepper asked Dot if it was me that hid the pepper. Dot acted disgusted that she could even think such a thing.

11/10/13 Near Calais-Nord, Nord-Pas-de-Calais, France via Mobile.

I have never felt so humiliated in my life. I have had my luggage searched and all my 'ready for laundry' larges spread out over a counter for all and sundry to see because ... it transpires I am travelling with four prolific smugglers. Who were all over the limit with ciggies. Causing a 4 hour delay at the port. Well did those people have some tongue sandwich from me? Twats! Thinking a wheelbarrow type walking frame was gonna put customs off the scent. I don't fink so...They had been told if they came out of the UK within a year and purchased tobacco they'd be in the kack. I tell you the DWP would have a field day. They are all on benefits. I tell you I thought I was street wise, compared to most of this lot I could pass off as royalty.
This holiday is likely the worserest I have been on thus far. Fortunately some of the people on board were out for a good laugh and we made the best of a bad job.
I have never met such dirty, unkempt, stenchy, devious, attention seeking, vile and ill mannered Herberts in my life.
I will be hitting M&S/Waitrose with a vengeance. I must be at least 2 stone lighter which has done nothing to help the fear of anorexia I have.
I don't need palliative care, I need palate care - and fast.
Hugh has been alerted.

10

ST IVES

15/03/14

Good morning.

Alighting from my pit at 0545 was not easy this morning. My last holiday was 6 months ago and it is apparent I need more practice getting up early.

I was ready by 0715 and managed to sink a few pirate ships at paradise cove before the arrival of our designated driver Amazonian Russell.

Imagine my shock when both Amazonians arrived 5 mins early. First for Ridgers! SFFU. I have already been referred to as heavy baggage! The St Ives express is due to arrive at 1130 am.

15/03/14 Here! Just checking in, view from hotel bar...

15/03/14 Fab day at St Ives...

15/03/14 Have enjoyed a most fabulous dinner at the Sea Grass restaurant to celebrate Ridgers birthday.
Finished up at the Sloop Inn.
The one man entertainment was all a bit of a dirge. (To be honest you couldn't even play his tunes at me funeral and get away with it. So bleedin' depressing.) I mean c'mon, songs with lyrics like my girlfriend left me for another man leaving me with six kids, and her new partner has taken Jeremy's advice and puts something on it is hardly Saturday night entertainment is it?
Anyway I have been abandoned by the two Amazonians who are heading off to Foreskin Street or was that Fore Street to a club for the under fifty sixes.
After 2 bottles of Prosecco Rosé and several pints of Bud I decided to head for home. After all I am only six weeks clear of chemo and don't wanna overdo it. I have been up since early morn and have done well to last this long.
Having a cheeky Bud in the hotel bar with two Adonis's that Viv is more than capable of dealing with. — With Vivvy Anne Le Fey at Chy An Albany Hotel.

15/03/14 Red sky at night...

16/03/14 Fabulous day. Walked along the coastal path to Carbis Bay. Followed a couple of aged Yanks off track who led us up a very precarious path to the train tracks. Bloody idiots. (I can say that as my brother is aged and resides in the US. He's a lawyer.)
Lunch at the Cornish Inn.
Pudding at Pels.
Shopping in Boots, cheap Durex at the mo. Three for two. Pre bed drinks at the Sloop.
If them Amazonians tell me once more they are too young to remember, they are going in the drink... Been educating them not to look at the flashy cars and to pretend they are oblivious. Looking is just what the male drivers with small willies want them to do!

17/03/14 The Torrey Canyon — at Porthmeor Beach.

11

SCOTLAND

21/03/14 near Cam.
A bit excitative today. I'm off on a traincation to Edinburgh Old Town for a six day stay to celebrate my birthday.
I am going by train using the pre booked tickets I ordered on line at a substantially reduced rate utilising my disabled railcard. Get me!
I am taking my imaginary friend Hugh with me purely because it's cheaper than hiring an escort. Needs must and all that. And I do need someone to carry me bags.
I have chosen the quiet carriage, facing forward and close to the luggage rack. Seat 5, carriage F.
I have decided to spend my time away to go in search of Gerard Butler but likely I will end up with Carrick Fergis whoever he might be.
I have three changes of train and am currently on the 2nd heading for Birmingham New Street.
The journey from WSM was eventful. One poor chap started his journey reading a copy of some French newspaper 'Le Metro'. It was hard to tell if he fell asleep through boredom or was in fact dead. I decided it was far too early into my holiday to be administering first aid so I left him. He is now the problem of the Welsh as he's heading for Cardiff Central... He was due to alight the train at Temple Meads...
Another couple were delighting in having foiled their respective partners, heading off to London for a dirty weekend. Smog and all that... I wanted to comment that they hadn't yet gotten away with it. I refrained. The female spent the whole 30 minute journey rubbing illicit partner's inner thigh. There was no sock available to hand that would cover the bulge in his trousers. I was most upset giving Hugh ideas...
My Scottish friends will be delighted that I have been learning Scotch all week. I did however have a head start as I am able to sing in Scotch. Being a huge fan of the Bay City Rollers, Paolo Nutini, Texas, Deacon Blue, McFly, Average White Band and Susan Boyle to name but a few.
SFFUL.

21/03/14 Just managed to catch my connecting train with seconds to spare. I get off the cross country train at Birmingham which arrived 10 minutes late and then have to leg it to platform 6 and a half to catch the

Virgin train. (Very apt.) Stupidity of it all, the cross country train was going to the same bloody place. I will be writing to Mr or Mrs Great Western Railway to point out a problem with the logistics dept.
I managed to cause major problems on the Virgin train. Uprooting an elderly couple from their seats, settling myself down, refusing their offer to move from the window seat before realising I'm sat in the wrong bloody seat. The numbering sequence on the chairs is all to cock. I will be addressing this with Virgin upon my return home. Most embarrassing.
The journey was pleasant and from Lancaster on the scenery is amazing. Very beautiful. There is also some seaside resort which looked beautiful. Need to check me atlas to find out which sea it is.
The elderly couple seemed to know where everyone got on the train and didn't shut up until they got off at Warrington. A pain really, especially as we were seated in the quiet carriage.
The sayings they were coming out with. WTF does 'there is enough blue sky to make a sailors trousers' mean?
My hotel is situated minutes away from the Haymarket and, despite falling over on the tram tracks and breaking a wheel on my suitcase, I arrived safely. My room is adequate and clean and so as not to disappoint me has no curtain over the loo window again. I have to leave the light off to avoid my ass being displayed to the numerous commuters and also my bod as I step from the shower...
The staff are friendly and after a few pints of Tennants I settled in.
My evening was spent at La Bruschetta, a fabulous Italian restaurant. The maitre d' is putting the Prosecco on ice for my birthday meal tonight. A treat from Hugh... (And not the only one may I say!) SFFUL.

With Hugh — at La Bruschetta.

21/03/14 I have been assigned a task by Blo aka Becky Ozzy Lewis; should I choose to accept the mission (and I have) it is to discover what Scotsmen wear under their kilts. SFFU. I am on the case...

22/03/14 On a mission... — at Royal Mile.

23/03/14 near Dalry.

Faux pas of the day, asking a blind person if I was on the right road for the castle. Absolutely mortified. The dog should have been the giveaway in his fluorescent jacket. Felt pretty bad at my stupidity all day.

It cost £16 entrance fee to get into the castle; which I have to say, once inside the castle walls, was a bit too perfect and lacked atmosphere. I didn't get any sense of history. The views from the battlements were however spectacular.

Princes Street Gardens are glorious with an abundance of Spring flowers in bloom, as well as some spectacular gnarly old trees.

The Royal Mile in the old town had beautiful buildings and there is a lot to grab your interest. (Men in kilts.)

Flooded the bathroom last night - and I mean majorly flooded. I left the shower on to heat up the bathroom; it's so bloody cold in my room. Water wasn't draining away. Oops. The room had only just been renovated, although I must say it's hard to tell and is very basic.

The staff are wonderful and very friendly and make up for the old fashioned digs.

Had a birthday meal at La Bruschetta, absolutely divine.

Off to the underground city today and hopefully an open top bus ride.

Not really much to report regarding other hotel guests. I appear to be the only one here...
SFFU.

23/03/14 near Dalry.
Oot 'n' aboot.

23/03/14 Mary Kings Close checked out and no kilts...

Tour bus checked out. No kilts...

23/03/14 Love playing what's your story?
Quote of the night. 'Sometimes all a woman has to hold onto is being a bitch'.

24/03/14 near Dalry.
What an eventful day yesterday was.
Decided I would use the bus as my knees were killing me and the attractions are all at the opposite end of Princes Street from the hotel.
Took the city tour bus, driver opened the door squashing and trapping my fingers.
Visited Mary Kings Close, a series of underground streets. Convinced I saw a chair move.
On the bus back to the hotel a Quasimodo 30 stone lookalike fell on me squashing my already swollen knees. Twat!
Arrived back at the digs, seeking alcohol for medicinal purposes in the bar. There was 1 other person there who spent the three hours chatting to me non-stop. Couldn't understand a bloody word he said. He attends the hotel bar daily, has been a regular for 26 years and is a customer who is allowed to keep his own tab. (There's a recipe for disaster.) He is allowed to serve himself and must've drunk about 6 double Bacardis in the space of an hour. When the barman came on duty at six he could see by my face that I was more than pissed off with this guy. I was told the likely reason I couldn't understand him was because he was drunk. Apparently he has a wife and a girlfriend... God knows what the attraction is.

Later that evening I met up with a lady who was holidaying from Connecticut, someone who enjoys a drink like I do. Got evicted from the bar...

Anyway I had a date with Gerard Butler at 0015 on BBC1 so
I wasn't too upset.
The kilt challenge is going well. Evidence will be posted on Weds.

24/03/14 Another fab day...

25/03/14 near Dalry.

Well it appears today I am resting up - having developed man flu with a sore throat thrown in, just as an added bonus. My knees have also given up the ghost too...

It is imperative that I recover by 1900 hrs. as I have a table booked at La Bruschetta. I also think I have a date. I am of the opinion it was more taken for granted on his part, but when I replayed what he'd said in my mind I think I agreed to meet him. Obviously delirium bought on by the flu.

I appear to be getting more Scotch like daily. (Must be all the Tennents I am drinking!) My ticket for the city tour bus was valid for 24 hours. With only half an hour to spare I managed to get two uses out of it.

There was a short wait for said bus and I believed I was stood waiting at the bus stop alone. That was until the bus arrived. This man appears

from nowhere and accuses me of pushing in. Hello. There was no one else there. He was extremely abusive and it was pointless arguing with him.
Anyway more on me date. Having lost my drinking partner Erin, who was well on her way home to Connecticut, I headed to the bar believing that I would likely be in the company of Bacardi George (A Dave Alan lookalike with all digits accounted for.) How wrong was I. George had fallen out of the bar earlier and in his place was a lone book reading male whose name I can't remember. We get chatting; he buys me a drink, I buy one back. This continues until I decide it's time to head to bed. And yes in case you are wondering I went alone. As I left he said 'so I'll see you tomorrow then'... Oooooh errrrr!
He is 50 years old and works as a logistics manager for Asda. Working in the car park in the trolley department...
I will keep you posted on assumed date.
The 'what's under a Scotsman's kilt' challenge is going well and the dossier containing my evidence will be released tomorrow. SFFUL.

25/03/14 Last night in Scotland. Has to be La Bruschetta. — With Vivvy Anne Le Fey at La Bruschetta.

26/03/14 near Dalry.

After resting up all day and dosing myself with man flu medication I must say I feel better. Also my knees are less painful.

Had a very lovely 'last supper' at La Bruschetta. Possibly the nicest food I have ever eaten.

I was a little nervous about going back to the hotel to meet my date and decided to prolong my stay at the restaurant using my new BFF Mr Prosecco.

Anyway, transpires I needn't have worried because Mr Associated Dairies was not there at agreed RV...

BTW for all you youngsters Associated Dairies is Asda and was its former name. Almost puts it up there with Waitrose don't you think? Just trying to think which dairy owned Tesco but the name escapes me right now.

I did not ask the hotel staff if he had already been in and assumed he was off getting 'trollied' elsewhere. Lol!

Phew, sigh of relief. Didn't wanna upset Hugh. He's been such a love.

Anyway my reports from Scotland are coming to an end. All I need to do is to compile my report for BLO relating to the mission I was assigned. Watch this space for full report later.

26/03/14 near Hemsworth.

What's up Jock?

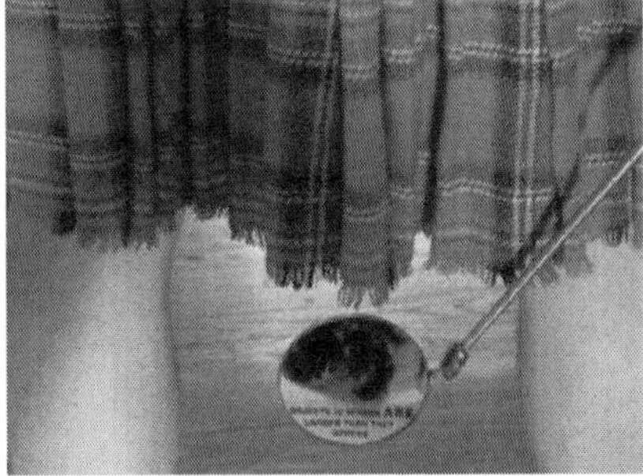

12

TINTAGEL

05/04/14 We have arrived.

My imaginary friend Hugh and my good self arrived in Tintagel early pm. Our journey was without incident. Just the normal bickering that goes on between a man and woman, you know what I mean!
Room is adequate and clean and although our room looks out over the car park you'll be pleased to know my ass won't. Fortunately for the holiday makers the en suite is without a window.
Have been shopping and bought several trinkets in a very unusual shop. The owner is a witch and has the longest nails I have ever seen. I came out reeking of Patchouli oil and now I keep getting strange looks from passers by. I stink.
Been on a recce down to the castle and have decided to attempt the ascent on the morrow. It's stunning and I've gotta give it a go.
We are currently sat outside the pub drinking and where 90 million bikers have just arrived. The bikers are members of the Great Western Chapter. Our peace has been shattered by thousands of Harleys. Having been a bit of a biker bird in my youth I got all nostalgic. Although I have to say I still favour Yamaha and Kawasaki. They were easier to ride around the island... (I won't tell them that. Some of them look a bit mean and grizzly.) They are all drinking in our digs, think it's gonna be a bit lively.
Hugh has just rushed up to the room to put his leathers on. (The

Weston Chapter just ain't got the same ring to it!) I'm hoping those 'Chopper' books I read 40 odd years back weren't true stories.
SFFU – with Vivvy Anne Le Fey at Tintagel Castle.

05/04/14 near Tintagel.
Feet on a seat!

Ride, ride, ride hitchin a ride or She loves you yeah, yeah, yeah?

05/04/14 near Tintagel.
Worrying!

With Vivvy Anne Le Fey at Tintagel Castle.
05/04/14 at 19:49 Tintagel.
The arrival of the Western Chapter caused quite a stir. I'd say 95% of them were over 50. They sat quietly, drinking their coffees and Colas, discussing hip and knee replacements. Transpires it was a loo break before they headed off to Bodmin. Perfect gents.
As you know we are here to celebrate Viv's birthday, after all this is where she hails from... So today we have spent doing what Vivvy Anne Le Fey wanted to do. She is so at home here.
I am proud to say I made it up to Tintagel Castle. The early start paid off and I didn't get in the way of any other mountaineers. It was comforting to see people who were totally unimpedimented struggle to climb the steps. I have a fear of heights and the steps are as close to the cliff edge as they can get. Hugh felt I ought to be used to it. He was referring to the heady heights he takes me too. Hardly the same. He likened the state of the wooden handrail to his back. Claims I left my nail marks permanently ingrained in the wood.
The view at the top was breathtaking. Had it not been for the Sahara Smog I'm sure my photos would be much better. (Hugh will be writing to the African Nations Desert patrol) if they need to dump sand I'm sure there are more needy locations!
It was extremely windy at the top and I feared at times I'd be blown off

the cliff. Hugh said he wouldn't have minded...
I was quite concerned about the size of the rabbit poo that littered the castle. Helluva lot of constipated bunnies I'd say. Later we learnt there are 27 sheep up there. Duh!!! Saved calling the vet.
The fog caused quite a stir at lunchtime, when through the mist seemingly heading directly for us was what looked like a pirate ship. As it got near all became clear. 'Twas our very own Royal Navy, patrolling the shoreline I was exploring.
After a cream tea après noon, we climbed the steps on the other side of the castle which took us to Glebe cliffs and St Materianas Church. I literally fell into the church despite having read the 'mind the step' notice, but not realising the minute you opened the door you were on them. The church lacked natural daylight and we couldn't find a light switch. Needless to say I had to light a candle for everyone I knew so we could bleedin' see our way round. They are now clean out of both tea lights and votives. Getting out of the church posed a bigger problem. Guess who got locked in. Yes you got it, me... I went into a blind panic. Had to use me puffer. Earlier I had found a sign in the cemetery that said 'Cornwall's living churchyards'. Fortunately some nice man heard my screams and let me out. I was in the process of calling the police but luckily my phone had no signal. If I had hair it would have turned grey.
The graveyard has numerous snazzy grave plots. If anyone is stuck for ideas well worth a visit.
Now back at the pub trying to rest my crocked knee ready for the cliff top walk to Boscastle tomorrow to celebrate Viv's birthday.
SFFU.

06/04/14 near Tintagel.

Tintagel to Boscastle.

The three of us set off on foot bright and early, our destination Boscastle for Sunday Lunch. A three mile walk. Well that's if 10 o'clock is early! We were waiting for Viv again who had the hangover from hell. Christ she can sink more pints than I do pirate ships in me Paradise Cove game!

I had decided that despite my crocked knee and joints (not the joints I roll BTW, great source of pain relief, although not recommended if one is gonna be stood on the edge of a cliff-top) I had to make an effort for Viv's birthday. This chemo stuff plays havoc with yer tendons, although age, wear 'n' tear and the fact I have Mulligan coursing through me veins doesn't help. The Mulligan clan have always suffered with dodgy knees. I was gonna wear me knee brace, but I came over all unnecessary when just the thought reminded me of someone from my past. That idea was discarded in an instant and relying totally on my Timpson's floral stick we set out. Let me tell you, have I become the mistress of the stick or wat? Although I must be honest, upon my return home I will be investing in a climbers pick and spiked walking stick - which can always double up as a weapon to ward off would be attackers. A very practical accessory. An every girl must have...

I was in considerable pain before we left the digs. I had brought my 4 x mirror with me this trip and whilst applying my slap noticed an abundance of new growth in my nasal cavity. Perhaps it wasn't such a good idea to use Hugh's nose trimmy thing after a heavy sesh the night before. I have sustained quite a severe injury and look as though I have been on Coke all weekend. My septum is severely damaged, and no amount of BB Cream is gonna cover it...

Anyway off we trotted, spirits high. The young guy at the pub pointed us in the right direction and assured us it would take, in total, about an hour and a half. From previous experience I knew it was gonna take a lot longer, what with Hugh wanting us to pose for pictures on precarious overhangs. Of course Viv was no help. The weather was a mixture of wind and rain and I likened the scenery to that in a Brontë novel. Viv got all dramatic and threatened to throw herself off the cliffs like Britomartis!

The name Rocky Valley should have been the clue and maybe we should have turned back. But no, we battled the elements and went forth. (We are all past the age of multiplying so no danger of that.)

Every time we thought the path couldn't get any steeper it did. The views were spectacular. The coastline was infested with fish robbing Cormorants, I knew I should have brought me gun. Ideal spots to pick 'em off. We passed very few people on the trek which I found was a tad worrying. Especially if I got into difficulty.

I needn't have worried.

Four hours later we made it to our destination. I was absolutely soaked and plastered in mud. We stood watching the three seals in the harbour; the waves dramatic, and the foamy surf retreating hastily as

they broke and crashed against the rocks.
After a few minutes I was approached by a guy kitted out in a red bodysuit. He told me that they had been made aware of a lady struggling along the cliff path, walking with difficulty. Numerous interfering busybodies had reported it Boscastle end. Said female was me. I explained I was fine and although I walked with a strange gait at times this was because I suffer from neuropathy. I was extremely proud that an obese asthmatic, with stage four cancer, had managed to complete the Acorn trail. He accused me of being irresponsible and if I had needed help it would have been his team that would have come to the rescue. Hello - I was 400 yards from the end of the trail FFS. Would have been nice if he could have hauled me up out of the valley two and a half hours earlier or been there to assist when I became wedged, straddled over a turnstile, injuring my lower abdominals further. (Which were already chafed from walking in wet jeans.)
Much to my chagrin he started to give me a lecture on cliff walking safety. Unwise move Murray. Was it my fault that in all the guide books there is no reference made to how treacherous the walk is? The young lad in the pub was adamant I'd be able to walk the trail easily. Was I the one who devised the walk placing the Acorn trail so close to the cliff edge? No I was not. Said red suited rescuer was given my opinion without breath. My parting words 'Jog On.' Most inappropriate when by this time I was dragging my left leg behind me and couldn't have run if I tried.
We lunched in the Cobweb but my day had been spoilt by being told off. It got worserer.
We had a few drinks, mainly to top up Viv's alcohol levels. She was in withdrawal and had started to shake.
Very wet, muddy and bedraggled, we ordered a taxi to take us back to Tintagel. It transpired that the driver was a volunteer coastguard and had heard all about us. (I know my clothing was distinctive but this beggars belief!) Needless to say I received another lecture all the way back to base camp.
Tomorrow we are off to Port Stanley where Doc Martin is filmed. I am hoping he'll be able to sort out me chafed chuff and my swollen joints.

I will report back dreckly...

07/04/14 Merlin's Cave and if you look closely a seal...

07/04/14 There on a chair...

13

IRELAND

13/04/14 What an early start. Up at 0315 for 0445 pickup. The taxi dropped me off at Tesco Eastgate where a minivan awaited. Bags loaded, we headed off up the M4 to Gloucester.

I have to say, at one point I was a tad worried that I was on the wrong feeder coach as all the documentation on board had the name of another coach company at the top. I was holidaying with Leger which was probably one of this company's biggest competitors. Nothing like a journey into the unknown.

First stop was at Gloucester Bus Station to collect a very elderly gent who I will call Dr Foster. He fell onto and into the minibus having totally missed the doorway and the step. Of course I had to suppress my laughter by burying my face in my coat. I cannot thank the anonymous person who sent me the emergency plastic pants enough. (Addressing the package to Bertha Bennett was a tad embarrassing though. My new neighbour - who is hot, hot, hot - had taken in said package and now thinks that's my name.) I am unsure whether Dr Foster is drunk or visually impaired. SFFU.

Next stop was Chester where I was twinned with Ms Puffalot, a Nana Mouskouri lookalike. Hopefully this will change at the port.

At the port I was reseated, thankfully I am sat on my own. However I am on seat 13...

13/04/14 En route to Holyhead.
So I am off to the Emerald Isle in search of Liam Neeson. Knowing my luck I'll end up with Shamus O'Shaun.
While there I'm planning to do some re-enacting of the Tommy Steele film. I hope to find a brook with stepping stones and sing and dance to the famous Irish song, 'How are things in Glocca Morra'. I also want to sing the Dana classic All Kinds of Everything. Will need to find a rainbow with a pot of gold at the end for that one.
So this trip will be like going back to my roots. Being part Irish 3 times removed on me mudders side. (Note the bit of Irish I threw in there.) Yes hard to believe but there is Mulligan running through me veins. I think maybe my drink problem is the giveaway! Well is it any surprise when I had a family of aunts and uncles weaned on Potcheen. Used to suck it from a barrel through a piece of straw they did fer sure, fer sure. Called themselves devout Catholics they did. Well I suppose there's enuff letters there to form part of the word 'alcatholics' which is nearer the truth...

13/04/14 We have arrived. Room with a Hugh... — at Seven Oaks Hotel Carlow.

14/04/14 near Carlow, Ireland.
The giveaway was always gonna be seat 13...
I boarded the Ulysses and positioned myself in front of the big screen with a pint ready for the match. Man City v Arsenal. Now you tell me what shipbuilder in their right mind positions a big screen in the walkway?
I must have missed every bleedin' goal. And to top it all Ms Puffalot sought me out and invited herself to join me. I wouldn't mind but her delirious tremors puts Shakin' Stevens to shame. She claims to be a special needs teacher which I found hard to believe. Her special needs were copious amounts of Sauvignon Blanc, and the lunch time sesh ended up with her drinking a total of 8 small bottles during the three hour crossing. Ossified is an understatement!
Kath and Phyllis joined us mid crossing (again uninvited) and before we

knew it we were hosting quite a party. I'm getting a déjà vu feeling. Feel an entourage coming on.
Back on the coach it has become evident that I am travelling with a load of 'in bed by eights'. However I am hopeful that several will break from their cocoon and reveal their true selves later in the week. Still this is only oiling me up for the biggie next Saturday. 16 days in Italy.
Mrs He Said She Said and Mr Wikipedia are trying to work out what nationality I am. He reckons I am Egyptian because of the green tinge to my skin and she states I'm definitely Dubai'ish. They then proceeded to argue as to what they felt my religious beliefs would be.
Hello... Is chemo a religion now?
Once at the hotel Hugh and I dumped our bags and headed for the bar.
Dinner was a pleasant affair where we were joined by two women who had sensibly left their husbands at home. Supper consisted of lots of mashed up food on a plate, was I thankful I was able to wash it down with a few Proseccos. I'm guessing a lot of the guests are either babies or dentally challenged.
It became evident later that I'd had far too much to drink when I ended up taking a wrong turn. Having summonsed the one lift which serviced the whole of the three storey hotel, we waited patiently along with several other guests for it to arrive. The familiar ping sounded, announcing its arrival. In my haste I mistook the lift door for that of the cleaning cupboard. Buckets, brushes, mops and stuff went everywhere. Hugh was most embarrassed and as of breakfast this morn' is still not speaking to me. Says I'm a right Holy Show.
Off to kiss the Blarney today.

14/04/14 near Ballincollig, Ireland.
Kissing the Blarney Stone...

14/04/14 near Bantry, Ireland.
Glengariff - Arrived at 2nd hotel. A 17th century hotel. I'm on the third floor.

15/04/14 near Bantry, Ireland.
We started the day with a visit to Cork. Not such a good idea. Let loose for 4 hours. Only consolation was I spent Euros and not Pounds. Lol..
To get to the Blarney Stone we had to climb the 90000 steps first. Well 126 to be exact in a confined space with people behind you all the way. The steps spiralled up to several landings where one could rest if required. The windows were covered with bars so there was absolutely no chance of losing Hugh... Who I hasten to add has had a puss face all morning. Yer man was being a right Bowsie.
It was just my luck to be stuck behind a very large lady from our coach

and her husband. (I'm not being largess after all I'm large meself.)
Mrs Herniated Disc decides to have a panic attack. I can't go forward and can't go back, there was literally no gap to mind.
Mr No Top Teeth, her husband, tells her to sit down. Now there's a problem. I'm in a confined space, claustrophobic with me numerous other impediments. This was not what you'd call a wise move Murray. She then starts to cry and begins discussing her ailments with the people in front of her who were kindly trying to help. I tell you cliff top rescue would have been a blessing on this occasion. After what seemed a lifetime the Yanks came up trumps, managing to coax her up to the final landing. By this time me puffer had been administered to me and all behind, and I'm clean out of Prozac and Diazepam.
Once at the top we were assisted to the ground by a gentleman who delighted in grabbing you around the waist. (Yes I do have one.) I had already applied barrier cream liberally to my lips, being immuno compromised and all that. Couldn't be sure what I might pick up. Hugh the langer thought it funny to shout ' Rapunzel, Rapunzel let down your long hair'. Might help if I had some. Today was the last time I will be laying on me back for a man I can tell Hugh. For me the Blarney kissing lark was a Eureka moment and a huge achievement.
Getting back on me feet was an even bigger challenge; whilst I might still be able to get down, getting up was a different matter. A hip and knee replacement seem likely.
On the way back to the coach Mr No Top Teeth was praising his wife for being brave and managing to turn onto her back and get kissy, kissy with Mick Jagger. (Now then; I have numerous friends with back problems and I know there ain't no way any of 'em could have got up the steps, let alone get down to do the deed.) He said she could now prove to all the sceptics at work who didn't think she could do it by showing them the official photo he had purchased. To show work colleagues photographic evidence might be a tad stupid me finx.
Apparently she had been off sick for a while with a work related back injury. Doesn't take a lot of working out does it? I wondered if I ought to warn her not to show the photo, but decided to keep me nose out. (There is no helping some people is there? Although I find gin is good

and there were several with my name on, waiting for me back at the coach....) Stand by broom cupboard...
Off to Garnish Island. Seal searching.

15/04/14 near Castletown Bearhaven, Ireland.
At McCarthy's Bar on the Beara Peninsula for the first pint of the day. Original marriage snug and bar. Doubles up as a grocery store.

The Beara Peninsula and Garnish Island. Spot the seals...

16/04/14 near Bantry, Ireland.
Have met several lovely people on this trip. One is a step clog dancer and an acapella singer. We're trying to coax her into doing a turn but at the mo she is resisting. Another is an opera singer who doesn't realise yet that she can't sing. Hugh spilled his guts and told her that, after a skinful, I was a much better singer and I proved it this very eve.
Last night was a tad scary, in more ways than one. A hilltop controlled gorse fire went very out of control and came dangerously close to the hotel. I was sat in the bar at the time (silently wishing to be rescued by a hunky fire fighter) and managed to order in more provisions just before the smoke detector alarms went off. The fire brigade battled through the night to bring the fire under control. This is a usual occurrence here and no-one seemed in the slightest bit bothered.
I was last out of the bar as per usual and had a damn good laugh with the locals who insisted I try various local drinks. Fortunately there wasn't a broom cupboard in sight.
The hotel is 17th century and looks out over Bantry Bay. Maureen O'Hara's house is a stone's throw away. I'm anticipating an invite in the

next day or so. My room had to be situated on the top floor didn't it? Accessible by lift only, no way was I climbing six flights of stairs. To get to floor three you press the button for floor one, it's all a bit back to front, and then you have a 1/2 mile hike to the end of the hotel and room 316. I am the only one from the coach, and likely the only guest, on this floor.

My sleep was disturbed by a mysterious banging noise (not of the sexual variety) and other ghostly goings on. I frightened me self to death throughout the night. You could tell all was not well 'cos of the state of the bed in the morning.

Hugh is not best pleased with me, reckons I ought to have made the bed and not left it in such a state. No! I am on holiday, I ain't making no bed. So as a result, following a heated argument, he's not talking to me. Bothered? Not!

Mr Wikipedia has now decided I'm probably a NAT (new aged traveller.) Not sure how he came to that conclusion. But has been heard to tell the other coachcationers that I'm very funky.

Went on a trip today around the Beara Peninsula. Fabulous views. After a liquid lunch we went seal spotting, on a boat, before being dumped on Garnish Island by a drunken boat captain. Playing chicken with a bigger boat was a tad concerning and the row between the two captains hysterical. Both were out of their faces.

Mrs Herniated Disc is being a pain. Told everyone she fell over. I wanna say fell overboard but I won't. That's wishful thinking. She's after the sympathy vote and ain't getting it. Upon further investigation we found out she only tripped. Oh I hope it wasn't over my foot. Lol... If she turns on the waterworks once more I'm gonna give her something to cry about.

The people watching is fun but the eavesdropping is depressing. People trying to outdo each other with their various ailments and disaster stories. The material is poor and none of it worth using in any of me books. A need for mayhem is required and I'm on the case.

Off to the Ring of Kerry and Killarney today.

16/04/14 Ring of Kerry and Killarney.

17/04/14 near Bantry, Ireland.

The unmade bed row continued this morning. We had to be off on a trip by 0730. Did I have time to make the bed. Did I hell? Are you allowed say 'hell' in Ireland? Anyway, Hugh's verbal attack was venomous and has resulted in me having to hide my toothbrush. Hide yer toothbrush I hear you ask?

Let me explain. I have a friend who, if and when she was pissed off by her numerous luvvas, and that was often, would scrub the toilet pan after a number two using their toothbrush. I have such quality friends... Anyway I made the mistake of telling Hugh a while back so I had to take steps to avoid having a mouth like the inside of a bog pan. He can be so getyerownback'ish sometimes. Let's hope I can find it later after a few pints of the black stuff.

As the saying goes 'love is blind, marriage is an eye opener'!

The ring of Kerry and Killarney were beautiful. Took a jaunty ride to Ross Castle. There were lots of trees down following a winter of 150 mph winds. We had a leisurely liquid lunch at the Red Fox and then headed to the hills.

Back at the hotel there has been a bit of an incident. A very inappropriate fess up by Mrs Herniated Disc and her hubby Mr No Top Teeth. It's not often I am shocked, but today that changed. I now know why Mr No Top Teeth has no top teeth.

The story: We are all sat around drinking and having a laugh when, bit by bit, we became aware that the bar was getting quieter and quieter and people were listening to a story that Mrs Herniated Disc was telling in a very loud voice. She had obviously had way too much to drink.
I thought I heard her say that she was a mechaphile. Absolutely no chance of that! My belief was that she had just seen the film 'The Counsellor' you know the one with Cameron Diaz, where she gets up close and personal with a car windscreen. There was no way Mrs Herniated Disc was gonna be able to climb up on the bonnet of a car, do the splits and get all suction paddy with the windscreen without doing severe damage. And that's just to the car. What she had in fact said was that her hobby involved cars. She asked people to guess what it was and Mrs Scrape Your Plate Clean suggested she was a mechanic to which she replied 'sort of'! My table of eight listened intently to find out more, joining in with the guessing game. I thought she might be a stripogram chauffeur. Had to be something weird. Anyway, it happens she and he are doggers. No wonder her frickin back is bad. The 79 year old Mrs Bunion bought us to our knees by piping up 'We call it Kennel Club'. (Woof, woof.) There were others who also didn't know what dogging was and it was left to yours truly to delicately explain. Delicate is not normally a word I'd use to describe my good self, as I am known to be void of any filter. However, delicate I was, waiting until the seventy pluses went to bed before I allowed people to view the Wikipedia definition of dogging... Needless to say most of the coach party stayed up way past their bedtime discussing this unusual hobby. Who in their right mind tells a room full of strangers about their sexual preferences?
To top it all; when they said if they could use the coach they would draw bigger crowds, the drivers turned puce. We were in bits and I might have wet meself.
I have also sustained a major injury and am even more crocked than I was before because Mrs Herniated Disc, in her drunkenness, fell on top of me. They were leaving a bar full of shocked people, to retreat to their room and sort each other out with lavender oil... The picture this conjures up is not a good one. Hopefully she'll need to pay special attention to her left rib following my two finger pronged attack. This

successful manoeuvre alleviated the pain her fat ass had caused when she landed in me lap.
Off to Dublin tomorrow. Hugh is still angry and is shooting me looks. Better watch it 'cos I've got his credit card and his number.

18/04/14 near Ballyfermot, Ireland.
My day started badly. As previously reported, the buttons in the lift were all back to front. A rather elderly well-spoken lady, who put me in mind of Mrs Richards from Fawlty Towers, landed on floor three having pressed the button for floor one. A normal occurrence. I am waiting for the lift on floor three. 'Is this reception?' she asks. I tried to explain that this was a peculiarity of the hotel. Big mistake. She told me 'in England the lifts don't do that' and kept repeating that she was English and just wanted the reception area. It was a waste of time trying to explain further so I just pressed the button for floor three knowing we would descend to floor one. To me this was the far easier option. Wrong!!!! Mrs Richards obviously thinks I'm trying to rob her or abduct her and she presses the lift alarm. Surprisingly it works and it's deafening. Eventually the world and his wife come to the rescue, this includes numerous people including the chef and the drunken boat captain who I now know is called Ted. I explain what has occurred to the male receptionist who I have gotten quite friendly with over the last few days. He tries to explain the anomaly with the lift but Mrs Richards can't understand his accent. Then Ted gets involved and nobody can understand him. Bear in mind the alarm is still sounding and everyone is stood inside of the lift. I manage to squeeze past everyone and leave them to it. I ache where I have laughed so much. Mrs Richards has not been seen since. Worrying...
Well I have had major, majors this morn. A friend of mine bought me a circular pill dispenser with the days of the week on. As most of the time I never know what day of the week it is she believed this device would help me. My dilemma is which way round do you go. Clockwise or anticlockwise? I think I may have taken me pills twice on a couple of days and today I'm fearful I've overdosed. I am very hyper and excitative, and I must declare I'm even getting on me own nerves.

Mrs Herniated Disc told Hugh that he and I ought not to dismiss her hobby too rapidly and maybe give the D word a try... Do I look as though I can manoeuvre around the front of a car with ease? I think not m'lud.
Visited Cashel for lunch, the highlight was the Cashel Stone which was covered in scaffolding and plastic.
Dublin this safto and it was heaving. The easiest option was to head to a bar. My god, shit faced doesn't cover it. Mrs Herniated Disc won the pole dancing competition and it took three of us to persuade her to tuck her chest away and put her clothes back on. We, as in ten of us, missed the coach - only four hours late. Had to ring the tour company to find out where we were staying and get a cab.
One of the girls received a text from her husband (who she left at home) asking her if she knew where two videos were. Her drunken, well no not drunken, poleaxed friend suggested the response she should send. Hugh reckons she'll be very lucky if she is still married upon her return.
These women have booked numerous holidays. They started off initially as one night away and over the years this has slowly increased to nine days. Their next holiday is a 14 day all inclusive to Ayia Napa. They have yet to tell their husbands.
Despite my knees giving me jip I am coping surprisingly well. Drinking instead of walking does of course help. Today we are going to find an authentic Irish bar.

19/04/14 It all started to go horribly wrong when we got dropped off in Dublin for the day. The sheer number of people made it difficult to manoeuvre around the streets so the ten rebels decided to hit the numerous bars.
We were having such a fab time we missed the coach back to the hotel. No-one knew where we were staying and we didn't have the telephone number for our tour drivers. When we realised we were stranded I telephoned a driver from another coach trip whose number I fortunately had stored in my phone. He said he would get back to me and to await instructions. Well that was after he'd told me off and took the piss.
How we progressed from beer to Veuve Clicquot I have no idea. I will

not forget it however. Our bar bill cost more than a month's mortgage.
I received the return call from our Knight in a shiny coach, however I believe I was getting at one with a slippery pole at the time. Thank god for voicemail. He had fortunately left details of the name and address of where we were staying.
We eventually got back to the hotel where we were greeted by other revellers. Perhaps it wasn't a good idea for me to change the words to the song 'On Mother Kelly's Doorstep.' I don't really know what the problem was; they loved my rendition of Cockles and Mussels.
One of the ten hens reckons it was the bit where I changed the lyrics to: 'she's gotta hole in her stocking, a hole in her shoe, a hole in her drawers where her arse peeks through. Oh Nelly....' etc. etc.
Needless to say the boring old farts asked us to leave the hotel bar.
I vaguely remember crawling along the landing unable to stop laughing. Absolutely hysterical.
I awoke late morn in severe pain, not only in my knees from the injury caused by Mrs Herniated Disc but also my inner thighs. The pain was excruciating. I managed to make it to the bathroom to inspect said area in private. I find my stomach gets in the way more than it used to and I had to use a mirror to see what was occurring in me nethers. OMG. Where I had gripped so hard to the pole with my legs I had a love bitey type bruise measuring about 5 be 5. And third degree carpetburnytypemarks. If Hugh had seen it there would be no convincing him that I hadn't been up to no good. I quickly applied some WD40. The relief. A wonderful feeling when the pain stopped.
We were all late for breakfast but that was nothing compared to the next revelation.
Several of the single girls travel with a married female friend. Barb, a singleton, had been taking pictures of us all behaving badly and innocently places the pictures on that site that JK is always going on about. The sister of one of the married women sees the posting and shows the pics to the husband of Barb's married travelling companion. The husband is not amused, and tries to reach his wife by telephone. As you would expect there were numerous missed calls. At brekkers the driver asks if he can have a word with the hen ten. We thought we were

gonna get told off for the noise we made and for missing the coach. Oh no. When Mr Ignored, left at home hubby, can't get hold of wifey he decides to ring the coach company demanding to know what sort of holidays they are organising. We were asked not to post any further photographs on that site or else there could be serious consequences and Barb was asked to remove her posting A Sap. When we viewed the photos even I cringed. We were also asked to apologise to the hotel manager.

Most of us don't know how we kept a straight face. We all look awful and have hangovers from hell.

I'm absolutely fuming. In the days prior to this trip I worked hard to try and get my knees sorted. Massages, ice packs, using me stick, keeping my leg elevated and of course resting. I'm gonna have to visit the doc and get some strong pain killers, and likely a tripod walking frame after that bloody pest of a woman fell on me. Even alcohol ain't helping anymore. She has totally crocked me and I know if I hadn't had this impediment I would have won the pole dancing competition without doubt. To say I'm livid is an understatement.

The need to take drastic measures to ensure that I don't get told off like a child for embarrassing myself was always on the cards. I have promised Hugh that on my next holiday I will refrain from drinking and only report on the weather and the places we visit. Word!

20/04/14 The weather today is sunny with lots of fluffy white clouds dotted around in a beautiful bright blue sky. There is a chilly wind and you do need a coat if stood on street corners for too long. There are numerous young people wandering around Ireland's capital this day, not too sure what they're up to but will try and find out.

As it's Easter we all felt that before we hit the pub we should go see a couple of the sights. Maybe get a bit nearer to god after our outrageous behaviour. Not my words or views, they are Hugh's.

Well it didn't take long and Lordy Lordy have I been insulted or have I been insulted. Went to walk into St Patrick's Cathedral and was asked, no rather instructed by Mrs Herniated Disc to remove my hijab. Now a lot of people wouldn't know what this is. My powers of deduction worked out it was my head scarf.

If anything it resembled a mantilla, which I understood to be acceptable head attire in a Catholic church. There was also doubt in my mind that this cathedral was for Catholic supporters. I thought it changed to a place of worship for Protestants. Google was absolutely useless and although Siri was better even the Wikipedia pages didn't help, we still couldn't find out. Regardless, the god that lords it over both of these is the same so I can't see what the problem is. I explained the scarf was to cover my partial baldness and was asked to refashion the style. Feckin eejit!

I now look like Mrs Brown.

Once inside we sit in the pews reading the history of the place but mainly because my knee was so bad and we all felt a tad lightheaded. All of us unable to eat breakfast due to hangovers. The anti-freeze that's just cost me an arm and a leg, that's supposed to numb the pain, hadn't kicked in. Probably haven't applied enough of the stuff 'cos the twats on the coach were inhaling the bloody fumes.

We are sitting there all lovely 'a few on a pew' and I'm recounting the story about my friends daughter who attended church and had used the holy water in the font to splash on her face to cool her down. Remarking afterwards to her mother, 'that's better.' The story was extremely funny and we were having a good old giggle. The Reverend also thought it was funny. No doubt hiding in a nearby priest hole eavesdropping on us sinners.

He asked us where we came from and what we'd been up to and hung out with us for a bit of a goss. Bit rude really, could have offered us some wine and crackers.

Once our hearts, souls and minds had been cleansed we headed off to the pub - after all it was our last day.

The other coachcationers are of the opinion Mrs Herniated Disc speaks loudly to attract attention. She is always looking around to see who is listening and her stories are told to shock. Everyone has had enough of her. The ache in my knees is a constant reminder. I still have the imprint of her arse on me upper outer thighs

Barb had heard enough of Mrs Herniated Disc moaning about everyone

and everything and had finally made her mind up. Successfully having interrogated Mr No Top Teeth she found out where his wife worked and has forwarded last night's photos of her pole dancing to a generic work email address. She delighted in pressing the send button and was most impressed with how easy it had been to find an email address. Oops.
This is my last posting until my next assignment which commences 0730 on Saturday. It's a sixteen dayer and I'm hoping to find some interesting items to write about.
Until the next time.

14

PUGLIA

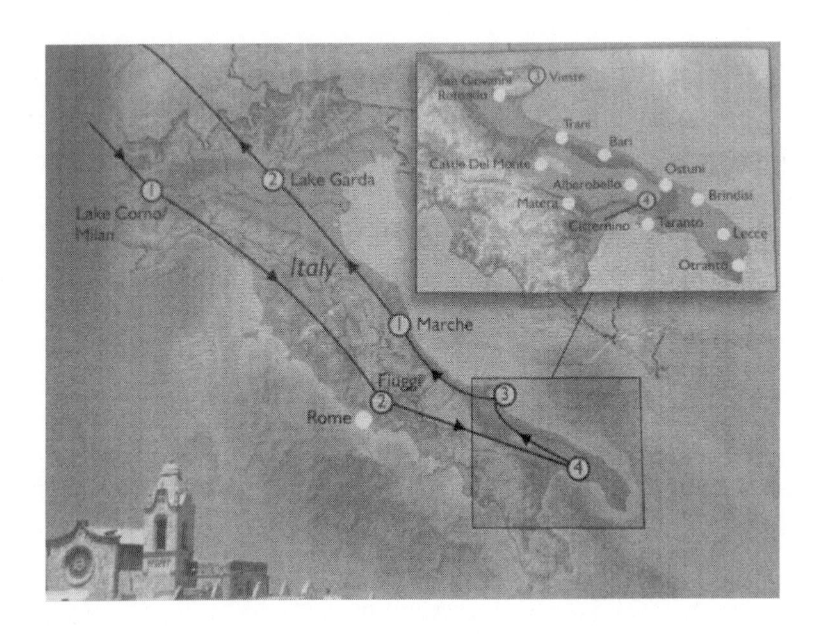
Vieste
Trani
Bari
Castle Del Monte
Ostuni
Alberobello
Matera
Brindisi
Cisternino
Taranto
Lecce
Otranto
Lake Garda
Lake Como/
Milan
Italy
Marche
Fiuggi
Rome

27/04/14

The weather today is overcast. There is dampness in the air and evidence to suggest it has been raining during the night. Currently 9 degrees in new money.

I suppose I shouldn't have really hidden my holiday money for safe keeping. Big, big mistake. Problem was it was in a wallet which also held my passport. By the time I left Worle I was a sweat ball!

My holiday started at 0700. BB cream check, Durex thin feel condoms. Check. (Had you worried!!) and of course my CK shades. Check.

Looking good in my ankle huggin' Levi's and my new navy and white Vans. Of course a matchin' t-shirt. I looked the dude. That was dude not dud.

On the way down to Dover I was sat behind Mrs Inconsiderate. A lady who was hell-bent on decapitating me. First, by lowering the window blinds with my head in the way, then by dropping the top box lid onto my head.

Mr Insecure? An elderly gent who felt he was perhaps out of his depth and had travelled too far. Bear in mind at the time of his declaration we were only in Maidstone. He felt unwell and had to be coaxed off the coach. Guess who had to dig deep to find her inner angel?

Boarding the Pride of Dover, spookily in Dover, I headed for where I belong. 'Club Class'. 'Twas there I was introduced to the captain Andy Vincent. A very, very nice man. I was lucky to be amongst a group of tee totallers and ended up with numerous glasses of complimentary Champagne. Obviously duty free. Got told off by the waiter. Whatever...

As stated in my previous holiday blog I intended to write about the weather and other mundane occurrences. However whilst talking to a gent who was more interested in me than he was his wife I found myself in my first lot of bother. And to top it off we were only talking about the weather and other mundane occurrences. Wifey remarks that 'he was her husband'. Like I was interested in son of Michael Berryman. Me finx not. Needless to say wifey was dealt with by way of a forked tongue... Legendary dialogue. Some of my finest. Champagne induced.

We have all been provided with the coach seating arrangements and the names of who is sitting where and with whom; loads of Mauds,

Mavis' and Ednas.

You may be interested to know I am yet again the youngest on the coach. However it was inevitable that my piss taking regarding peoples impediments was gonna come back and bite me on the ass. Earlier this week in a severe state of crockedness I thought I was gonna have to bring me tripod walking frame with me. One that I have been provided with until I am considered capable of driving a mobility scooter. Having discovered that I can be done for DIC whilst using one of these I am not too sure whether I want to be the proud owner of a pimped up lime green motorised shopping cart. Anyway, after a restful few days I am pleased to report my knees are much improved. May not be up to out 'n' runnin' standard but at least I can climb the stairs now. Most important if invited.

There is a single gent on board who is giving me the eye. Not too sure if it's evil or a nervous twitch. Standby for further update.

Off to Milan today — with Vivvy Anne Le Fey at Hôtel Mercure.

28/04/14

The sky was brilliant blue and the sun was high this morn. Temperature around 10 degrees at 0630am. The iPhone app promised a fabulous day and I suppose it would have been if I hadn't had the hangover from hell. The hotel was parked in the Champagne region of Reims. The Veuve Clicquot Champagnery was just down the road and round the corner and there was a special offer on this delicious nectar in the hotel bar which I took full advantage of. Excessive advantage. Until 0140 this day. I am most unwell and grumpy.

My schamps must have been laced with something causing me total disorientation resulting in me ending up on the wrong coach. Not really my fault...

The story: I get on what I believe is my coach to find some gormless looking female sitting in my seat. Thinking I was on the wrong coach I get off, and make my way to the other coach in the car park. Find seats 11-12, park me arse, and settle myself down for a siesta under my coat. About an hour into our journey I get rudely awoken by an unfamiliar face. 'Do you know you are on the wrong coach?' he asks trying to suppress his hysterical laughter. The coach exploded, people cheering and shouting, not helping my poor head at all. I had been oblivious to the fact both drivers were male and not the man and wife team I was supposed to be with. The coach I was on left an hour before the one I should have been on. My coach drivers know me well and knew instantly that Gawdyshocks who was sitting in my chair was not me. I do not shop at the centre of Naffness or wear a tea cosy on me head like she did. When the error was realised they instantly telephoned to check if I had mounted the wrong coach. The exchange of passengers took place just prior to the Gotthard Tunnel. The precious cargo, that being me, is back in her rightful seat on the correct tour. The alternative was unthinkable. The Alpine Slopes of Lucerne doing a bit of cloud spotting and name that goat! I hasten to add with not a bleedin' bar in sight. I am highly embarrassed and am now drinking Bovril. Transpires Mrs Wonga-Dot-Com and Mrs Grouper-Fish-Mouth had seen me get on board the wrong coach but did not think to alert me. They are brilliant fun. They whack back the booze on the coach.

When we stopped for food, next to the food hall was a shop called Magic X. This shop is similar to Ann Summers. The window has numerous sexual accoutrements on full display which delighted Mrs Wonga-Dot-Com who was most insistent that we check it out. Hugh would have been in his element.

On the subject of Hugh I'm hoping he'll join us at Lake Garda following his 8 day business trip.

The single guy looks a bit like Groucho Marx. He wears ill-fitting denims equally as saggy as his arse and his jumper needs de-bobbling. He keeps staring at me and today he sought me out. Well after I'd been found he did. Trying to make conversation he was. Must remember to look at the seating plan to check out who he is.

The cost of going a pee here is one Euro. This extortionate charge has caused something I have never witnessed before - just heard about. A mad dash to the coach loo just prior to stopping. The coach drivers, like me, think it's hysterical so I have called this spectacle Euronate Gate... — at Hotel Parma & Congressi.

29/04/14 near Fiuggi, Italy.

The temperature this morning is a pleasant 12 degrees. Cloudy overhead but not bothered as it's not affecting my beer and we have a good day ahead of us. The plan is; travel south through Italy passing Bologna, the Tuscan capital of Florence. Then head south east of Rome to Fiuggi.

My promise to stop drinking was broken from dinner time onwards, however I decided to stick to lager. The water content is higher...

There are several singles on board; 3 women, one of whom is my good self and 2 men. Anthony or Boney Tony is my stalker and then there is James aka Mr Chocks Away an officer and a mental man.

This holiday is a revelation and the people watching material is of the highest quality. While waiting for dinner I observated the singles (excluding my single self I hasten to add) standing near the bar, but behind the husbands who were dutifully purchasing drinks for their wives. Several of the husbands turn and speak to the singles while waiting to be served and then as an act of kindness, through gritted teeth, feel obligated to offer to buy them a drink. James the officer and a mental man and Dilly Dally Sally have this ploy perfected and have yet been seen to buy a drink. Boney Tony knows I've sussed him. Earlier while I'm at the bar purchasing my alcoholic beverage I ask him if he's waiting for a drink. 'Yes, if you're buying' he replied. Sharp of tongue and quick of wit I reply. 'Nah, the only mug here is the one containing my drink.'

The singles were all seated together along with the Wonga girls and several couples. Mr and Mrs Chiselled Haircut, Mr Gromit and his wife Mrs Tightly Belted Jacket and Mr and Mrs From the 18th Century.

Happens there was a bit of a Watergate scandal at dinner. Details of the occurrence as below:

The Wonga girls are on the Chianti and me and another couple are on the beer. Dilly Dally Sally orders tap water, which we have been pre warned not to drink. Waiter brings bottled water and breaks the seal ready for her to pour. She kicks off 'cos she will have to pay for it. Mr Chocks Away an officer and a mental man asks her if she wants him to take the problem on. (Her hero.) I have never felt so bloody

embarrassed in all my life and all over 1 euro. The poor waiter. I have told them both today to kindly sit away from me at dinner this eve as their behaviour was not what I was accustomed to.
I have spoken to Hugh who is missing me terribly. I can't wait to see him later this holiday. It'll be comforting to cop a load of a nice firm ass in those snug fitting jeans he wears. Being 42 and working out daily I gotta say he's got it all there.
This morning was a struggle getting up out of bed. Bit of a late night with the Wonga girls. They start drinking at 10am and just carry on. Something about the sun being over the garden. Whatever that means.
All the coachcationers reckon Boney Tony is after me... Watch this space. I have alerted Hugh. Gotta keep him on his toes. Tony in his youth (and bear in mind he can remember rationing) was an oil riggers rigger. More like rigor if you ask me!
Off to Rome...

30/04/14 near Fiuggi, Italy.
Patches of blue sky and 17 degrees. Ideal weather to visit Vatican City for tea with the Pope. Apparently he has just had a makeover and some kind of beautification. I must say I could do with a bit of that following a devastating discovery. I am mortified. I seem to have developed a cleavage that starts just under my neck. 'Impressive. A helluva pair of tits', I hear you say. No... Although me nipples might be kinda central, the rest rests on me stomach. All a tad worrying. I know I'm a hefty bird but this smacks of old woman. I noticed this deformity while checking for age spots in the mirror this very eve. Too late to be addressed, it has already occurred.
Boney Tony reckons I'm wearing well and Mr Pushing His Luck the wannabe straying husband is of the opinion we could make a firework the like of which has never been seen before. Twat, the Catherine Wheel has already been done years ago. Anyway Hugh might have a problem with this guy, he adores me and will get very jealous - says for an old gal I've got it all going on. Bless him. All I'm hoping is that the magical blue tablet doesn't show up on me next blood test.
I've been near slashing me wrists these past couple of days. Mrs Dilly

Dally Sally is slashy wristy material. My ears are bleeding from the pain. No wonder she's never been married. She asked me tonight how many men I'd had, like it's any of her business. Anyway after 30 does it really matter? I'm dedicated to Hugh now. She keeps going on about how lovely everything is. The Hotel Dei Pini can hardly be compared in any way to the Cipriani. Come on, she doesn't even know cutlery etiquette. Thought the dessert spoon was for soup she did.
The policewomen in Fuiggi have got to be seen to be believed. They went on strike over the state of their uniforms. They won, and now look as though they have stepped out of Gucci. Red lipstick, red nails, hair coiffed and high heels. Oh and not forgetting the gun. How the hell they chase crims I don't know. Must just shoot them. Thought provoking.
Off to Puglia via Tranny.

01/05/14 near Cisternino, Italy.
101 things to do when in Rome. Go when there are 70 million other tourists. Drive like a bleedin' lunatic. Act as tour guide to the crinklies who were too stingy to pay for the official one. Get told off for climbing the Trevi fountain to take a group photo. It was actually my portrayal of Sylvia in the fountain. The policeman who assisted me from the rocky edge fortunately had a sense of humour. I told him under my turban I was long, blonde and a siren. Do not use the yellow buses that use a different route to the rest of the hop on, hop off, buses. At one point I didn't even think I was in Rome. Make sure you're able to hop on and hop off before you part with your dosh. They do not hang about. Clog the pavements up checking your map while trying to work out where you are. Hardly anything is signposted or marked on the maps. Never give way to oncoming pedestrian traffic on zebra crossings, just fight your way through barging and ribbing people as you go.
Met a lovely American as we were strolling around to the Spanish Steps he thought I came from the States too. Really nice eyes, nice teeth and good looking. When I eye him up and down he's only dressed in a brown monk's habit. Really funky guy for a monk. What a waste...
I have queue jumping Wonga's, they won't wait for anything or anybody, they just push their way to the front. Both are 84 year old

Mancunians, so you can't really tell them off. They are extremely well travelled, love a drink and are a great laugh. Dilly Dally Sally says it smells of Christmas when they hit the brandy. She of course does not partake in an 11am shot like we do. She was late back to the coach. Despite being given concise instructions she went to the wrong floor of the coach park. We were nearly suffocating in Sahara like conditions while we waited for her and the coach drivers incurred a penalty cost for overstaying.

Me cleavage that I was moaning about did me proud today. I was being all trendy and had my designer CK shades (to match my CK bag) hooked over the neck of my t-shirt. Got up to leave and discovered a prescription lens missing. A quick frisking down and discovered it had fallen in between me boobs.

Mr Gromit and his wife Mrs Tightly Belted Jacket got lost in Rome claiming I marched off without them. I am not marching material, my impediment has seen to that. And how the hell he can get lost wearing the get up he wears god only knows. Cowboy hat, green rolled up trousers, black lace boots up to his knees, walking stick and hand on his hip. Picture to follow.

Boney Tony broke his tooth on the bread. Found a Spar shop in Rome and has bought some super glue to fix it. Picture to follow...

01/05/14 Because you deserve what every individual should experience regularly...

BUDWEISER ... — at Alberobello (Bari.)

02/05/14 near Cisternino, Italy.

Not a cloud in the sky and it's 13 degrees as at 8am.

We travelled south into the Puglia region of Italy's boot. En route we stopped at Trani, 'The Pearl of Puglia'. Trani has a pretty medieval quarter and cathedral, literally perched on the water's edge. This is a perfect place to watch the rich and their yachts. No sign of 'The Wet Dream' though or it's good looking owner...

Talking of Perch. We got fed this at supper time. My understanding was that these fish ate crap off the bottom of the river. Tad worrying.

Our journey was one of wonder and delight. Poppies in abundance adorned the fields like the broken hearts of lovers spurned. Olive trees gnarled and twisted with age, stories of old, locked deep in their roots.

Am I poetic, or am I poetic?

Carers licence has been revoked following an incident. Me and the Wonga's decide to eat lunch 'al fresco'. I accidentally stand on an elderly dog that was just lolling around. Apologising to dog I walk around it. It wasn't bothered. Wonga 1 falls over dog, pushes me, I fall over and Wonga 2 lands on top. Wonga 1 has broken wrist. I have a broken finger tip (distal phalanx, well that's what it says on the form) which apparently is very common, and two broken toes. Reaching out and grabbing the massive umbrella was not a good idea and nearly impaled several unknown people as it crashed to the ground. Wonga 2 has scraged knees. We have received medical attention and will live to see another day. I am splinted and Wonga 1 is in plaster. Bloody waste of half a day if you ask me. We are both on the gin to numb the pain.

Dilly Dally Sally won't have an ice cream because it melts, obviously not used to getting her mouth round things. If she says lovely, beautiful, amazing or fabulous once more we are gonna stick her in the hold.

She can't make a coffee in her room 'cos she's bought the wrong plug, my lord did she moan and go on. It was down to me to sort her out with one borrowed from reception.

James the officer and a mental man complained about me and the Wonga's being too noisy. Tad worrying cause he's on the floor above us. We reckon he complained 'cos I told him to get a life. He was moaning about having no view. I said 'give me a minute and I'll run naked across

your balcony'. Po faced git. Everyone else thought it was funny. Think he wanted to get his own back. I mean we weren't even that loud, we may have had a few for medicinal purposes, but we were only tap dancing across the tiled floor. Caused a bit of a stir when we thought we were stuck in the lift, didn't realise the door opened each side of the lift. We all thought the lift had broken down. By the time I had made the discovery we were helpless, screaming with laughter...
Wet meself again.

03/05/14 near Matera, Italy.
Mafia out 'n' about...

03/05/14 near Cisternino, Italy.
Today we are heading for Ostuni, a charming town - perhaps one of the most stunning in Southern Italy. The bright whitewashed houses create a perfect contrast to the green of the surrounding countryside and its maze of well preserved, winding streets with hidden delights around every corner.
Our next stop is Alberobelo where the landscape is dominated by 'trulli'; whitewashed cones made of stones and built without the use of mortar. There are over 1300 'trulli' houses here. These cylindrical buildings with grey conical roofs reflect the true image of Puglia, one of the most unique towns in Europe.
Next and final stop is the Castellana Grotte where we visit the famous

network of caves created by underground rivers. These caves are amongst the deepest caverns in Europe... (had to be!)
Getting down to the bottom of the Castellana Grotte was fun. Not!
200 steps that take you into the bowels of the earth. A right yomp... I've got crick neck from continually looking up and down. Checking the crazy paving flooring for divots. (I wonder how they got all that crazy down there. 3km of tunnels and there are no emergency exits.) Continually being told to look up to check you weren't walking into a phallictite. You are not allowed to take photos here. Well rules are for fools and I've sneaked a few that will preview on FB.
Only two other people besides my good self have a mobile device. Those being the two drivers. The others claim not to need them and don't know how to operate one. So, when the coach drivers handed out laminated cards with a contact number it caused quite a stir. This is believed to be the reason I have an increasing number of crinklies to manage. I have to prearrange a meeting place before I'm allowed to leave them. They have been told to find a public telephone or ask a restaurant to use their phone in the event of an emergency. This very day an incident arises where Mr Commando 45 and his wife Mrs VPL are lost and are gonna be late back to the coach. They ring me. 'Where are you?' I ask. 'Zona 30' That's the bleeding speed limit not a location. Bloody idiots. Anyway after interrogating them we managed to find them and they have been retrieved.
Had a delightful lunch in Alberobelo. Crepes and a beer. When we left a young boy, no more than seven, said 'ciao bella' and blew me a kiss. I didn't know whether or not to take that as a compliment.
Wonga 1 broke the coach loo, and came out holding the bit she broke in her only working hand. For the while we have no on board loo.
Major, majors at dinner time this eve. When we arrived on the first day we were asked to keep to the same tables when eating breakfast and dinner. I and several others did as we were told (unbelievable but true.) Most didn't. This left Mr Spivvy Brum and his partner Ms Designer Outlet unable to sit together. Now these two are real smoochers, snogging at every available opportunity. A bit like Hugh and my good self I suppose. It gets worserer. That evening the same thing happens

again but this time it leaves Dilly Dally Sally without her seat. For a dimwit, did she kick off or what? Mr Officer and a mental man comes to her rescue. I tell you it was better than watching the Wonga's on full throttle.

04/05/14 near Cisternino, Italy.
Today is a trip to Brindisi, a city rich in Gothic and Baroque style churches, cathedrals, battlements of Swabian castles and fortresses.
Among the sights, the church of San Giovanni al Sepolcro with a beautiful and finely decorated marble portal. We continue on to Lecce more commonly known as the Florence of Southern Italy. Lecce is the main city on Puglia's Salento Peninsula. We head onward and forward to Otranto which lies at the most easterly point of mainland Italy, on the Adriatic Sea. The imposing castle with its robust towers and thick perimeter walls dominate much of the town.
The air force were out in abundance today dealing with their ongoing operation 'Mare Nostrum' rescuing illegals from Afghanistan that were trying to sail into Sicily.
Group 1 used to call me the 'bag lady', regularly taking bets as to how many bags I would bring into work. Well Dilly Dally Sally could beat me hands down. Daily she comes onto the coach loaded down with bags. She brings coats and shoes for every type of weather and her packed lunch which she makes at breakfast. What's worserer is she carries them with her wherever we go on the guided tours.
Putting on my makeup the past few days has been a bit like applying it at Studio 54. The energy saving light bulb was continually flashing on

and off and I was concerned ships would mistake my room for Oak Island. Anyway using a prezzy gifted to be by Mrs N (a manicure kit) I was able to fix the loose connection. When I told the others I discovered they had the same problem, so I have spent over an hour fixing their lights.
Tonight it's Pizza night in the hotel Tavern, where we will sample numerous local dishes including Pizza. There's a surprise.

05/05/14
Sorry for delay in posting today's drama. Sorting major majors. Standby for update. — at Spiaggia Rodi Garganico.

05/05/14 near Rodi Garganico, Italy.
Moving on ever so slightly to the sunbed.

05/05/14 Matera.

05/05/14 Taranto.

05/05/14 near Rodi Garganico, Italy.
The pissa night gave the Wonga's a golden opportunity to misbehave. As we were eating in the Taverna the dining rules of sticking to the same table did not apply. They rearranged the seating so I'm sat next to Boney Tony. He's a lovely guy but not my type at all. (If they had sat me next to The Captain and a mental man I tell you I would have jumped!) They weren't aware of Hugh and if I had told them, as he isn't here with me, would probably think that he is a figment of my imagination. Anyway the Wonga's decided to matchmake and thought that as he has a yacht he was suitable material. If he has a yacht then I'm a size 8. #Bullexcrementmefinx..
The evening went well despite having to listen to 'way back when' songs from the Saturday morning club at the Gaumont. We used to have loads of sing-a-longs when I was a kid with my Uncle Edgar playing the piano but I've never heard the song they were singing before.
The Wonga's hit the wine and were well into their second bottle before heading off to bed. I asked them if they wanted a cork to put in the bottle. 'What do we want a cork for, we are gonna drink the rest upstairs.'
This morning Wonga 1 says 'how did you and Tony get on? (bear in mind I was drinking beer, he was on coffee.) I said he sat up talking to me in

the bar. They both give each other a knowing nod. 'Did he take you up the snicket?' They enquired. 'What's a snicket?' I ask. 'You know up the snicket, up the ginnel'.
Wonga 1 said look it up on that fancy thing you've got.
Snicket and or Ginnel = a narrow passage between houses; an alleyway.
A fabulous urban example of this put me in mind of an old adversary of mine;
Al: Where's the pub, mate?
James: Down t' road, first snicket ont' right, past t' badger and ont' left. Near the white picketty fence, and yellow house on the corner Blue.
I explain Boney Tony and I have had a conversation about his teeth. They are false, top and bottom. If you know me well then you will know I have a thing about teeth. He also told me that all the doings from train loos are dumped on the tracks when you pull the flush. He said the brown colour of the bottom part of the train's carriage isn't paint, its excrement. Vinyl Shat... What a load of crap. Riveting stuff. Do I look like I'm into Polygrip and poo?
Off to the cities of Matera and Taranto today.
We start off on Matera, one of the oldest towns in the world where we can explore the fascinating Sassi region. It's here where there is the most intact example of a troglodyte settlement in the Mediterranean region.
Later we continue on to Taranto one of Italy's oldest and most beautiful ports. Taranto is also known as 'the city of two seas' due to its location on a spit of land that separates the open sea into what is known as the Mar Grande and Mar Piccolo. The artificial channel that connects them is surmounted by the famous swing bridge. Beyond the bridge lies the heart of old Taranto, an ancient medieval town comprising the Cathedral of San Cataldo and the Castel Sant' Angelo.
Discovered Wonga 2 is blind in one eye which explains why at lunch I got red wine all down me white linen trousers. Second pair ruined in 2 seasons.
They all reckon I'm outrageous. I think one of my nephews might have called me that... Bothered? Not!!

06/05/14 Castel Del Monte.

06/05/14 Bari.

06/05/14 near Rodi Garganico, Italy.

Last night's entertainment was provided for us by a local dance troupe. We were all invited to join in at various stages throughout the performance. I had been expecting a night of sensuality and was hoping for an Italian Tango dance display. No chance. It was all scarves, bloomers and hankies. The night came to an end with a very demonic Tarantella dance performed by my good self which ended in rapturous applause and cries for more. The Conga Wonga bought down the curtain literally and our evening ended abruptly with the waiters frantically trying to retrieve Wonga 2 from underneath 10 tons of chintz...

We headed for the bar. The conversation was no better than yesterday. I learnt that if you suffer from incontinence you don't need to buy Tena Ladies, you can get an alternative on the NHS.

Does anyone know if you can get cystitis from drinking too much? Felt like I had a bout coming on. I am trying to monitor the amount I drink but keep losing count or forgetting. Unthinkable impediment to have when Hugh's due to arrive in the next few days. Can you imagine? My mum used to say it was a newly marrieds problem, so it's hardly surprising. I wondered what 'feeling the burn' meant now I know. Should I be buying yoghurt?

There is a god... Lovin' the bum washers in the en suite, I'm finding the whole experience a very pleasant distraction from my pain. I tend to sit there and while away the time writing my blog. My dedication to my fans, and I suppose also me fanny, is only to be commended. After all both have such high or should that be Hugh or even huge expectations!

Off to the Vieste area of Northern Puglia today for a 3 night stay. We stop at Bari, the capital of Puglia. Its labyrinth of seemingly endless passages weave through courtyards and under arches where local artisans peddle their wares. We continue to Castel Del Monte the highest point in Puglia where we will visit the most splendid of all Puglia's castles and one of the finest surviving examples of Swabian architecture. Commissioned by Frederick 11, Duke of Swabia, the castle is an outstanding example of medieval architecture.

We arrived at Villa Americana Park Hotel. Yet another hotel where you press the wrong button in the lift to get to the right floor. This room is by far the worsest, smacks of a seventies style Cartagena brothel. All that's missing is the waft of smoke from a Cohiba Behike and the sound of gunfire.

I'd like to be all dramatic and say I have bullet holes in the walls but I won't. The holes are just missing plug sockets.

When I opened the door to the Pley Club (aka room 110) I expected to see Hombre del Overol from the Norte del Valle Cartel sitting on the bed awaiting favours.

I am a very positive person as you all know and I love to embrace the

local culture. But the only culture going on here is bacterial. And I'm not referring to me nethers either.
Three nights here ain't gonna kill me. Well at least I hope not. Worry if there are no further postings.

06/05/14 Content and fulfilled... — at In Centro A Vieste.

07/05/14 Rodi.

07/05/14 near Rodi Garganico, Italy.
Firstly I must apologise for my late postings. There have been numerous events requiring my expertise to sort that have taken precedence over everything else.
We definitely chose the wrong table to sit at for dinner last night. This was my first encounter, and hopefully my last, with Mr and Mrs Shropshire. There are other names I could give them but I'd probably be arrested for some kind of -ism.
She has a dislike of all things edible and he couldn't give a toss and just ignores her.
The table consisted of me and the two Wonga's, Boney Toney, Dilly Dally Sally, James an officer and a mental man and these two.
I was only trying to fill out the menu choices for the following night. What happens? I get her life story. She's not allowed to eat red meat 'cos as a child she had asthma. Her father used to make her chew chicken bones. If you ask me it was likely in the hope they would choke her! The day before I learnt she had told the driver she can't eat eggs. How funny. I've just organised an omelette for her dinner tomorrow and she has three fried eggs and chips in front of her which she is ploughing through quite happily. Attention seeker me finx.
Anyway, as a result of organising the menus I am now dinner monitor. This was something I always aspired to be at school but never got the chance. I'm sure it wasn't as difficult as this though.
The list of injuries is rising daily. Mainly where people have fallen over.

Numerous scraged knees and mosquito bitten ankles.
On the subject of knees you will be delighted to know mine are improving daily. I am climbing steps a lot more easily. Getting up out of chairs is still a problem but hoping this will also get easier as time goes on.
Of course I've had the mickey taken out of me because I have brought 32 scarves with me. 1 for every day and 1 for every night. I can hardly go around smelling of sweat head can I? Hoping that I will be able to abandon them soon. It will stop the speculation as to why I wear one.
Today we were supposed to be going on a boat trip, but allegedly the captain has had his licence revoked and so it's been cancelled. This caused major, majors today and an uprising of my fellow coachcationers. I think it may have had something to do with Juventus winning but, hey ho, nothing we could do about it. Other boats claimed not to be sailing due to the sea being rough. Looked fine to me.
We spent the day down by the marina and in and around the town. Ended up sat by the pool drinking.
Quote of the day: Wonga 1 to Caff
'I don't know how you manage to drink all that liquid'. This was referring to my beer.
This day the Wonga's have downed 3 litres of red wine and are on their 4th nightcap. Hello...
Spent the evening listening to music from the '70s. Shirley and Company 'Shame on you'. Fab tune.

07/05/14 Lunch: — at San Benedetto.

08/05/14 near Porto d'Ascoli, Italy.

Off to the fabulous coastal city of Vieste, with its ancient centre; set above towering, sheer white cliffs. The old town sits on the easternmost of the two promontories, at the tip of which stands the Chiesa di San Francesco, once a thriving monastery.

After lunch we head to Peschici, perched on top of an impressive cliff overlooking the bay and filled with whitewashed houses which cling to the rocky headland. The old town of Peschici climbs from the harbour to the fortifications of the Swabian Castle. For me Peschici and Taranto have so far been my only disappointment. Yes the views are fabulous but there is very little to do or see. A half day trip would suffice.

On this trip I have met some of the rudest people I have ever encountered. Too much trouble for them to say please or thank you.

They just can't seem to do as they are told. I spent ages organising the menus for people on our table and three defected to another table causing mayhem. The 3 were Mr and Mrs Shropshire and James an officer and a mental man. We weren't complaining, quite frankly we were glad to see the back of them, but it cocked things up for the waiters.

Took me ages to sort it out.

Today Mrs Shropshire has been wearing a prototype sun hat that she has customised. It's style I'd say is very reminiscent of a Boonie Desert Hat with a broderie anglaise affair attached on the back. See photo. Limited edition.

Mr Shropshire thinks its okay to fart like a 98 gun salute all day, regardless of who is behind him. He has been advised having let rip one too many times. Disgusting individual.
Looking forward to seeing Hugh in Garda on Thursday.

08/05/14 Vieste.

08/05/14 Peschici.

09/05/14 near Garda, Veneto.

Today we left Rodi. The hotel staff made our stay better than we had expected it to be.

Heading north and leaving beautiful Puglia, next stop Marche.

Wonga quote of the day. Referring to my new very trendy Monsoon top that I'm wearing. 'Have you spilt something'?

I check my frontage.

My reply: 'No it's the pattern'.

This hotel is by far the best yet.

It is clean, spotless in fact, and you can turn around in the shower without your arse changing the temperature. 100 metres from a beautiful promenade and beach with numerous restaurants where al fresco dining is at its best.

If I have a criticism they could perhaps relocate the motorway and train line from off my balcony.

10/05/14 Pie 'n' a pint at Ferrara Centro Storico.

En route to our hotel on Lake Garda we visited Ferrara, an outstanding renaissance city rich in history and regarded as one of Italy's hidden treasures. The San Giorgio Cathedral dates back to the 12th century and the Este castle is complete with towers, moat and drawbridges.

Very emotional driving into Lake Garda. Never imagined being able to return. Feeling blessed...

11/05/14

Today we explored along the shores of Lake Garda visiting some of the picturesque villages.

Removed my head scarf today. Had to hit the chemist for a comb and gel.

11/05/14 Lazise.

11/05/14 Sirmione.

12/05/14 Heading home...

I feel very fortunate to be well enough to go on these coachcations. Pending the oncs permission I have booked two more. Both 19 dayers; one to Morocco and the other Transylvania. Becoming a bit of a coach setter.

I know I take the rise (better not say mic) out of people but I do it in jest. When people relax and get to know you they tell their stories. Most people have one to tell. Some are very sad, others quite shocking. Having worked in the job I did for twenty years and with the knowledge I have gained I have been able to refer 1 couple to a bereavement councillor, and give best advice to others who are and have been suffering in silence. The Wonga's have been given the telephone no for Alcoholics Anonymous. There have been a lot of laughs too. Flattered that so many people wanted my email address to stay in touch. I'm even meeting up with Dilly Dally Sally in July.

You may not receive further blogs now until my holiday later this month in West Bay.

I have to disclose I'm off to Cardiff on Friday to stay with me chemo bud; however I'm banned from posting on FB. She doesn't want people knowing she's a bit of a lightweight when it comes to a drinking sesh, or that she's in her onesie by six and on the sofa snuggling with her Yorkie. Still once I have prised her Kindle away I know I will have a fab time. I understand the Prosecco is chillin'!

15

CORSICA AND SARDINIA

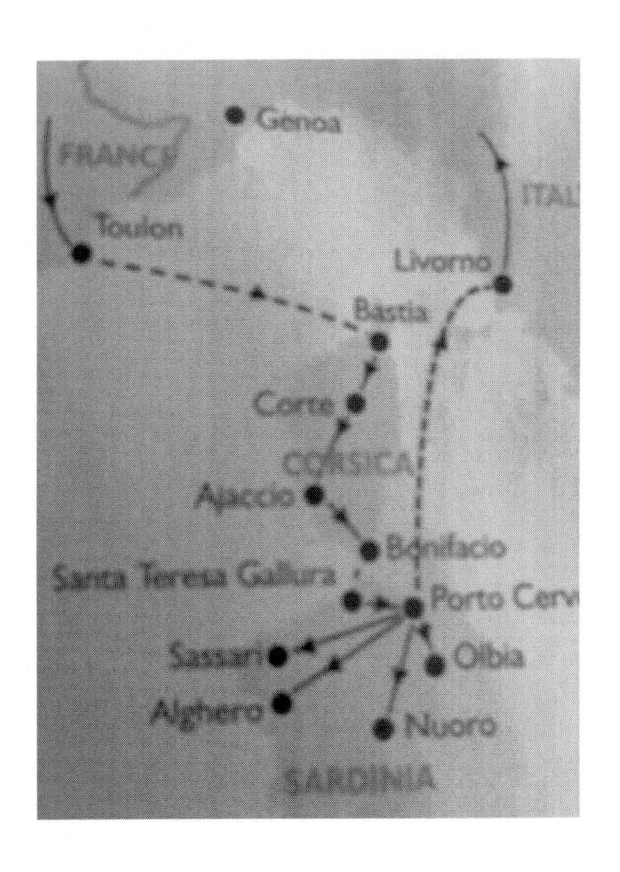

09/06/14
Day 1
After the mega wax fest yesterday, I am able to declare I am suitably coiffed from top to toe and ready to depart on a two week coachcation to Corsica and Sardinia. I will be leaving San Georgejay at 0650 and heading down to Dover where I will meet my fellow travellers.
Also, and more importantly, today a funeral will be held for a very dear friend of mine. I will be thinking of his family and friends and sending them my love. Tonight I will raise a glass in his honour.
RIP Mr H.
Such fond memories which I will cherish always.

10/06/14 near Les Ulis, France.
Day 2
Once at Dover I was assigned to coach number 48 and was seated alone in seats 21/22. Right royal result. Once again I am the youngest person on board coach.
There are numerous unkempt people on this trip. Several with dribble stainage in both upper and nether regions. Both Eau de aisselle and Par Fam du fanny have already introduced themselves to my nasal receptors.
Bad haircuts, colorants, trackky bottoms and cheap trainers seem to be the order of the day.
May need rescuing at some point. A while back, on a previous trip, one of the feeder coach drivers was very rude to an elderly WW2 vet. He had just returned from a very emotional visit to The Somme. This coach driver shouted in the ear of the elderly gent, 'I told you no water bottles in the behind seat compartments.' The elderly gent jumped a mile and was extremely shaken. I was not going to allow such bad manners so challenged the driver. I believe I may have made reference to the size of his dick at one point. Remarking that men with big mouths normally had small dicks and as he shouted so loudly his must be a micro penis...
Guess who my tour coach driver is?
Caught the Pride of Burgundy at 1440 to Calais. As always I enjoyed several complimentary glasses of Champagne in the company of Capt.

Andy Minter.
The crossing was good, sea like a mill pond. Sky was weird, strange hazy light. If someone had told me we had been beamed up I would have believed them...
Once off the ferry we headed to our overnight hotel, Mercure Les Ulis.
The A25 was invaded by a fantastic spectacle. Fabulous sports cars involved in the Gumball3000 rally. Heading to a secret location. French police in hot pursuit. Numerous dummy cars led them a merry dance.
The people I am travelling with are hard to call at this time. Their antics in the bar were funny. A posse of them complaining to the only member of bar staff on duty about the lack of service. Hello dimwits it's a French bank holiday...
Today our journey continues South through central France and to our overnight hotel in Millau in the Midi-Pyrenees region.

10/06/14 near Saint-Chély-d'Apcher, France.

And a backup!
Got a ling a long a Caff going.

10/06/14 near Millau, France.
Day 2 cont'd.
Well I can't say that hotel would win hotel of the year. The air conditioning was past its sell by date and for most of the night I

resembled a very large greasy sweat ball. Attractive not... I even managed to miss a spectacular thunderstorm. Numerous half naked male Japanese tourists obviously had the same problem, arriving at breakfast in their vests. The mind boggles.

Back on board people are beginning to come out of their shells.

So far we have the spotty Monk, Mr Hair by Alistair, Mr Benny Hill (he is a ringer for him) and his wife Mrs Quarter Past Three, Mr Invade Yer Space and Mrs I've Been Everywhere Man... Oh I nearly forgot Mrs Weight Of The World. A lone female I'm steering clear of. The ability to depress a person with just a look.

Our tour guides/drivers are a husband and wife team. The female has one of those voices that put me in mind of a weather girl. Very bleedin' annoying. She also rolls her r's. Once she gets hold of the mike she don't shut up.

People are also being told off about putting large objects in the behind seat compartments. Bit of deja vu me finx. BTW. It's not me Being chastised I hasten to add. The male driver is really OCD.

11/06/14 near Millau, France.

Day 3 - 0711

The sky is blue, the sun is shining and I'm glad to be alive.

Them Gumball3000's are giving the police the run around. Hundreds of cars going to Barca. (I knew I'd find out where they were headed. My investigative skills are second to none.) Thoroughly enjoyed seeing all the different cars, so much so I'm now on their FB page. One of the cars I remembered from my childhood, a pink and blue Corvette Stingray. Fabulous car. The eye candy has improved at the service stations and rather than queue for the loos I'm spending a lot of time in the car parks. Not going a whoopsie or a onesie mind you, just flashing me ankles, cos I have a lovely turn of. Lovin' scouting the area for hot Gumballers and very hot coppers. M&R to say the least.

Temperature reached 32 degrees yesterday. Bloody lovely.

Bought meself a fancy gadget today - 'kit' it's called. Dead handy fancy thing.

For a 2 star Ibis hotel I gotta say it ain't half as bad as I thought it would

be. Food was good and beer chilled to perfection.
Leaving our hotel we are heading towards Toulon, where we get the overnight ferry to Corsica. En route we pause at Avignon, one of the major cities of the Provence region. Located on the banks of the River Rhone, Avignon is a charming Roman town famous for the Pont d'Avignon or broken bridge. Originally the bridge had 22 arches, but now only 4 remain.
I am being constantly annoyed by a Mr I Can't Sing For Toffee. (Not everyone is lucky enough to have the voice of an angel.) The on-board ear phones don't work which means the drivers play the music to the whole coach. Normally you have the option as to what you listen to, be it music or DVD.
I have my iPad mini with me and a vast selection of tunes. However to block him out I need to have the volume up so loud I believe I may have perforated my ear drums.
Anyway after lunch we got things livened up. Singing along to a Barry Manilow sound alike. Reminded me of the Pickwick LP's you could buy for 50p all those years back. It was like a ling a long a Max sesh; singing to Everybody Loves Somebody Sometimes. I may well have been two bars in front of unknown singer but my descant was truly outstanding. And my rendition was better by far. What with me new funky do I kinda look like Sheena Easton, all I need are some shoulder pads and six inches off me height and I'm there.

11/06/14 near Millau, France.
Girlfriend style trackky bottoms...

11/06/14 near Avignon, France.
It's getting hot out here...

12/06/14
Day 3 cont'd.
First visit of the day was to The Millau Viaduct. The world's highest bridge which spans The Tarn. Seven steel pylons rise majestically toward the sky. The viaduct peaks at its highest point of 343 m. Designed by a Brit, Sir Norman Foster. The build cost 400 million euros and took 4 years to build.
Next was Avignon, Aix en Provence where at 1500hrs it hit 36 degrees. Passing through Aubagne where I was hoping to sign up a few of the knobs on board for the French Foreign Legion. Finally ending up in Toulon. Action packed alcohol fuelled day.
Christ knows what's going on with this bloody trackky bottoms lark. It's like some kind of heinous 90's revival. Half the coach are wearing them. Am I missing some kind of fashion trend? Do I need to invest?
Teamed up with a lady called H. Nice person from Wigan with a sense of humour.
After doing some people watching I started to think that Mr Benny Hill and his wife/partner Mrs Quarter Past Three were brother and sister. They have the same eyes. You never quite know who they are looking at! Anyway after dinner, unable to quell my curiosity, I asked.

Turns out they met on a coachcation 7 years ago. He fancied her and told her. Scary...

Mr Spotty Monk and his wife Sarah are from New Zealand. Got invited to have a beer and sit in the square with them. Needed to drown my sorrows so was glad of the offer. (Saw a D & G ring I liked. The sales assistant said it wouldn't fit my fingers, but she and I tried anyway. I guess - fat arse, fat fingers!) Anyway the conversation developed and we ended up talking about architecture. Mr. Spotty Monk said I had raised some interesting points. Do you know I bloody amaze myself sometimes?

Nearly caused megas today. Suitcases had to be out at 8am. Got a bit flustered trying to find one of me little Vans dappy socks (they match my blue 'n' white Vans Converse. C'mon you blues.) Eventually I found it. On my foot. Anyway this hindered me somewhat and as a consequence delayed putting my case outside the door. End of the world!

12/06/14
Day 4
Over the last day or so several new people have come into the mix. A single, Mr Hairy Ears, who wears his belt over his trousers instead of through the tabs. He speaks French fluently and if you close your eyes could almost imagine Maurice Chevalier. Well if you have a good imagination you could.
Mrs La Rue (as in Danny) you gotta see the make up to believe it. With this heat I'm surprised it hasn't slid off her face.
Mr Joe Pas-Squeal, another single gent, has Frank Spencer mannerisms. He's hysterical.
Spending time on the Cote d'Azur was very nice, however not as glamorous as I had imagined. Numerous yachty type boats. (No sign of The Wet Dream however.) The Navy base docks their vessels there and numerous women of ill repute peddle their wares very close to the harbour.
We sat eating crepes and drinking beer until it was time to board.
The ship is called The Mega Express Five. Sounds like a runaway train and has a Corsican pirate as its logo. Tad worrying. The cabins are more than adequate, kitted out with three beds. As we set sail music blared out of the speakers, all very dramatic. Put me in mind of the type of music played when the North Korean army do that marching thing.
Only one overnight incident to report - a minor tsunami in the cabin. Drainage from the shower is very poor.
The sunset was spectacular - watching the sun go down as we sat up on deck drinking yet another ice cool beer. The mistral wind cooling us down. The temperature still showing at 28 degrees. The music being played on the upper decks was mainly by British artists from the '80s and by midnight several of us were strutting our stuff up there with the youngsters.
This morning at 0530 back up on deck it was fabulous to watch the sun rise. The sea calm and the warm wind drying my moussed hair.
My overnight crossing may have been better if it had not been for Mr and Mrs Flemmy Chest in the cabin next to me who coughed all night.
The noise of the engines on Deck 8 was minimal, just aware of the

womb like rocking every now and again.
We safely docked in Corsica at Bastia at 0700. A mere 27 degrees.
We continue by coach to the ancient capital Corte. Situated in the heart of Corsica's regional nature reserve, Corte's upper town is picturesquely situated on top of a hill.
Our free time was spent exploring the maze of narrow streets before heading off to the Sunbeach Hotel for a two night stay and more beer.

12/06/14
Day 4 - Corte.

13/06/14

It would be so rude not to carry on from the night before.

13/06/13

A load of Bolognese... — with Vivvy Anne Le Fey at Port d'Ajaccio.

13/06/14

Day 5

Mr Hairy Ears has adopted some kind of very strange ritual. First thing in the morning he dons a thick coat and wears long socks over his hands. I initially thought he was drying his socks as it was 27 degrees and rising. Trying desperately to find out why he does this. Discovered he does voice-overs. This explains his lovely accent and a really nice voice. He reckons his accent is English but people don't believe him and keep questioning him, which is really funny as they ain't subtle.

Tried the local Chestnut patty-cake which is spookily served on a chestnut leaf. Very moreish.

Caffs Coach Crisis Centre hasn't opened yet this trip. However I have been sorting out people's mobile phones and cameras. Good job I have been paying attention to my niece who has been helping me to understand gadgets and their workings. It's more luck than judgement though, believe me.

I'm also mosquito bite expert and have been treating people's bites with toothpaste. A very good remedy from old.

The moaning started today at breakfast. We were told brekky started at 0800. Nobody could understand why they couldn't go in earlier. Did they shut up asking each other why? Did they hell? Now then, I'm a firm believer that rules are for fools but why get so wound up over something so trivial.

I can tell you I've been quite glad of the Muscadelle at 0830, it dilutes the moaners and numbs me mozzie bites. Currently Corsica has numerous blood sucking insects flying around that are a luminous fluorescent green, having been gammo rayed after biting me.

Trouser braces and wearing the same clothes every day is the in trend with this lot. Or else they've bought three of each with them, which I doubt. I may be the hander outer of soap tomorrow. Bloody stink bombs.

Mr Benny Hill aka Dennis and his wife Mrs Quarter Past Three are real love birds, he's so caring. He keeps a daily diary on the events of the day in an A6 notepad and has done since the day they met. Apparently he has hundreds of them.

Back to the interesting stuff. Today we visited the beautiful coastal town of Ajaccio. Famous for being the birthplace of Napoleon Bonaparte. The imposing Citadel dominates the town and the harbour area is a maze of yellow ochre houses.
After being frog marched around the town by a very scary Corsican tour guide I am fit for nothing (except a beer.)
I feel as though I've been on the GR20 trail. Must have lost at least two stone.

Day 5

14/06/14
Day 6
Today we visit the charming village of Propriano on the Gulf of Valinco. We then continue to the Southern tip of Corsica and to the town of

Bonifacio. This was once a hiding place for pirates and then later became a major trading centre. Here we board the ferry to Santa Teresa Gallura in Sardinia, the second largest island in the Mediterranean. We spend 5 nights here at Hotel Li Graniti.
Major majors late afternoon yesterday. Only took 6 days before I'm injured due to no fault of my own.
If I had witnessed this I would probably have been in dire need of a change of nicks and likely hospitalised for having an acute asthma attack, however as I was on the receiving end it is far less funny.
Back in my day, when kids went on holiday we played on the beach building sandcastles and went swimming in the sea. Well let me tell you this was not the case this afternoon.
Several children felt it very funny to spin the hotels revolving door. I was unaware this was going on and stepped through the cylindrical enclosure as it revolved. My timing was not good as the next thing I know is that I am trapped and wedged between one of the four partitions. I slid down the glass and ended up in a burbling heap on the floor of the foyer. The three little shits responsible made off in haste, never to be seen again. Now, most people who know me understand I have difficulty getting up from a sitting position. Trying to get up off the floor, with a large audience who had come to my aid, well you can imagine. Not a pretty sight...
The accident has left me with severe contusions to my left boob and arm. In fact if I was a doctor I'd say I have major multiple hematomas. Needless to say I have hit the gin big time in order to numb the pain. (BTW I have been checked over by a medical professional.)

15/06/14

Day 7

The excursion today takes us to the Barbagia area which is also known as the heart of Sardinia. The name comes from the age when the Romans conquered the islands. The Romans themselves were unable to subdue the fierce inland population so this part of the island was named 'The land of the Barbarians'.

We visit the small town of Nuoro, which boasts some of the best views on the island. We continue through the local vineyards to Oliena, the 'murales' of Orgosolo, the famous bandit villages and many other attractions of the surrounding area. We spent lunch with the Pastori Shepherds whose sheep produce the famous Pecorino cheese. We were seated around in semi circles on granite benches, covered in oak leaves among the wonderful cork tree woods. Lamb and porchetta are roasted on the open fire and is served with local Sardinian bread and home-

made red wine.
This invite is such an honour. Quite honestly I doubt very much that even my Welsh friends have experienced this...
I was most put out today when several of my fellow coachcationers made reference to the fact they had seen me eating lunch close to the harbour. I don't deny this occurred, after all it was lunch time and as my impediment requires that I eat properly and regularly this is quite normal for me. I really couldn't understand what the problem was. By the time I got back to the coach I was the topic of conversation. Apparently I'd had lunch with a non coachcation man and had been seen drinking something sparkling which was chilling in a bucket of ice. That is not what happened. The male my stalkers made reference to was in fact sitting alone on the next table. Well let them think what they want. I ain't gonna deny it.
Have got H drinking beer, she had never drunk it before meeting me. Witnessed her order a bottle on the coach without being prompted. Proud moment.
My décolletage looks like Scaramanga with chicken pox. Bloody midges have performed march of the mods all over me.
Had to rescue numerous people today from being locked out on their balconies. Twats!
They sit out on the balconies and shut the patio doors behind them to keep out the midges and to ensure the room stays cool. The doors lock and they can't back in. There's me trying to enjoy a beer on the patio and all I can hear are numerous people shouting my name asking me to alert reception that they are unable to get back in the room. Up and down like a bleedin' Weston donkey.

RINASCITA

Orgosolo - Lunch with the Shepherds.

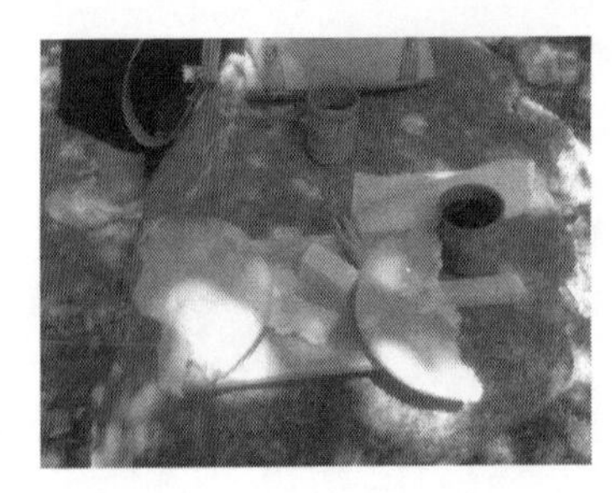

15/06/14 near Orgosolo, Italy.
Grappa is the new Limoncella. Word!

16/06/14
Day 8
Chasing with Grappa at the shepherds lunch was maybe not such a good

idea. Needs must. Being here in Italy after the England game has been a tad difficult to say the least. Anyway back to the Grappa. They just kept topping up my cork cup and forcing me to drink it. Bit grumpy this fine morn but up and ready for the off.

I have a vague recollection of being dust panned and brushed before being allowed back on the coach. Lucifer knows what I'd been up to.

All I know is we laughed a lot. H was out of it and Ms and Ms. Plastic Packers were laughing instead of moaning. Result!

Mrs Weight Of The World aka M'lady and Mr Hairy Ears think they are better than everyone else. He reckons he's the 'mind the gap' voice. She. Well. What would you be doing on a coach trip if you were dirty stinking rich? Reckons she's a professor with master degrees coming out of her ears. She holds court every day and as long as she's getting attention she's happy.

I knew I'd totally lost it when I started singing My Old Man's A Dustman, Me And My Buddy Gonna Pick A Bale Of Hay and Truly Truly Fare. Hello how old am I? #Reup

Give me a New Year's Eve dispatching on South in the control room any time of the week! I have never met a bunch of women who complain as much as this lot. Guess who's sat with them for the next 6 days? If only they would stop and listen to themselves.

Classic lines such as 'I couldn't even blow dry my hair because I was so flustered'.

Me: "Ok what can we do to change that? Is there anything housekeeping can help with?"

"Well the volume won't go up on the TV, I can't get world news, and I haven't got a view from my balcony because it's all overgrown with plants..."

We journey 50 yards through the bar area to reception who kindly replaced the batteries in the remote sorting one of the problems. There is no CNN channel which sorts another. The bougainvillea that is in full flower and absolutely stunning will, I'm sorry to say, have to remain there as it has done for the last 20 years... What are these people on?

The questions you get asked. Why can't we go up for salad? Why are we just sitting here waiting? Why is the hotel so far from the beach? I was

physically shaking by first course.
You wait until you are told to go up for food so Chef can monitor what needs replenishing otherwise he gets complaints there is a lack of food. This actually happened 'cos the women on my table wouldn't wait until Chef was ready for them.
The reason we are 45 mins from the beach (on foot) is that we are staying up in the Sardinian hillside in a 3 storey hotel that has been carved into the rock.
Read your effing brochure before you book you morons.
And breathe.
It's off to the exclusive and beautiful Costa Smeralda today. This being a coastal resort in the north-eastern part of Sardinia. Costa Smeralda is only 55km long and spreads into small and deep bays reminiscent of fjords. Pausing at the harbour town of Pilau before hopping aboard the ferry to the Maddalena Islands. We visit the town of La Maddalena, the only inhabited island in the archipelago. The town is perched on the hill of Guardia Vecchia.
I will post more pictures but the Wi-Fi is so slow.

Palau.

La Maddalena.

17/06/14
Day 9
How the hell I ended up with the German coach group I'm not too sure. I think it was because I removed Stephen aka Mr Joe Pas-Squeal from in front of the television while they were trying to watch the match. Stephen is one of those people who are totally oblivious to everything and anyone around him.
If I hear him hum anymore spaghetti western theme tunes I am gonna have to suggest he looks up the tune for The Great Silence. It is really annoying especially as he has that stupid squeaky voice.
This morning my knees feel like I have walked around all 120 Islands in the archipelago, I know I haven't as I'm still unable to walk on water. Yet! (I'm good but not that good.) My head is worse and I have 3rd

degree whiplash. I think it was dancing to Status Quo, doing the get down, deeper and down. My hair isn't long enough to swing it all about, but rest assured fellow Brits I did not let the side down. I introduced our German friends to Grappa to celebrate their win and at breakfast this morning their numbers were severely depleted.

Mrs Weight Of The World aka M'Lady is from South Africa and thinks she is better than anyone else. Her suitcase has got to be bigger than mine without doubt, as she has a hat to match every outfit. Yesterday on the way back to the hotel she decided instead of alerting the driver to stop the coach or averting her head she would puke all over me.

Apparently she suffers from motion sickness and she said the roads were too windy. I had to be hosed down and sit in bin liners until we got back. She didn't even apologise. Her card is marked.

I appear to be the only person on board with an iron. Just a little travel iron with steam and spray capability. Had it for years. I was asked by several women how I managed to keep my clothes free of creases. I told them about my handy little gadget, you could see the envy. Later M'Lady comes over and asks me in front of a gob smacked group of coachcationers how much I would charge to do some ironing. Back at home she allegedly has a maid (maid my arse, reasons her boyfriend's name is Roddy - smacks of similarities with one of our royal family me finx!) I was not ImPressed.

Mr Benny Hill aka Denis with one N is still wearing the same track suit bottoms that he has done for the past nine days. He has however removed the socks he's been wearing for eight days. Yukhowvile!

Mr Hairy Ears has had a massage in reception. I suggested he may like to see if they could wax his extremities which he found very funny. I remarked it might be a good idea to take Denis with him to get his feet seen to. Perhaps get his curly toenails clipped.

Our excursion this morning takes us through the charming landscape of the Gallura region to Tempio Pausania. Founded in 250BC, this is a beautiful spa town as well as being the cultural capital of Gallura.

The historical centre of Tempio Pausania is an important area for mining and the working of cork and granite. We also visit a family run Cork factory in Calangianus.

This safto we hit the jet set resort of Porto Cervo, where lots of celebs have holiday homes.

Calangianus.

Tempio Pausania.

Porto Cervo.

17/06/14

Drunken selfie. Afar in a bar — at Porto Cervo.

18/06/14 near Cannigione, Italy.

Nobody is gonna ever believe me. Get home from Porto Cervo only to find an infestation of cockroaches in my bedroom. I remove 8 before it all becomes a bit much. Receptions English is not good. However he offers to come to my room to see the problem, numerous upside down receptacles are covering the floor to imprison the critters. Here he is chasing them round my room... PMSL.

18/06/14 near Cannigione, Italy.
Day 10
Following the Coo Ka Ra Cha fest in my room early this morn the management are falling over themselves to make sure I am happy. They have promised me they will be looking at my room all day. M'Lady is green with envy at all the attention I'm getting. Couldn't get any more people in my room if you tried. The HazMat girls are in there with their sprays and cockroach impalers, and there are five men overseeing that the job is done properly.
Porto Cervo is right up my street. I loved it there, beautiful food and a lovely location. I could really do this celebrity lark. Still no sighting of the Wet Dream though.
Watched the footie, Brazil v Portugal, with a load of Adonises. Had a good excuse to be there as close to the very slow Wi-Fi connection. Had my bar bill paid for me by one of the German guys from last night. His name was Carsten - a very Vivvy Anne Le Fey type name. Not too sure why he did this. Left me his email address and telephone number on my

room door. I knew me Status Quo moves were good...
Everyone is dropping like flies. Likely due to M'Lady and her pukey buggy body. People have caught some kind of lurgy and are confined to bed.
Today, or what's left of it, has become a free day to allow time to prepare for the Gala tonight. I'm still recovering from Porto Cervo, I didn't get back till five this very morn with 18 Brits, 19 Germans and Carsten in tow.
Apparently Mrs Quarter Past Three arrived at dinner minus her teeth and in a more dishevelled state than normal. She has been in bed all day and it is thought unlikely she will rise tomorrow. Thank god I missed the toothless spectacle. I was told it wasn't good!
M'Lady has offered some cock 'n' ball story as to why Roddy isn't with her (most of the coach have been surfing Google to check if it's true.) I won't divulge the details at this time just in case it is true. The story is horrific and I don't want to be disrespectful until her claims have been verified by my source. Reckons he, that being Roddy, is gonna claim on his insurance. Don't quite know how that's gonna work as she has used his suitcase allowance.
You will be pleased to hear I have devised a system to ensure I'm protected from mozzies. Mix the mozzie spray with sun cream. Works a treat and ensures the crevices are covered.
Off to Baja Sardinia to mix with the rich and be infamous.

18/06/14
Hangover food. — at Baja Sardinia.

18/06/14 near Cannigione, Italy.
Rude not to.

19/06/14 near Calambrone, Italy.
Day 11
The gala evening went well - considering we got on the wrong hotel shuttle minibus and ended up at another complex. I was surprised I

managed to get ready in time.
Our hotel is set in rock as are most of the others in the area. After trips out we enter the hotel on floor two. Bedrooms are on floor one and Reception is on floor zero. Simples!
Today the minibus drops us off outside the rocky reception area. We all head towards the lift which had disappeared. I ask the receptionist where the lift is. Her English is not that brill, bit like my Italian really. Anyway, after an hour of gesticulating we find out we are in the wrong hotel. The other coachcationers I had in tow said the receptionist probably thought I was asking for a boob job the way I was trying to explain. Making rising motions with my hands.
The entertainment at our gala was a very good looking male singer, who couldn't sing, buttons on his shirt undone to his navel, windswept hair and wiggly hips. The food, well let's just say it was difficult to tell what it was we were eating but it tasted better than it looked.
I think I may have been threatened today. An alien bottle of red was left on our table at dinner yesterday. We sit at table 51. The bottle had been opened and there was about a quarter missing. The number 51 had been marked clearly on the label. We knew the wine didn't belong to any one of the 8 on our table. Regardless, one of the Plastic Packers starts to pour the wine - sharing it with her friend. The bottle was drained of its contents and disposed of. Today we find out that the table next to us was missing a bottle of wine, purchased by Mr and Mrs Flemmy Chest. There was a big hoo ha and various people were accused of nicking it. The Plastic Packers just sat there and said nothing. It was suggested by H, to stop further upset they should admit they had drunk the wine and offer to replace it. They refused and said to me 'and you make sure you keep your mouth shut.'
Luckily I had plenty of anti-venom with me and was able to bite my tongue. Bloody cheek. Up until this remark I hadn't had any involvement. I have however made it clear that if they don't come clean then I'm gonna spill the beans. I will not be intimidated by two seventy six year old thieves.
Today we explore Northern Sardinia with its varied landscape. We pass through the province of Sassari to the attractive coastal town of

Alghero. Surrounded by the ancient town walls, Alghero has a delightful mix of architecture. We also visit Neptune's cave. The Grotta di Nettuna is without doubt one of the most popular day trips for visitors to the town of Alghero. Discovered by fishermen in the 18th century, this sea level cave complex has numerous stunning stalactites and stalagmites.
The tranquil blue bay of Porto Conte and the vertical cliffs at Capo Cacciatore are spectacular.
Quote of the day, 'can I borrow your iron?'
I reply 'yes of course, I just need to run the iron over a few things first then you can have it.'
'Well that's not fair; you've had it all week.'
'Yeah, well that's because it's my iron'. Hello...

Sassari.

Alghero.

20/06/14

Day 12

The boat trip to Neptune's caves was eventful. Fantastic scenery. Had to climb 160 steps inside and bend double, which I don't do with ease, to move through the caverns.

On the way out the wind wouldn't allow the boat to dock. Soooo, we had to climb up 650 steps to get back to land. It was like walking the Great Wall of China in 32 degrees. There is no acorn trail in England which comes as close to the cliff edge as this does. I should know, I've walked a few. What with me fear of heights and my impediment I thought I was gonna have to stay there and camp the night. If it wasn't for the two Adonises helping me, cave rescue would have been required. I'm in need of major surgery to my hips, knees and ankles and have been on a lager drip all day. It gets worserer.

We reached Orgosolo ready to board the biggest ship I have ever seen, for our overnight crossing. The whole thing inside and out was plastered in Disney characters. Angry Disney characters with unsmiley faces. The cabins had mirrored tiles on the ceiling, not too sure what the purpose of that was. Ahem...

Watched the England game in the bar. A tad difficult as most of the passengers were supporting Ukraine. Still there was no incident and if an excuse was needed we had one, to hit the bar and drown our sorrows.

We docked in Livorno an hour earlier than we had been told. So it was a mad panic to get dressed following the 0445 tannoy announcement to get out of bed. I, plus others, initially thought it was some kind of emergency.

Once off the boat we headed past Pisa, and Genoa to Aosta for lunch. Then it was up to Mont Blanc, using the tunnel to travel into France.

Most of the passengers have decided not to listen to the announcements of departure times and places we need to be to meet the coach. Instead it's let's ask Caff she'll know.

We spent the evening in the Trunker Truckers bar across the road from our hotel, where the beer was cheaper. Having met up with several Trunker Trucking Brits who asked if they could join us, we finally hit the pit at 0200 hrs. I'm gonna need to sleep for a week after this holiday.

21/06/14 near Roissy-en-France, France.
Day 13
And so today the journey home continues. Onward to Paris where I am meeting Hugh, while my fellow passengers continue onward without me. Just a little surprise he arranged. I hope I will be able to do him justice. I am still battered and bruised from the revolving door incident, everything from my hips down ain't working proper. I'm talking bone wise here.
I don't want to labour on it too much but my getting out of the bath this morn was hilarious. If it had been recorded and sent to Jimmy Hill we would have won first prize. Performing the whale like roll so I could then get into a kneeling position, nearly flooded the bathroom and almost drowned me in backwash.
I have listened to enough Foster and Allen to last me a lifetime and I won't miss the moaners and asinine questions I was asked daily.
I have had a great holiday. Up there on my top four. Met some lovely people and some right nutters.
So folks till my next holiday it's ta tah from me.

21/06/14 With Hugh... — at Tour Eiffel. Phew. Hugh... That's all.

24 June

Paris with Hugh...

16

BOURNEMOUTH

11/07/14

I suppose it was a foregone conclusion that this holiday was gonna involve 97 thousand hills. It is not H for holiday it's H for hill.

When I recced the area none of the maps showed 1 in 13 hills. Talk about crocked. I nearly croaked coming back up from town. Thank god for Next where I managed to catch my breath over a new top or two.

The students who are out in force offered to put me in a shopping trolley and wheel me up the hill. I wasn't banking on the suspension holding out so declined the kind offer...

My morning was eventful. BT which stands for bloody twats decided to change the email address again, from Yahoo back to BT.

Managed to change my passwords on my numerous fancy gadgets and tested said apparatus to ensure I could receive emails. However despite being a bit of a whizzo I discovered I couldn't send emails on my iPhone. After a lengthy conversation with BT the problem remained unresolved and I came away to Bournemouth before my day was consumed any further with technicalities. I could give talks on IPOP and IMAP. I'm qualified to degree standard! Word!

Google had assured me there was a store on Westcliff Road so I was happy the matter could be resolved at my journeys end.

The drive down was delightful apart from the 50 million roundabouts you have to navigate. The scenery stunning and what a glorious day.

Google was wrong and I ended up in the Vodaphone store where I received a first class service. Thanks Naeem and Matt. If I hadn't been in fear of being arrested for paedophilia I would have kissed you.

Listen up BT customers with an iPhone. When you change your password for the incoming server if it doesn't work change the password on the outgoing server too. You have to drill down to find it. Don't start messing around with ports or you'll bugger it all up.

I am now free from all stress and enjoying a late lunch and a pint. People watching with Viv

12/07/14

Well I survived the night. Just...

The hotel has no air conditioning. If I hadn't been saved by porter service with an oscillating fan I'm sure I would have dissolved. Several other things I have observated thus far. No best before dates on complimentary tea, coffee etc. in the room. Sink in en suite only reaches me nethers and is far too low. I'm only 5ft 4 so vertically challenged, but I draw the line at kneeling to clean me teeth.

The hotel is clean; staff friendly and efficient and the food, although expensive, is clear your plate standard. Oh, nearly forgot those knee cracking hills.

Breakfast al fresco was delightful in the sunshine. Nothing like an F.E.B. to start the day. The stroll down to the beach was pleasant. Lots going on. A cheer leading competition which had over spilled onto the beach and was very entertaining. I can cheer and I can lead but my hair wasn't long enough to wear the mandatory sparkly Minnie Mouse style bow.

Loving the people watching. Evidence of numerous cosmetic alterations going on. Mainly upper torso and facial. Really surprises me how insecure people are about themselves and their bodies/looks. The eavesdropping has been a revelation and a real eye opener. The women having the conversation had nothing to worry about as far as I could tell. But had severe hang ups. Some issues they had hadn't even crossed my mind. I need to seek advice from Hugh. Women never cease to amaze him as in yours truly; I'll be interested to hear his spin on the wrinkle.

Loads of totty to watch from behind me CK's and stacks of grotty.

There's a chest fest going on with the men. Walk around bare chested but carry your T-shirt. I'm not grumbling mind.
I took a leisurely stroll along the beach; collecting shells from the shoreline as I went, and which were in abundance. This pastime always reminds me of Sare Le Bare and Ridgers for some reason. Came across the biggest jelly fish I have ever seen. Must have been spectacular in the water.
There is an ice cream boat that patrols the shore playing an ice cream style ringy bell Benny Hill theme tune. Although I like the idea could do with some alternative music. Gets on yer nerves after a while.
The sea water theraputed me crocked knees and eased my pain. 'Twas probably the shock of the freezing Channel waters. 15 degrees today when I checked.
Love how Bournemouth is helping the bees and butterflies with wild flower meadows along the cliff line which I must say look absolutely stunning.
Gonna have to hit Boots on the moro to get heat itch stuff.
Just eaten two mouthfuls of the worst cheesecake I have ever tasted, overwhelmed with some aniseed additive. Yukhowvile.

13/07/14
May have unintentionally caused a bit of a domestic today.
Breakfast was a busy affair with numerous guests who had stayed over following a wedding ceremony.
A couple sit on the next table to me 'al fresco'.

The female is busy running backward and forth to fetch her husband's brecky. He, being a most rude character, was making remarks about how stupid she was and that after 22 years she ought to know what he eats for breakfast. Said female turns to face me and the crowded patio and says 'no pleasing some people, don't know what to do with him'.
'I do' I replied. 'Park your ass, enjoy your breakfast and let the miserable git get his own. That or starve'. The patio erupted. The female takes my advice and sits down; her husband couldn't believe it judging by his face. She then says 'you heard the woman, get your own breakfast or starve.' Tail between his legs he leaves and gets his breakfast to rapturous applause and cheering.
Spent the day down on the beach. Well after I had been to Boots and purchased anti-itch cream I did.
Walked through the gardens and had a wonderful day people watching and enjoying the sunshine.
Came back up from the beach using the rock lift. Considering I'm scared of heights I did well.
Now enjoying dinner al fresco. Fajitas. Not too sure I get the chicken 'n' cheese thang but trending. Having scones and cream for pud.

17

TRANSYLVANIA, BULGARIA & THE BEST OF THE BALKANS

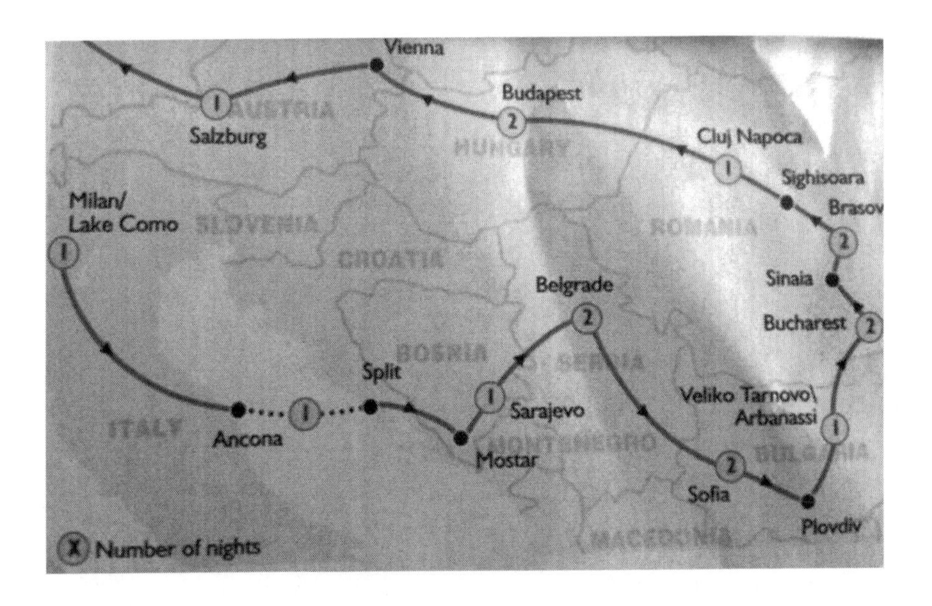

04/08/14 near Dover.
I have a bit of a confession to make. I haven't been able to say anything until I was sure me brother was well and truly on his way back home to the good ol' You Ess of A. Well you know what expats are like about our National Health Service and I didn't wanna cause a heated debate. Prior to embarking on this holiday I had a meeting up at the health centre to discuss the tests I had following an earlier appointment with the onc.
Anyway I met a new out of the box doctor, (if she resigns it's my fault and I'm sorry and I'll never go to heaven for sure) who, after taking 30 mins to find the computerised report, reassured me that my bloods were ok, I don't have gout and my thyroid levels are good so no need for drug adjustment, and me CA19-9 will always show normal because of an anomaly with me and me genes. Now with regard to me knee joint, initially there was concern it was the onset of cachexia. (I won't bore you with the ins and outs.) Anyway, my knee isn't broken but the doc can't tell me what it is as she's not a radiographer. I was offered patch style opiate based pain killers so it goes directly into my bloodstream. Where else would it go?
I was not best pleased and stated my case. 'Well that's not gonna work is it? I'm going on holiday and don't wanna be monging out all day at the back of the coach and I wanna be able to drink!' The shock on her face would have made a fab Mee Zee or Her Zee. You can guess where the conversation went next. A discussion relating to my alcohol unit intake per day. Needless to say I administered a large dose of Bennett's Tongue. Bloody cheek. I refused the opium and told her I'll use alcohol to numb the pain. She's now writing to the onc to suggest I see a health care councillor who deals with alcohol dependant patients. It would be fair to say she needs to find a sense of humour and learn how to deal with people who have misplaced their filters.
Anyway you know me - always a backup plan, thought I'd phone my hospice nurse. Not a wise move Murray...
After I was located on the computer it was discovered my hospice nurse had left for pastures new months before and I had been archived. The nurse on the end of the phone assured me I could be resurrected at any time... Is my name Jesus? If that option is open to me I'd like to hang

onto it for as long as poss - might come in handy... bloody dim wits.

This particular holiday blog is dedicated to my good friend Adabank. This is in a bid to cheer her up while she recovers and recuperates from breaking her foot.

I have had a lot to think about before this holiday. Firstly having to organise all the different currency I needed was a nightmare. Then, as if that wasn't enough to up my stress levels, someone finds a flaw in my fatal plan...

It's comforting to know you can always rely on a special friend to flag something up over lunch that you may not have previously thought about. On this particular occasion it was repatriation.

When I go on holiday I travel without insurance mainly because no company will touch me. Irresponsible? No...this is normal for people in my position. Being extremely organised, or up until the 1st of July I thought I was, I have a contingency plan in place to get me home should I fall ill. I was asked the 'but what if' question. Hadn't given it a bleedin' thought.

Reference was made that I could end up like the character in 'Weekend at Bernie's'. Said friend volunteered herself to be official fundraiser if the 'but what if' occurred to ensure I make it back home. Comforting.

I was not happy I had cocked up.

Upon returning home I got on it straight away, determined to rectify the problem.

Using my BFF aka Google I found a company that will post you back. (See attached pic.) I didn't fancy being parcel wrapped so have found an alternative very nice company who will deal with me for a fee of £3500 to £4500 (dependent on where I am in the world.) They kindly emailed the form I needed to sign and it is now with the other documentation I carry and take on holiday with me. People can now sleep easy.

The bonus I suppose on this trip is everyone sleeps in coffins in Transylvania. So I've spoken to the driver and we plan to nick one and bung it in the hold just in case I get a 'but what if' occurrence. Drawing on a positive at least I get the opportunity to get a practise run in.

My luggage is much heavier this trip. To be honest I'm a bit put out. If I hadn't needed to prepare for Vlad the Impaler I could have brought more clothes with me.

The stakes I whittled are not only in my hand luggage, I have another stash in me case. Along with a bible, crucifix and garlic.

I have calluses you have never seen the like of before. I'm still picking splinters out. Some are so deep I've had to buy some magnesium sulphate which has stunk the house out. Let's hope it works.

I nearly killed myself yomping across the fields at the top of the road to get the wood.

You try climbing over fences in the dead of night with a chain saw, torch and ladder with all my impediments. Not easy.

And this whittling lark is equally as difficult. I whittled down too far and the wood kept breaking when I tried to carve a cross in the point.

Turns out it was all a bloody waste of time anyway. The stakes need to be made of oak, hawthorn and rowan. Next day I ended up going to 'buy and queue', where I got an assortment of wood which should cover all types of vampire. Sorted.

Trying to buy Goth purple clothes in summer has not been easy either and if I'm honest it is not a colour I have a lot of in my wardrobe. I certainly will not be wearing any Petulia oil that's for sure.

Gotta say my eyebrows look very Goth like, might have left the dye on a bit too long but I'm sure it will fade, well that's if my eyebrows don't fall out first. Had to dye my hair to match them.

The coach number is 13 and I'm in seat 33 toward the back lhs.

I am the only lone female on board, there are 9 lone males. Divided by 19 days. My maths ain't good Lol..

Spending the crossing up in club class where I belong and where I can people watch.

Off to Northern France to the Hotel Ibis in Reims for an overnight stay.

05/08/14 — At Lago di Pusiano.

Our stay at the hotel Ibis was rather a pleasant one. Soft double bed and plush pillows. Best night's sleep I've had for a long while.

On the suggestion of a good friend and former colleague S.S-P I hit a rather large church in Reims late last night, under the cover of darkness obviously and I nicked some holy water. Came in dead handy those little plastic bottles Boots sell in a three pack.

I just hope 'cos it's nicked that it will still work the same on those pesky vampires.

Gotta try not to get it muddled up with me gin bottles.

Breakfast was with John, an elderly lone gent, someone I met in Ireland earlier this year. Had to help him undo his butter. Thank god it weren't anything else.

This lot are taking a while to unfold. I'm the only one drinking alcohol on board coach. Most of the others are drinking vegetable soup. Hidden message there me finx...

It was comforting to find my gin and tonic had pole position in the on board fridges and my lemon was frozen in the freezer awaiting the sun over the garden... Still not too sure what that saying means...

Several characters have emerged today like pupae from a cocoon.

Sat in front of me Mr Click Away, with his Kodak instamatic who takes pictures of anything, Mrs Plaster Cast who by the end of this holiday is gonna wish they made one for noses. Mrs Catch the Bus, who can't understand why anyone drives. Lucky someone does otherwise she

wouldn't be on this holiday, and as I pointed out to her the bus driver does too. Ruined me G & T wittering on. Mr and Mrs Hart To Hart, Mr Lounge Hogger, Mr Leave It On Display, Mrs Plume Of Smoke and Mrs Bridge Over The A2 - a twat of a lady who came down the wrong stairs from the café and ended up on the opposite side of the A2. Kept us waiting for 20 minutes while a posse was sent to recover her. She was a burbling wreck by the time she'd been found. I had to keep quiet as didn't want the Gotthard tunnel incident bought up. Same drivers and Pete loves a wind up.
Numerous controlling husbands, got 19 days to sort them out but biding my time.
Continuing on to the Milan/Lake Como area, staying at Albavilla.

07/08/14
Well the 2nd day turned out to be eventful.
Travelled down through Switzerland into the Gotthard Tunnel, Italy and then Lake Como. A long day.
Dinner was spent with 7 racist, homophobic, opinionated bigots.
My tongue was split in two where I bit it so hard. Used up all me anti-venom too.
Here is the text the driver sent me whilst at dinner. Yes it was that bad.

'Please don't hit her on right just yet she has a bad arm and leg and knees and hurt her head on screens be gentle Xx'

In fact it was so awful I had to leave the table and make haste to the bar...
The main culprit, Mo**Ron,** sought me out and had the neck to say that he hoped I hadn't left the table on account of him.
I stared him right in the eye and said 'for purposes of clarity let's be clear. You would never be responsible for anything I do. I am my own person and I do what I want, when I want. However I refuse to listen to an opinionated bigot who has clearly outstayed his welcome on this planet and perhaps should have opted for the coach Dignitas trip.' The patio went silent.

I was given a wide berth and lots of supportive nods from other people.
I spent the rest of the evening looking at the sky and the lightning flashes, and thunder without rain, over Como as well as trying to Fugly watch. There was no shortage of material. Most of them are from Coach 13.
This morning was novel. The electric in the room is on a timer. I managed to have a shower ok, it was when I came to do me face the problem arose. With only my makeup on one eye complete and ready to face the world, the lights went out - there was no amount of flicking on and off of light switches that was gonna make any difference. With CK shades on (to cover my embarrassment) I made haste to reception. I can make haste by the way, as there has been a vast improvement in my knee joint since I had the worsest cramp in the world the other day.
Anyway back to my plight and lack of light.
The manager, a rather good looking 50 plus'er accompanies me to my room where light is thrown on the problem... 'twas all my fancy gadgets that had used up my electric quota; iron, charger, iPad, phone, oh and I was watching the tele which didn't help. Thank god all me other fancy gadgets are battery operated. I could have caused a major black out. It was not possible to give me more electric unless I paid for the room for another day. Have you ever heard anything like it? Anyway, the short of it, I had to use the coach wing mirror with the piss being taken out of me by the driver who insisted on making funny faces as I tried to perform a work of art.
It gets worserer. An elderly gent, who was sat next to Mo**Ron** on the coach, has left the trip. He suffers from diabetic comas and is partially blind. He was discovered this morning in a dreadful state, extremely distressed and shaking. A flight home has been arranged.
Yesterday he had been verbally bullied by Mo**Ron**. This disclosure came from Mo**Ron** himself at dinner last evening, where he relayed in great detail what he had said to our fellow passenger. At the time I didn't know who he was talking about. I do now and I am disgusted. This guy Mo**Ron** and Mrs Plaster Cast are an evil combination. I feel a double staking coming on and the repatriation of two, who unlike my good self are without a fundraiser!

Making our way across Italy (470k), past the cities of Milan, Parma and Bologna and onto the port at Ancona for overnight ferry to Split in Croatia.

08/08/14 near Bistrik, Bosnia and Herzegovina.
We arrived in Split and disembarked the ferry at 0630.
The crossing on the Marco Polo was pleasant enough. Didn't get much sleep due to the noise from the engines. Sounded like one of those boats that John Rambo uses chugging up the Salween River.
I spent dinner with a Maths teacher, Mr Minus One, Mrs Good Morning Class, a headmistress, and her husband a Scottish bank manager, Mr RBS and not a fan of Martin Lewis. The conversation however was better than the previous evening.
I got into mega trouble. Three of us decided to share a bottle of red. As it was Croatian wine which I know nothing about, I suggested we go for the most expensive. 36 Euros for 15:3%. Still tasted like paint stripper.
Mrs Good Morning Class was seething that it was gonna cost her husband 12 euros. He wanted to order another bottle but she was having none of it.
The people on this trip are the strangest yet. They hardly speak and most only drink if the wine is free.
I then spent the evening in the bar with Red Ed, a seventy something electronics engineer, who is recovering from prostate cancer and drinks red wine straight from the bottle. I got to hear about his E.D. and the

implant he has, which apparently mimics the change of life. At one point it got so graphic I thought he was gonna show me.
Loving the Fugly watching. Most of the husbands and wives don't even speak to one another. One goes off in one direction and the other in another. I have observated that several of the husbands continually put their wives down, and do it loudly in the company of others. However the wives have control of the money and the amount their spouses drink.
We commence our journey south crossing the border into Bosnia and Herzegovina, pausing at the city of Mostar situated on the Neretva River. During Turkish occupation a bridge, known as The Stari Most, was built across the river. Only 20 years ago, 90% of the city was destroyed. The Stari Most itself became the symbol of the city when it was totally destroyed during the Croatia-Bosnia conflict in the early 1990's.
Loved my time in Mostar, another place I never thought I'd be lucky enough to see again. After refreshing my memory with a revisit to the touristy bits I found a fab café. The waitress kept asking me to say 'lovely' in a British accent. Bit difficult as I'm Bristolian but not wanting to disappoint and all that.
Spent a fab few hours upping my vitamin D in the 35 degree heat. Later the tour guide joined me; Bruno, a nice guy who remembered me from my previous trip. Should I be worried or should I be worried. Then Bryan the Maths teacher aka Mr Minus One ruined the moment. Oh sorry, I meant joined us with his water and double scooper ice cream. Told us all about his diaries and the research he does following a trip. Told me he thought I was a real character... Okay... Think he might want me as his plus one.
We continue to the capital, Sarajevo where we stay overnight.

Mostar.

Chillin' — at the Old Bridge, Mostar, Bosnia and Herzegovina.

09/08/14 near Sajmiste, Serbia.
At dinner the singles were seated together on 2 separate tables. Not too sure why. I am the youngest on the coach again and the only single woman. Anyway I ended up sitting with John, who I have to keep reminding to do up his flies, and Bryan aka Mr Minus One - who I'm sure is gonna put me in his holiday diary. John is so sweet, complimented me on my necklace and outfit. And no, it wasn't a pearl necklace before you ask.
Joined the Pratt Pack last eve at the bar (not out of choice might I add) who consist of Mo**Ron** and D**Ron**e (yes there are two of them), Red Ed, and Mr Minus One.
Mo**Ron** was showing off to the others and being sexist. Told me that I looked nice and that I had raised his flag to full mast. Fortunately I was on form and managed a rapid response. 'Oh I didn't think that dead birds left the nest.'
The look on his face indicated the blood had drained from somewhere and it wasn't his face.
Going back to the room was scary, the lights are on timer control, but don't give you enough time to reach your room before they go out. Another electricity problem to deal with. Kept having to go back to the start of the corridor to reactivate the lights, then make like Jodie Williams to my room which, yes you've guessed it, was at the end of the corridor. Took me six attempts!
This morning's breakfast was disappointing; tinned fruit, vacuum packed meat and scrambled egg made with powdered egg. The coffee was worserer. So for me it was off to the Caffe Bar where after a quick lesson in the art of coffee making I can proudly say the Bosnia Hotel can now make a decent cup of coffee. After breakfast we discovered an attempt had been made to break into our coach. The offenders damaged a lock which wouldn't allow the coach driver to start the coach. Mercedes don't operate repair and recovery in Bosnia, so while we were out sightseeing a local garage attended to fix the problem.
Sarajevo is one of the most historically interesting and varied cities in Europe. It has been an example of historical turbulence and the clash of

civilisations, as well as a beacon of hope for peace and tolerance through multi-cultural integration. Today the city has physically recovered from most of the war damage caused by Yugoslav wars of '92-'95. It is now a cosmopolitan European capital with a unique Eastern twist.
I have to say, this is not a place I would wish to revisit. It's like a time bomb waiting to explode. You are not allowed to say the T word here and you daren't ask for Turkish coffee. It's Bosnian coffee.
No one smiles; a lot of hard faces and dead eyes, very sad.
Following our guided tour we headed north from Sarajevo to Doboj; the landscape and view was far less depressing, none of the houses were the same and were much improved. Seemed to be a much wealthier area. Only three weeks ago most of the roads had been underwater, evidence of this was extensive. Measures are already in place to prevent this happening again. A levee is being built all along the river's edge.
After passing through three borders, and miles and miles of queueing traffic, we continued to Belgrade for a two night stay. After a 7 hour journey, you can guess where I'll be heading.

Bosnia.

10/08/14 near Sajmiste, Serbia.
My first hour in the Queens Astoria Design Hotel was eventful. Air con in my room wouldn't work and I thought I was going through the change

of life again.
Two maintenance men, plus ladder, attended my room - followed by another 3 men when the problem couldn't be immediately rectified. I didn't tell them I'd climbed on the chair and tried to fix it myself with me fancy gadget, gifted to me by a lovely friend. Not a wise move. Fortunately I had removed my hand as the contraption shot a thunderbolt across the room. Melted a white plastic, not so fancy gadget, on the ceiling - blackened the white vinyl matt and singed my hair, giving me a look of someone out of a Laurel and Hardy film.
I also have numerous naked young men who are running back and forth across the corridor. Thought I was seeing things. Well I was, but you know what I mean. Depravation can cause strange events and, missing Hugh and all that, I could have been hallucinating. There aren't many men with a nice ass over forty, are there. How lucky am I? Anyway, I have a feeling sleep will be minimal judging by the head banging music coming from their rooms. Unless of course Mr and Mrs We Shall Be Complaining who are in the next room put a stop to it. They are obviously far too old to remember fun.
Dinner was a lively affair. Sitting with Red Ed, Mr Sidecar Racer and his wife, Mrs Quiet As A Mouse. Mr Sidecar Racer is an expert on everything war, stocks and shares and property. And so is Red Ed. Both had sunk a bottle of red each and tried to outdo the other with their knowledge. When it became evident Red Ed was the less knowledgeable of the two he decided to get personal. Telling Mr Sidecar Racer how lucky he was to have such a young wife. 'How old do you think I am then?' asks Mr Sidecar Racer. 'Same age as me, about 75.' Red Ed replies. Oh dear he was about 20 years out and got ruder and ruder when challenged. Ended up with me having to split them up and Red Ed storming off.
As usual I was the last one in the bar, I needed to chill, and what an occurrence occurred. I'm sat minding me own business in the lounge/foyer enjoying me pint. Mo**Ron** and D**Ron**e arrive back from a strip joint and are asked by the receptionist if they know where the coach drivers are. They say no but told him I would know. Then 3 police officers arrive; big muscly baddies with clan tatts and chiselled designs

in their hair, oh and guns - as in shooty things, demanding to see the guest list. The receptionist had one but did not have our coach parties' details and needed to speak to one of the drivers to get it. (The coach drivers had already agreed with the early tour receptionist that said list could be produced the following morning, so the drivers had gone to bed. It was 0045 by this time.) Guess who had to wake the drivers up; texts first, then continually ringing them. Yes, you've guessed it - me!
This was the text I sent;

'The 3 very big police in reception want the list of people on our coach LIKE NOW and the receptionist is gonna try and find out your room number by whatever means necessary. TORTURE!!!!! They tried to get the info out of the two Ron's who have just arrived back. I have refused to give your tel no, told them your name is Petro and I have now gone into hiding. Following a domestic, and 4 people storming off, I have had to settle their bar bills in order that I could leave the restaurant; fortunately my maths is crap so don't know how much it's cost me. Just sat quietly in the foyer enjoying me drink and I get pounced on. Also sorted out another row. Red Ed told the guy who sits across from me on the coach that he thought he was 75 and his wife was 40. Bryan got upset and started crying when Mr Sidecar Racer mentioned death and shooting himself (he has only just lost both parents) and I've had to 'there, there, never mind' him. Couldn't write it... I am not drinking or staying up late ever again. Going back to weather duties and toilet monitor. Lol, lol.. GET OUT OF BED. Oh and the lift's broken 'cos I pressed Floor 4. Can I Read Serbian? Can I ---- ends in a K...'

A sightseeing tour of Belgrade's main attractions is planned today: the imposing Kalemegdan Fortress, dramatically situated at the confluence of the Sava and Danube Rivers; Republic Square and Saint Sava Temple and of course, Tito's Memorial.
During the middle ages the town became a Serbian stronghold until the Ottoman invasion. Then in 1878, when Serbia received its independence, Belgrade became the capital.

Belgrade.

11/08/14
Went to bed at nine last night. Was totally exhausted.

Mr Sidecar Racer doesn't take breath, and it now explains why his wife is so quiet. My knowledge on WW1 and stocks and shares has vastly improved. It was when he started to loudly discuss a treaty organisation in a Serbian hotel foyer that I decided to retreat to the fourth floor (FB won't let me use the four letter acronym.) Well, in fact I took the lift to the fifth and walked down a floor. Didn't wanna bugger up the lift and have to deal with the security militia again. There are so many similarities between the people on this trip and my previous trips. Mr Minus One aka Bryan keeps diaries about his trips and writes in the tiniest writing you've ever seen; he documents everything, so he reminds me of Denis. He is able to tell you which border it took the longest to go through, to the millisecond. Mrs Pink Plaster Cast is another Mrs Cru C Fix; Red Ed is a cross between a more well to do Jim, and a Wonga. He sticks his camera in front of me, with a picture of a Serbian wine label Radovanovic and demands to know where in the UK he can buy it. 'How do I know?' I ask. 'Look on that gadget of yours!'

He went AWOL today. Was angry that he had changed all of his Euros into Serbian Dinar. It's not a recognised currency and was no use whatsoever in Bulgaria. You'd think for someone who deals in stocks and shares he would know this. Hopefully the guide or the bank will have a solution in the morning.

Mrs Pink Plaster Cast has taken to sitting in the lounge area with anyone's husband but her own. Problem is because the lounge is at the back of the coach it means I've gotta listen to her giggling. I've developed tinnitus 'cos I've got the volume up to high on my iPod. She leaves her husband alone on seat 2, that being the seat he paid a hefty supplement for.

Personally I would have left him at home, but there we are.

Talking of left at home. No one else but Hugh is busy working hard back in Blighty. He's hoping to catch up with me towards the trip end. Such a love don't you think?

Our journey today takes us south through Serbia and over the border into Bulgaria, where I will be two hours ahead of the UK. We continue to Sofia, the Bulgarian capital where we stay for two nights. 400k.

13/08/14

Great night in the bar. Sat with an opera singer, Mr RBS, and his wife, Mrs Good Morning Class, who is also an opera singer and pianist.

Red Ed rolled in about 2230 - he had found a curry house. He was as pissed as a fart. On the form we all have to fill out he has listed that his special requirements/needs are 'must have curry'. Carried on drinking Rusty Nails (Drambuie and Whisky.) Think he's a very lonely man. People starting to open up. Lots of would-be photographers among the group; all with different, but 'the best', cameras and all trying to take that perfect shot.

Off sightseeing. The Levski Monument is first stop of the day. The monument commemorates the hanging of the Bulgarian national hero and major revolutionary figure, Vasil Levski. Continuing on foot we walk along the Yellow Brick Road. A bit like Dot did all those Christmases ago. And if I'm honest it's a hand painted mustard colour. Best foot forward, not that I have one anymore mind you. We pass the monument to the Tsar Liberator, an equestrian monument erected in honour of the Russian Emperor Alexander II who liberated Bulgaria of Ottoman rule. Onward and forward past the Russian Church, a magnificent example of a Byzantine style cathedral surrounded by picturesque gardens leading onto the Presidency Building, home to the Bulgarian Presidents official chambers. In the administrative centre of Sofia the streets are yellow. The pavement was laid at the beginning of the 20th century and was a present to the Bulgarian Tsar Ferdinand for his wedding, from the Austrian-Hungarian royal family.

Mrs Quiet As A Mouse fell over on a pedestrian crossing and her husband Mr Sidecar Racer just left her there and didn't even check she was ok.

Sofia.

14/08/14 near Ghencea, Romania.
Sorry for lack of postings but I have been under the weather. In fact R.A.F if I'm honest... mixture of tiredness, too much sun, late nights and Red Ed. On the guided tour around Sofia he went right up in the face of one of the presidential guards and demanded he smiled. He was moved on by the keeper of the guards.
Later, back at the hotel about 2300 we were enjoying a beer in the bar when Red Ed arrives back from his 3rd curry of the trip - drunk and feisty.
He plonks himself down in the spare chair next to me and waits to be served. He orders a Rusty Nail. It's evident he has already had a few; slurred speech, wobbly under foot and rude.
He tells the bar staff to 'talk in bloody English and not that communist crap' they speak and refuses to sign the bar bill as he doesn't believe he has been given a full measure. Bit by bit the company sitting with me disappear. This should have been my cue. I'm still enjoying my drink.
He then orders a double Johnny Walker Red and is extremely abusive to the staff. 2 huge, and I mean humongous, security guards from the in-hotel casino arrive and tell me if I don't take control of the situation both he and I will be removed from the hotel.
I explain that he is not with me and is merely a fellow traveller with my coach party.
They ain't having any of it. Demanded my room pass and passport and

instructed me that the confiscated items would only be returned when Red Ed left the bar.

He was served a further two doubles of whiskey and they weren't about to stop so I called for the manager. That foyer exploded, Bennett-on-form style.

I explained what had happened, and his staff's expectations of me, elaborating that despite Ed's condition and abusive behaviour they still continued to serve him.

The manager instructed his staff to stop serving Ed and retrieved my passport and room key, apologising profusely. Ed eventually collapsed and was carted off to bed by Mo**Ron** and D**Ron**e, and apparently just dumped on his bed. I got to bed at 0100, not that late for me admittedly but having had the shit scared out of me and battling with Ed and his behaviour had worn me out.

I had already set up an alarm call for him and just hoped he'd get up in time for the early start.

At 0730 I hear a hammering on a door. Upon investigation it's a porter trying to get an answer from Ed's room. Nothing. A room key was sent for. The porter and manager enter the room. He is out of it on the bed. I ask 'he is still alive isn't he?' I was then asked to accompany the manager into the room to check on his welfare. Out of it on his back, still wearing the shirt from the night before and green cartoon boxers, and yes - he was breathing. Phew! The coach driver had already been sent for and we left him to try and get some form of response.

I have managed to do all the trips but have slept in between which is unheard of.

Hugh, the love, has been in touch with the hotel and is dealing with the matter on my behalf. Bless him. The tour company has also been advised.

Leaving Sofia we head east to Plodiv, Bulgaria's second largest city, which enjoys a pleasant setting on the banks of the Marista River.

Plodiv is one of Europe's oldest continually inhabited cities, incorporating into its history a Neolithic settlement, a Thracian hub and a Roman cultural and economic centre. We visit the charming Old Town and the Roman amphitheatre, discovered by chance after a mudslide in

the 1970's. The theatre dates from AD98, and now stands on a hill overlooking the city set against a backdrop of the Rodopi Mountains.
Plodiv in my opinion is a much better place than Sofia. More trendy, cleaner and less oppressive.
Our journey takes us north through some beautiful scenery and across the Stara Planina Mountains. We stay overnight in Veliko Tarnovo.

Plovdiv.

14/08/14 near Ghencea, Romania.
Today we have time to explore Veliko Tărnovo. Located in the heart of Bulgaria, the town clings to a hill high above the Yantra River on the edge of the Stara Planina mountain range. This was Bulgaria's capital during the Middle Ages and the city retains many of its medieval features. The old part of the city is situated on three hills; Tsarevets, Trapezitsa and Sveta Gora. Later we travel to Arbanassi, once a favourite summer residence of the Bulgarian kings and queens and home to the Church of the Nativity built in 1637. Arbanassi is located in

a high plateau, sandwiched between the larger towns of Veliko Tărnovo and Gorna Oryahovitsa.
Following this visit we continue across the Danube, which forms part of the border with Romania, and onto Bucharest for a two night stay.
Great fun winding up the would be photographers. Apparently I have a good eye and have spotted some very good photo opportunities which have been used by the others. Bit of a standing joke. They are all tall and use me as a prop while getting the perfect picture. Today I just pulled out my iPad and took a picture of nothing in particular.
'What are you snapping?' several David Baileys ask in unison. 'Nothing, just winding you lot up.' Har, har and it worked'. Made my day - little things and all that...

Veliko Tarnovo, Bulgaria.

13/08/14 near Veliko Tărnovo, Bulgaria.
Hugh Jardon.

Arbanassi.

15/08/14 — at Palace of the Parliament.

Ok, just stick me on the 6th floor of the Ibis Hotel where the only mode of transport is two scenic lifts why don't you? Luckily they let me use the staff lift at the back of the hotel - but that was a ten mile hike, with no air con, weaving through tiny passageways. I would have rather used the ninety million stairs, probably have been far less sweaty. If I was considering using this as an alternative, I was told that every time I went up or down I would need a staff escort. Judging by the service here it would be a long wait.

Anyway, by dinner I had talked myself down and am now using the lift. Another fear conquered.

We are in prime position overlooking the Parliament building and a 15 minute walk away from the town centre.

Just prior to dinner we all congregated in the bar. Mr Sidecar Racer put his drink down on a table while he went to use the loo. By the time he came back his drink had been removed. After much fuss, and me and the driver being questioned, said beer was found being necked by a female on the table behind us. She was among a party of South American Harley riders touring around the world, pretty much on our trail. The Nicking Necker apologised, claiming that she thought it was a complimentary beer put on the table by the bar staff. Mmmmmmmm, unlikely. She offered to replace the beer, and did so. Mr Sidecar Racer weren't happy - he went on and on about how he should have just picked up his drink and spat in it and said 'drink that', and that the replacement drink was smaller (it wasn't) blah, blah, blah. He didn't shut up.

Strange man; very, very slim but walks like he has muscles. I have bigger bingo wings. Wears a vest top, cowboy hat and leather heeled boots. Thinks he's a dude... dud more like.

The Romanian capital has a long and turbulent history, but in recent years has transformed itself to former glories. Once known as 'Little Paris' tranquil parks and gardens fit alongside wide, tree lined boulevards, contributing to Bucharest's beauty. Off to Parliament Palace today; the world's second largest building (after the US Pentagon) and certainly Europe's largest building. The palace spans 12 storeys, 3100 rooms and covers 330,000 sqm. Just a step out the door...We continue past Piata Universitatii where some of the fiercest fighting during the 1989 Revolution took place. We see the 11m Triumphal Arch, built in 1935 to commemorate the reunification of Romania in 1918. This is currently enclosed in scaffolding and has a covering over it.

The Romanians have a close association with the French, and a lot of the streets are named after French people and places. There is no similarity to Paris whatsoever, although our tour guide kept making comparisons. Obviously not been to France then!

I think her finest and funniest moment was when she pointed out an obelisk on their equivalent of the Champs Élysées (not.) She said it resembled a potato on a stick and she didn't know its significance. We get off the coach to take a closer look and it obvious. It's a heart that has been impaled on a stake. There was red paint dripping from it (meant to be blood) big clue...hello... Vlad the Impaler. We delighted in telling her... duffer!!!!!

Bucharest reminds me of Berlin, very noisy with lots of building work going on. There is no health and safety evident here. All flip flops and no hard hats, pedestrians are free to meander around the huge machinery which litter the pavements. Most of the sights or tourist attractions are spread out so you need a good four days here to navigate around all of them.

Had a 'weekend at Bernie's' moment on the way back to the hotel. By late afternoon it had hit 37 degrees and it's a very dry heat here. Despite the constant spraying of the roads with water the walk back to the hotel from town was a real struggle, no shade whatsoever. I fell into the hotel and practically had to crawl to the bar. You'll be pleased to know I reached it...

16/08/14

Last night after dinner we spent the evening singing around the piano. Great night just chillin'.

Today we leave Bucharest and head to Sinaia, often referred to as 'the Pearl of the Carpathians'. It is located in a beautiful mountain region at the foothills of the Bucegi Mountains. While in Sinaia we visit the

Monastery and Peles Castle, considered to be the most romantic in the world. Next it's off to the village of Bran and to the spine chilling Bran Castle. According to legend this was once the home of Count Dracula.
We stay here for two nights.
Today, the 15th, is a public holiday to commemorate the death of Mary.
Her birth is also celebrated with the same in September.
For us it's VJ Day, and the birthdays of Napoleon and Princess Anne.

The Monastery and Church at Sinaia.

Peles Castle at Sinaia.

Bran Castle.

17/08/14 near Brasov, Romania.
Another energy saving hotel, except this time there is no way you could get to your room before the lights go out. You have to do everything by touch... Hugh tells me I'm very good at this!
Quite a quirky little place close to The Black Church. The hotel has no restaurant and so you have to walk 300 yards across the road to a restaurant, the same applies to the bar which is in the square. Hopefully it won't rain as there are limited umbrellas to sit under.
There is no air con in my room and no space for my case to be left open without me falling in it, or over it.
The shower is another revelation. Getting out I felt like I'd done the Hokey Cokey on full view to guests in the overlooking hotel. Left boob turned the tap to cold, right boob to hot, stomach to off and backside to on. Hilarious.
Woke up a bit grumpy after listening to the 90 millionth encore of the 'cockerel squawked and the dog didn't shut the ---- up'. I was not the happiest to be around. Although I discovered most of my fellow coachcationers were feeling the same.
I heard several of the guests discussing the hotel; I thought I heard them mention coughing which bothered me. The air conditioning on the coach makes me a bit wheezy first thing in the morning and I thought they were complaining. What in fact had been said was that there were 'no coffins in the bedrooms'. Course my sense of humour, I couldn't stop laughing.
Fringed by the peaks of the southern Carpathian Mountains, Brasov contains some fine examples of Gothic, Baroque and Renaissance architecture. The Rope Street (Strada Sforii) is approximately four feet wide and links Cerbului Street with Poarta Schei Street. We visit the famous black church (Biserica Neagra) which is the largest Gothic church in Romania. Its name derives from damage caused by the Great Fire of 1689, when flames and smoke blackened its walls. The interior is impressive and houses one of the largest organs in Eastern Europe. Bit like Oaktree Place. PHugh. Later we get to explore the Old Town Square.

18/08/14 near Cluj-Napoca, Romania.

No amount of BB cream was gonna work this holiday. My Benefit waterproof mascara has become my new BFF.

I have, for most of this trip, resembled a sweat ball and as Hugh pointed out this is not a look I am able to carry off well. Slicked down hair, looking like some freshly tarmacadamed road surface with makeup sliding down off my face, and dropping down from my chin onto my décolletage like a mudslide, is not a particularly fetching look.

Loving drinking in the square after the sightseeing and before dinner.

The people here put a day aside each year to celebrate their family dead. Each family chooses a significant date. They take food and wine to church which is blessed by the priest and then, after the ceremony, given to the poor.

Absolutely hilarious watching the 'poor' stumble down the church path out of their faces.

Watched about thirty weddings take place throughout the day. Extremely glamorous brides and guests. The vicar must be earning a bloody fortune.

The local beer here is called Ursus and it is very strong. As it got darker and we were getting drunker we started to explore the possibility that Dracula could be among us, disguised as a coachcationer. You never know. Are the people I'm with, the people I'm with?

Anyway I remain bite free and my stakes remain blood free (only because they have been forced from my hand mind you.) Still awaiting a visit from Jonathan Rhys Myers, he has several more days to make contact before I'm off territory.

My impediment is improving daily and my knees have become better with each passing day. I am coping well with all the trips despite all of the attractions being at the top of a 1 in 96 hill or at the top of 96 million steps. Every day a challenge.

Brasov is a beautiful place. £20 a night for bed and breakfast. Lots to see. Well worth a long weekend.

Today we were due to visit the pretty medieval town of Sighisoara, pronounced Siggyshora, a tranquil village nestled within stone city walls. Behind it's charming exterior this town holds a dark secret. According to legend, it was the birthplace of the notorious Vlad the Impaler (Dracula.) Later we continue by way of Tirgu Mures to Cluj Napoca, the historic capital of Transylvania for an overnight stay.

En route our coach broke down. The air brakes snapped, we all heard the noise, probably caused by the horrendous bumpy roads over here. Likely there will be an increase in operations for Pilonidal cysts when we all get home. That or replacement fillings.

Our tour guide came to the rescue and we transferred over onto 2 battered minibuses which took us onward to our next destination.

The coach was eventually fixed and we have been reunited.

Sighisoara.

Cluj Napoca.

19/08/14 near Budapest, Hungary.

We commence our journey west, crossing the border into Hungary. We continue to the capital Budapest for a two night stay. 460k.

It's here we meet up with Mike and Garry, drivers I know from previous tours that I have been on.

We are doing Budapest by night so should be fun.

Travelling down, we pass numerous fields with row after row of sunflowers and corn. White storks in abundance, picking up the carnage of wildlife after the harvester.

These people on this trip that seem to be into stocks and shares, my arse. Never got enough currency. Always asking to borrow until they hit a cashpoint. Bring it with you like I did, get organised. Even borrowing raffle tickets to buy drinks as not enough euros. Don't like using cards in cash points, or paying with a card. Hello it ain't free and I'm not the bank of Caff. If you don't like my rates of exchange, then don't ask me to sub you...

Mr Sidecar Racer the font of all knowledge. Not! Thinks he's the dogs lucky bits, don't know about that but as tight as a ducks ass. Told me I couldn't change the currency back in the UK. Total tosh, have a receipt that tells me different. Anyway I've got a good thing going if they borrow from me then they pay me back in Sterling. Saves me cashing it in when I get back home. My working out: example 2000 florint, knock off last two noughts then divide by 4 = 5€. Simples...

20/08/14 near Budapest, Hungary.
A long day today, just enough time for a quick shower before dinner.
Great to see the boys from my previous trips.
At dinner, due to the table layout, Ed was seated alone. I just couldn't do it and moved over to keep him company. He was perfectly behaved. Although that changed later. I kinda thought; give something, get something back from the universe.
Today I had an intellectual discussion, with John an ex civil servant who worked for GCHQ and speaks Russian and who is meeting friends in Budapest this very night, say no more. Really interesting guy. I merely mentioned that the horsemen beneath the Corinthian column in Heroes Square looked like Samurai. That was it. He has apparently been studying the connection between the Japanese, Turks and Romanians explaining that the word 'good' is a prime example of where to start his explanation. A word you must agree is synonymous with my **good** self.
Must be the only person to fall asleep standing in the busiest place in Budapest...
The boat cruise was great, the two coach parties merged together for the trip. And I think I'm with a right shower. Wanna see this lot. All beige trousers and polo shirts. After lunch I head up to the top deck and am sat all lovely on my own, building watching, when I am joined by an Indian gent (previously sat alone at lunch - who I felt sorry for, but now realise why no one was sitting with him.) He says 'bit windy up here.' Me: 'I quite like it.' He replies, and I think he said 'sorry for making a rude comment.' To which I reply 'You weren't being rude.' He then repeats himself and what he did in fact say was 'sorry for making a poo, poo comment.' Really? He then launches into an incomprehensible verbal attack that took someone else to intervene and tell him to calm down. I've been in shock ever since. He was last seen swimming up the Danube. Twat!
We had a full day to discover the Hungarian capital of Budapest. The city is composed of two historically independent communities, Buda and Pest, separated by the majestic River Danube. It's not blue BTW, bit Weston-Super-Muddish. Buda for bumpy/hills and Pest for plain/flat.
Lots to see here; the impressive Parliament Buildings, St Stephens

Cathedral, Heroes Square and the huge Citadel.

We start with a panoramic view of the city from the top of Gellert Hill, continuing on to Liberty Statue, built in remembrance of the Soviet liberation of Hungary from Nazi forces during World War II.

Travelling to the Pest side of the city we visit City Park and Heroes Square. Continuing down Andrassy Avenue to the Grand State Opera House and the beautiful St. Stephens Basilica.

Next stop is Castle Hill on the Buda side of the city, and time to explore the medieval city.

Our day is finished off with a cruise on the Danube River with a lunchtime meal included.

21/08/14 near Eisingen, Bavaria.
Leaving Budapest today we head towards Austria and the Imperial City of Vienna.
Later we continue to Salzburg for an overnight stay.
Great catch up with the boys. Stayed in the car park on the coach drinking up until dinner. Far cheaper than the bar. The conversation was all about a guy on the other coach who had made a miniature working V8 engine. The boys were going on and on about how they'd like to own it. Just sat there watching a video of the bloody thing. Then we progressed to man sheds. Hysterical. Very hung over hence the delay in posting.
Garry took a picture of me talking to Bryan aka Mr Minus One at the bar and sent it to mutual friends stating I'd pulled. Not my type. And I really don't need to know how many bridges we have driven over or how many statues we've seen. I know all about statues of horses with riders on. If the horse has two legs off the ground the rider died in battle. If the horse has one leg off the ground then the rider died after the battle but of injuries received in the battle (lesson of the day Pat Nott x), horse with no hooves in the air - rider just died!
John had a wonderful meet up with his friends in Budapest. Said there was so much love in the room for him. He was near to tears telling me all about it and made me cry too. Sharon Richards - revisited a restaurant in Vienna and had lobster for lunch, which was very lovely. Then explored the Graffiti trail along the river BANKS...

22/08/14 near Bierges, Belgium.
We have an early start this morning as we continue our journey north through the heart of the German countryside and into Belgium and our overnight hotel. 903k to travel today.
Major, majors last eve. Peter Pratt, one of the Pratt Pack, has caused problems. Every time he goes to sit in the lounge area on the coach he leaves his headphones plugged in to the coach system with the music on full blast so everyone can hear his choice of music. Not a good choice either. It's annoying and it's been down to me to get up from my seat and disconnect the headphones, ensuring he gets a Bennett look of despair and disgust as I do it. Transpires the rest of the rear coachers are also pissed off with this but only threaten to say something and talk about him behind his back. However the problem has been made ten times worserer due to an argument over whose round it was. He has allegedly been accepting drinks but hasn't been buying back. This caused a humongous row and explains why he hasn't been talking to anyone.
To make matters worse an alarm has been sounding every two hours and he is also being blamed for this. Most people believe he is doing it on purpose to annoy, resulting in a heated exchange. Following a thorough investigation by my good self I have tracked the alarm offender down and it is Mr Sidecar Racer. He is totally unaware of the annoyance believing the ringing in his ears was the tinnitus he suffers

from. His wife is also totally oblivious to the ringing, or him, as she just sticks her headphones on and goes off into another world totally ignoring him. Anyway, faulty cheap watch has been removed from his wrist and placed in his suitcase as he doesn't know how to reset alarm. Like they say 'buy cheap, buy twice'.

Watched the Sound of Music today, had to be done.

You can probably guess who won the backwards bingo. Bryan. The proper bingo. Bryan. I jest not I was waiting for one number. 69. And that's the truth. General knowledge quiz. Bryan. Mileage. Bryan.

Bryan, Bryan, Bryan, bloody Bryan.

Bread gate has reared its head again. Long uncut sticks of crusty bread. Watching people scratch their ear, flick a bogey from their nose, and then cut the bread without using the serviettes provided. More worryingly - did they wash their hands after their morning shit? Aaahhhhhrrrrrgggggghhhhhh. I am fed up of this and plan to start a campaign 'cos it bugs me so much. Ban Bogey Botulism Bread.

Lost it big time...

23/08/14

We leave our hotel this morning for Calais and the Channel port for our return crossing to YUK.

2 weeks until my next adventure.

A total 5798 kilometres this holiday.

18

MOROCCO

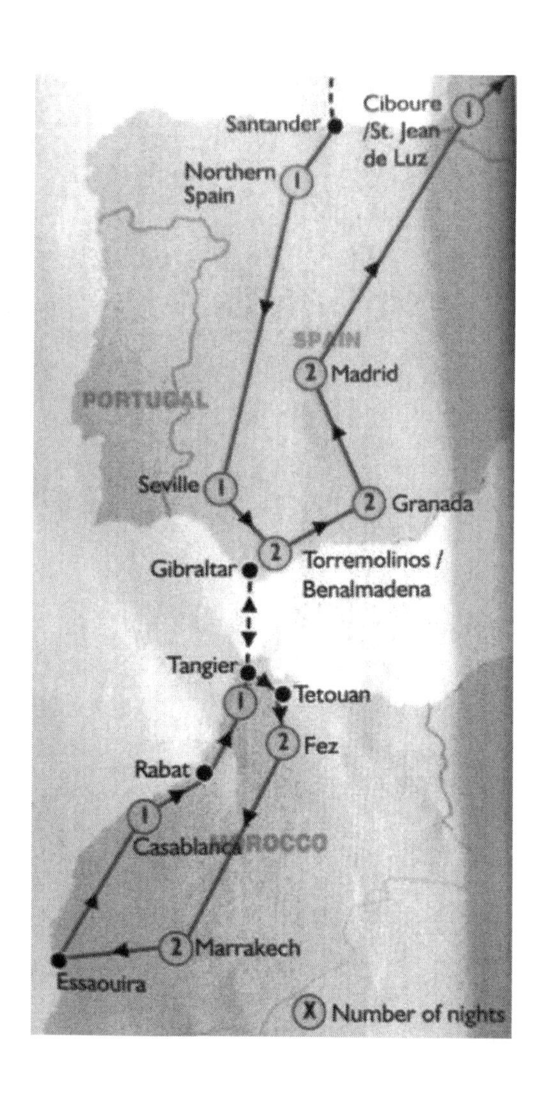
Santander
Ciboure
/St. Jean
de Luz
Northern
Spain
SPAIN
Madrid
PORTUGAL
Seville
Granada
Gibraltar
Torremolinos /
Benalmadena
Tangier
Tetouan
Fez
Rabat
Casablanca
MOROCCO
Marrakech
Essaouira
Number of nights

09/09/14 Wanborough.
So my coachcation begins. Departure from W-S-Mare to Portsmouth; where we board Brittany Ferries' flagship vessel, the Pont-Aven, for an overnight crossing to Santander.
Looking dapper in my lime green and burgundy blouse, contrasting jeans and trendy Toms.
A later start today which was fab. Even made me own packed lunch which included two of my five... Didn't even pack my cases until Monday which is so not me. The fact I hadn't been at home much, likely cause.
Anyway imagine my delight when on the last trip I am advised by the host and hostess that I had their full permission to bring a second case on the next holiday. It had to be smaller than my main case but enough to get several days clothes in.
The reason behind this was that they felt I would struggle getting into Morocco with my big Pinkie. This was obviously a subtle way of giving me an early warning and would indicate that Moroccan customs is gonna be high on a hill, on the edge of a precipice or that I'm likely to have to climb 90 million steps. What's new?
I have become good friends with Sandra and Pete, I think this is my 5th holiday with them this year. So we text to keep in touch (I'm so 21st century aren't I?)
Text - me to them:
Hey you two, bet you've been missing me.
So lovely to have 2 cases to pack but a real conundrum. What do I take? Me bedroom resembles a Shopping Mall at sale time...
I hope the quiz has been revised. I am really gonna try and win this trip.
Bryan (that being Mr Minus One from the Transylvania trip) has been in touch and has sent me a blow by blow account of our last trip. Even detailing what films we watched while on board Delilah and what drinks he had. Glad he didn't list mine... (Delilah is a coach btw.) Reading it was like reliving that holiday all over again. Really weird. Anyway this is your 7 day warning. I'm coming to get you... xxx
Text - reply:
Evening all, of course we miss you (like a boil on my bum. Lol.) Bryan

was going to send it to us as well, can't wait and as for packing just put stuff in case till you can't lift it like you normally do xx
What a cheek...
I have decided to be Viv the whole holiday, realising that a lot of coachcationers pretend to be something they are not. You know the type, allegedly into stocks and shares, have numerous properties and are rich, blah, blah, blah. So I sent a text informing/warning them.
Text - me:
Just to let you know I have decided to live out my alter ego and use my pseudonym for the whole holiday. If other coachcationers can be property magnates and stocks and shares boffs then I'm going to be Vivvy Anne Le Fey the mad author of two bestselling novels which in fact is true, however I'm not mad but am going to have a go at it. I'm bringing 2 hats to help with the portrayal of my character.
I did note the sarcasm in your text reply and you'll be pleased to know I will be taking your advice. Big bird, big case!! Can't wait to see you both. Take care. xx
Following info given to me from the good friend who last trip found a flaw in me fatal plan, I am going to have to discuss the banning of all pens and pencils on board coach. I will let you know the outcome. All a bit worrying actually.
My niece has given me something to do whilst travelling. She started to make me a bracelet with all good intentions but abandoned it and me for the pub. What a proud moment. Like aunty, like niece...

09/09/14
Waiting to float. Spinnaker Tower features in Viv’s novel. So it's quite special, even from a distance.

10/09/14 Los Corrales de Buelna, Spain.
Got stared at the whole way down to Portsmouth by a very strange individual. Now you all know that I'm not impedimentist, and how could I be with a list of them as long as the one I've got!
Wanted to say eyes front but under normal circumstances that wasn't ever gonna be possible. Literally impossible without surgical intervention. To say there were directional issues is a bit of an understatement. Put me in mind of a chameleon. Am I painting a picture here? Anyway I put a stop to it by asking if I could help her...
I didn't get to bed till one. The on board entertainment was good. We watched a Sheena Easton soundalike, who thought connecting with the audience meant sitting on men's laps and rubbing their heads, (the head where their ears are located...) a magician and the Candy Girls; a trio who sang 50s stuff. A bit Andrews sisterish.
I have a vague recollection of singing Fantasy with the biker boys toward the end of the night.
Having had it drummed into us that we would be docking at five I set me alarm, laid all my clothes out and tried to get some sleep.
I was the only one in reception at five this morn waiting to disembark, and have had dialogue with the reception Captain regarding his tannoy announcer using the 24 hour clock.
Use of the phonetic alphabet and the 24hour clock needs to be made compulsory. It would save confusing people like my good self who use these all the time. Bloody eejits...

I'm sure the last time I did this crossing it didn't take a whole day. I know I spent most of the crossing confined to bed due to the force 9 gale but I thought it was like half a day.
I was most grumpy this sunny morn when I alighted from my bed, the constant chuggy, chuggy noise and riding the swell has taken its toll.
Plus the fact I woke up with me new pink Jim Jams covered in melted chocolate. The state of the white sheets is unmentionable. Reminded me of Hugh and that always makes me emotional as you know.
Been up Whale and Dolphin watching with the on board experts. The only Orca I think they're gonna see this trip is the hungover, beached one on deck 9 who is currently soaking up the rays and replenishing her stock of vitamin D...
I have an afternoon of bingo to look forward to if I fancy a change.
We arrived at the port of Santander at 1830 after a smooth crossing, we continue our journey by coach for an overnight stop in Northern Spain.

11/09/14 Benacazón, Spain.
Our stay at the Eurostar's Diana Palace was a short one. I'm not into processed foods. Blame me mother, and I couldn't eat the breakfast; ham and cheese rolls don't do it for me first thing.
At breakfast one of our coachcationers was walking back to the table with a mug of coffee and, right on cue, the waitress comes through the swing doors knocking the coffee all over him and his shirt. They then go into a blind panic. Spray him with this stuff that's supposed to turn white, you brush it off and miraculously the stain's supposed to have gone; that didn't work but choked everyone sitting in an arm's length radius. Hysterical. Had to ram the serviette in my mouth to stifle my cries. Oh I mean laughter. Sorry it's the Viv in me.
The knob sat behind me on the coach is likely to be the first victim of my razor sharp tongue.
I'm gonna call him Mr Like The Sound Of Me Own Voice. I have had to leave my ear phones plugged in to drown out the drone. Says things loudly to try and impress. Lordy, lordy what a bore. The only decent thing about him is that his family name is Womack...
I am second youngest on board the coach and one of 5 other single

people. Three women and two guys; one from deepest darkest Wales, now known as Boyo Royo, that I need language line to understand. The other lad is Jason The Facilitator he 'arranges things' but is currently living off the money his rich father left him... Mmmmmm. He has apparently travelled with Pete and Sandra before and is known to have huge hygiene issues, noticeable more as the holiday progresses.
Someone on the coach is wearing a very vile perfume and I have needed to ask for a sick bag just in case (not in me case obviously but in the bag.)
Onward and forward to Seville for an overnight stay.

12/09/14
OMG it's all going on...
We arrive at Hotel Abades Benacazon in Seville. A bit harem-ish but I have a lovely room with a veranda overlooking the pool boys.
I get all lovelied up, and I have to say I looked the biz. There was I sat at the pool bar, people watching and enjoying my beer, when this fellow female coachcationer starts taking her swimsuit off and drying herself in full view of my good self, Boyo Royo and Jason The Facilitator (BTW I am still trying to get more info on this character... just be patient.) And I mean it's all out, and in quantity. She's gotta be late sixties easy; and not wearing well so you can imagine, it's not terribly pleasing to the eye at all.
In the meantime Jason The Facilitator comments that he would like to know who Anita is, and did I know? At the time I didn't. Initially, before being moved to a seat on his own, he was supposed to be seated next to her and had been looking forward to it. Anyway Aphromighty joins us on the patio and Jason asks if her name is Anita. 'It is' she replies, towel in hand, acting all coy and skippity.
I tell you The Facilitators moves were better than Jagger's, before you could say 'and it goes like this' he had pulled a chair out for her at his table, and was making haste to the bar to buy her a drink. Boyo Royo and I couldn't stop laughing and were both speechless. We hadn't even had time to recover from the provocative pool side display just moments earlier.

I have been asked to accompany Boyo Royo on the horse and carriage ride through the Yves St Laurent gardens and also to the caves where we will have an evening of entertainment. I have accepted. He's more Waldorf than Omar Sharif but hey ho. Now Hugh, if you're reading this there's no cause for alarm, he ain't my type. BTW I'm meeting up with PHugh in Madrid tour end...

Two women on the coach reckon they know me from another trip, said I was always late and held everyone up. Now those who know me will be fully aware that LATE don't feature in my dictionary. So ladies I'm afraid you have the wrong chick. Because they misheard my name they are calling me Naff. Funny to start with, but wearing a bit thin now.

Après dinner we all sat outside on the balcony. Jason was engrossed in rolling his joints. He must think we are all stupid. I know what cannabis smells like and I also know what a spliff looks like, you're talking to a Glasto' bird here. Anyway I knew that I could drink more than six beers and couldn't understand why I and several of the others started to act a bit weird. All I hope is that it's out of my system by the time I see the Onc next. Can't have her thinking I'm using alternative medicine can I?

Apart from being smashed outta me head, and my suitcase stinking like a hydroponics factory, the evening was most enjoyable (thank god for the drawer liners I brought with me and have now wrapped my clothes in.)

This morning was a revelation. The sinks were not for the vertically challenged, far too high and me boobs got in the way as I bent over the marble surround. It caused me a bit of a problem cleaning my teeth. To empty your mouth of toothpaste you had to be able to gob to reach the sink. Most uncouth and I have taken issue with hotel basin control to lodge my complaint giving them a fully clothed demonstration.

We spend the morning in Seville. Our sightseeing tour features all the major sights and includes the cathedral, the third largest in the world, and the equally imposing Alcazar Royal Palace. We then continue to the Costa del Sol for a two night stay.

12/09/14 - Seville.

12/09/14 Playabonita Hotel.
Getting ready for dinner...

13/09/14 Benalmádena, Spain.
I can highly recommend Seville. Once the early morning smog/mist clears, you get used to the 32 degree heat, the three million flies and the overpowering stench of horse doops, it's a lovely city to explore. I have to say I prefer the smell of horse doops to the smell of Mrs Parfam de Puke, offender of vile perfume located in the seat just in front of me.
The hotel is really nice and I have a room overlooking the Med. Reminds me a bit of an episode from Benidorm. Met some fab people unconnected to the coach, real characters. Get why people holiday here and I'm glad I've had the experience.
Once again I'm the font of all knowledge with my fancy little gadget: looking up where you can buy Seville Orange flavoured Gin, that one was simples, Waitrose, or make your own; finding out where museums are; how to visit the underground fortifications on Gib, problem is once

they know the cost involved that's when the moaning starts. Do I arrange entry fees? No I don't. For Christ's sake, due to age, the likelihood of them ever getting back here is a slim one. Just do it, it's a once in a lifetime.
Last late eve after dinner I spent my time people watching on the veranda with a few beers. Happy hour is all night here, although not the case for some guests.
What I really need to understand is how a woman can sit at a table drinking coffee with her husband/partner who is drinking wine? Not speaking a word, he then falls asleep. She has a face like a ducks ass. Hello FFS get out of dodge love.
Off to the famous Rock of Gibraltar, locally known as Gib, where we will experience a little bit of Britain on the Iberian Peninsula.
Oh and Jason The Facilitator went to bed early having got drunk on Bloody Marys.

14/09/14
Gibraltar, Gib, or the Rock, was fabulous. From a distance it just looks like a rock, which basically it is. The queue to get in wasn't that long and it kept moving. Once through Spanish customs, and then English customs, you have to take your life in your hands and cross the airport runway. 'Live dangerously' has fast become my motto. Through the centre of the rock are numerous shops, restaurants and bars. This is probably the cheapest place to get cigs too. £27 per 200, so the tourists are quite vulnerable here. You could be asked to be a mule getting paid 1€ for every pack of 200 you bring through customs. Every other shop is a duty free shop and it's big business.
Sir James Dutton was visiting Gib today, war hero representing the queen. The 10th of September is their National Day and they celebrate big time. Apparently celebrations go on for days. My kinda town... Shook my hand on the walkabout, I just happened to be in the right place. We knew someone important was around because of the number plate on a car parked nearby. A single crown... Press were out in force so I could be front page news tomorrow. He wasn't bad looking either.
These holidays I go on all seem to have a lot of similarities and follow a

pattern. Everything has to involve steps, height, hanging off precipices, drivers who look round at the passengers in the back seats rather than the road while they are driving, a distinct lack of barriers on extremely narrow roads (I will be writing to barrier control btw) and every kind of obstruction you can possibly imagine to force you nearer the edge of the cliff.
The monkeys are fab; if you follow the rules they're no threat, they just squabble amongst themselves. The males share the parenting of the young and are very good at it. Doesn't even have to be one they have sired either. They don't seem to mind sitting on the railings with a 60 million foot sheer drop behind them.
St. Michaels Cave is a natural underground cave which is used as a concert venue in summer; the acoustics are excellent in the auditorium.
The tunnels are extensive, all 34 miles of them, and are managed by the military. You can only go inside certain tunnels but it's well worth a visit, despite the gradient as you go deeper into the tunnel system. I managed it, stick and puffers in hand.
Take a look at the photos, another fear kinda conquered ish.
Mr Next Question is the guy who wants me to look things up for him on me fancy gadget, one question after another. I don't mind, 'cos I'm learning stuff as I research. His wife, however, is ignorant - she doesn't speak. My mission today was to get her to say hello to me. Mission accomplished.
Early start today, have been up since 0430, must be bleedin' mad.
My fellow coachcationers were all moaning about the noise from the bar last night. Yes, it's holiday makers on holiday enjoying themselves.
Pity you didn't all practice what you moan about this morning when you were all chattering loudly and laughing along the corridors where other guests were sleeping.
It was like bleeding arts and crafts in the seat behind me today. Mr Like The Sound Of Me Own Voice and his partner, Ms Can't Take Me Drink, were tasked with being the last through customs at Tarifa. This was so our coach drivers could use them as a marker. They sat there discussing what they could use to hold up in the air so the rest of the group could see them. By my reckoning if everyone was doing as they were told

there should be no-one behind them. So why would you need a makeshift brightly coloured paddle? Duh!!!

Nothing to report on the coachcationers as we have all done our own thing the last few days. But this is early days.

We take the ferry across the Straits of Gibraltar from Tarifa to Tangier, Morocco. It is here we meet our Moroccan guide and continue through the Rif Mountains for an insight into the lives of the Rif people, whose blue and white-washed houses with red sloping roofs nestle peacefully on the slopes of the Rif mountain range. It's here you can get hash and marijuana, undisclosed amounts a day are seized by customs!

We call at Meknes, one of Morocco's Imperial cities, before heading to Fez for a two night stay at The Pickalbatros Royal Mirage.

14/09/14

Gibraltar.

15/09/09 Fès-Ville-Nouvelle, Morocco.
The crossing over to Morocco was choppy; 45 minutes of trying not to puke while queuing, and attempting to keep your balance to get your passport stamped, not easy.
Security check point was fun; to get to it you have to climb Kilimanjaro, with suitcase in tow and all your impediments. Good idea to bring two cases. Subtle swap to the Baby Blue for towing up slope purposes. Then revert back to the Big Pinkie.

Mrs Ignorant is my new BFF, she is now speaking to me and hasn't shut

up since the ferry crossing yesterday.
Back on care in the community; money for the loo, tissues for wiping, hand sanitiser, watcher of loo doors. Get organised holiday people.
Last night was spent around the pool bar drinking. It was fun listening to people swapping their ailment stories. Also there is a lot of use of bong type things by the locals. Allegedly it's herbal teas...
The food is good; hotel is clean, although edges of skirting/carpet need attention.
Miss Daisy, a seventy something year old, fell over at the last hotel. At breakfast today she shows everyone her boobs which were black and blue, really bad bruising. Caused an outcry, as frowned upon here. We all got advised reference keeping things under wraps.
Our journey today is dedicated to exploring the city of Fez, also known as 'The Athens of Africa'. We begin in the Old Medina and the Andalusian and the Karaouine Quarter with its dyers, tanners and artisans working in the style of their forefathers. Later we also take in the Mellah, or Jewish Quarter, with its old cemetery and the Royal Palace.
BTW Aphromighty and The Facilitator are back on, following the standoff. Think she was playing hard to get. Was flirting with Naj the guide today and The Facilitator was not best pleased. Watch this space.
Hugh is missing me as you probably can imagine. We are speaking daily.

14/09/14 Royal Mirage Fes Hotel.
Just what I needed after a long day.

15/09/14 Fès-Ville-Nouvelle, Morocco.
Meknes, Morocco.

15/09/14 Fès-Ville-Nouvelle, Morocco.

Fez.

16/09/14

Yesterday's trip to the Medina in Fez was enlightening. I can now understand why you wouldn't wander around on your own. Firstly; you would never find your way out, there are millions of narrow streets which all look exactly the same. Shop after shed sized shop, full of men selling their wares. How they make a living is beyond my comprehension.

The streets are very claustrophobic; flies are as many as the humans that live there, and street peddlers who hound you all day and follow you around can be quite intimidating. You need to explore inside some of the shops, where they open up into the most beautiful buildings. The threat from theft here is apparently low, hard to believe though with such poverty around, hand choppy offy is still the punishment in some places and is a huge deterrent.

The leather shop is an eye opener, the smell is overwhelming and sprigs of mint are offered to you as you enter. And you need it. Once again it's hundreds of steps up to the tower balcony which overlooks men working in the most dreadful conditions. Waist high in pigeon poop which softens the leather to make it more workable. I have never smelt anything like it. Each man in an individual round bath made from clay, filled with either poop or dye. Each bath owned or rented by some rich business man. The locals breed the pigeons and sell the poop on pigeon poop market day. One kg of poop you get less than a pound for in money.

We stopped for lunch at a local restaurant, which was surprisingly stunning inside. The lunch would have been nice I'm sure, if only the mother and son combo on the coach hadn't nicked my portion of bread and chicken; they were unperturbed that I had nothing on my plate and didn't even apologise. They buy nothing on the coach to eat or drink, but certainly make up for it with the freebies.

The Facilitator got taken off by the locals to make a purchase. There was a lot of speculation it was some kind of illegal on the coach substance. He was seen marching swiftly back to his room, black carrier bag in hand. Our guide was sent to investigate, and discovered The Facilitator had bought magnets. Fridge magnets. We wet ourselves laughing. If he will walk around talking gangsta with a voice like James Bond, the Sean Connery version, and telling people he 'arranges things', what does he expect?

Alcohol here is expensive, £4:50 for a bottle. We stayed off the local beer for fear of stomach upset. It's cheaper to smoke hash and drink mint tea.

A wrap of hash here costs less than a pound and most of the locals use it to take their minds off the awful jobs they do. They rarely live a long life. It was strange to see that the government worry about concealing phone masts as shown in the photo, but allow their people to live in squalor.

Leaving Fez this morning we head towards the 'red city' of Marrakech where we stay for two nights. We have several stops en route which include Ifrane; a small town with many new houses, the style of which looks very British.

The drive through and over the Atlas Mountains is revealing. People live a solitary existence in the most basic dwellings, their only company the livestock who share the confined indoor space.
The abandoned litter is disgusting, mile upon mile of plastic bags and bottles.
Lunch was in Beni Mellal, a much more modern town with buses instead of donkeys.
The police were out in force with their new speed cameras; don't know why, the roads are so bumpy you'd take off at speed. The stinger contraption looks like a rusty bed of nails and is fully deployed at all times. You have to drive around them.
Driving through the countryside the landscape is varied; barren, almost desert like, rocky, fruit trees, oak and cork, grapes, wheat fields but very little greenery.
Dinner this very eve is at the fabulous Chez Ali Fantasia, bit strip joint sounding but I'm sure it'll be fab. Here we will be entertained by troupes of folklore artistes, and charging horsemen providing a tribal display of strength.

16/09/14 Marrakesh, Morocco.
Fez to Marrakesh.

17/09/14 Marrakesh, Morocco.

We reached our destination at 1830. The Kenzi Farah Hotel. The most back to front and inside out place I have ever stayed in.

Yes it involved a route march.

We were given two hours to prepare for dinner. I made it to the snack bar with 30 mins to spare. The cost of a small can of beer here is €5.

The staff are rude, when I asked where the bar was I was told it was closed for repairs. Hello! When I asked where I could get a beer I was given the Moroccan shrug and told by the receptionist it didn't bother her 'cos she didn't drink. Behaviour breeds behaviour and I couldn't help myself replying 'yeah and I don't smoke hash!' I was pointed in the direction of the snack bar where I was assured by the manager, who had heard the exchange, that I'd get a beer free of charge.

The evening at Chez Ali was fabulous. The venue extremely well thought out. Overcame my fear of heights and did the magic carpet ride, and had my picture taken on a camel. I'm sure there were more being taken of me getting off. I had difficulty getting me leg over. Never seen anything like it.

The food was very good; lamb to start, chicken and couscous tagine, fresh fruit, mint tea and macaroons, and two bottles of the vilest red wine I've ever tasted.

The display consisted of horses thundering around the arena, with their riders performing very dangerous acrobatics. Plus there were the dancers from several different tribes, wailing, screaming and gyrating. Bit like our Morris dancers I suppose. Old traditions kept alive by a minority.

The people here pray 5 times a day, I would have to stay there all day. With all me impediments I'd never get up off the ground after prayer 1 let alone 2, 3, 4 and 5.

It's bad enough getting on and off the coach. I'd be smoking whacky baccy within a month.

Our guide Mohammed is a Moroccan Arab, but for him more importantly Muslim.

Everyone born here is Moroccan be they Jewish, Berber or Arabic.

The people here live by French law and the language here is mainly French, English and several dialects of Berber and Arabic.

We were treated like royalty when we arrived. I thought Barack Obama was in the royal box as all you could here were the security shouting Barac, Barac. I took loads of photos hoping to pick him out, standing nearby in the hope it would be another photo call and hand shake; it turns out Barac, Barac means get out of the way.

Today we have a full day exploring the 'Red City', called this because of the colour of its red earth ramparts, monuments and houses. Our guide takes us into the Medina, which is a labyrinth of small streets and alleyways all filled with shops and stalls producing amazing aromas of saffron and orange blossom. We also visit the Bahia Palace, providing the king isn't in residence, and complete the day in the Djemaa El Fnaa Square, where I am expecting to be enchanted by the snake charmers (a talent I fail in continually), fortune tellers, dancers and water sellers.

19/09/14 Tingis, Morocco.

The birdsong first thing in the morning can be a bit annoying. The staff open up all the windows along the corridors and from five onwards you hear this overly chirpy noise. I believe they were just playing chirp noises on a tape to wake people up for breakfast. All a bit chirpy, chirpy, tweet, tweet. Got right on my nerves.

Marrakesh is cleaner than Fez and the poverty not so evident. The Medina still has the windy, narrow streets but it's not so claustrophobic. People use donkeys, camels, mopeds, cycles and cars to get around. No-one gives way, they don't wear helmets, they drive at speed and have no regard for pedestrians. They bomb through the Medina four up, choking everyone to death with the fumes from the exhausts. They don't need a licence or to pass a test, so you can guess the standard of driving. There isn't one.

The guide went on a bit, repeating himself three times. His English was good but not good enough to keep us interested. We all ended up wandering off; not advisable, as reconnaissance was required to find us all. I was with the cobras...

The herbalist was informative and I have cures and potions in my suitcase for everything. I'm keeping the cream for piles for myself as that helps with bags under your eyes. Same vein apparently, all the stars use it. B1 500mg for mosquito deterrent and cube of chocolate for tickly cough.
Marrakesh comes alive at night, gotta be seen to be believed, truly amazing. Indescribable.

Colonel Blimp and his wife, the Lame Dame, have pissed everyone off. They have been asking Mohammed, the permanent on board guide who sits up front, for drinks. There is on board coach etiquette which needs to be adhered to. The guides don't serve drinks. You wait your turn until the host gets to you. No queue jumping allowed.
Now Colonel Blimp is not the name I allocated to this character. It is the name that Mrs Parfam de Puke gave to him.
Another coachcationer calls the lady travelling with Miss Daisy, Joan Le Mesurier because she looks the spit of John Le Mesurier. Proves I ain't the only one that does this name association game. The in crowd, of which I'm one, were discussing this last night over a very expensive beer and we had a right laugh. They loved the names I had given them although I had to think off me feet and change most of them. Phew!!
I'm known as the helpful lady, the one sat by the drinks trolley that never wears the same clothes. Mr Wanders Off said he calls me Origami. When I asked why, he said because I'm obviously very good at folding to be able to get all my clothes into such a small suitcase (obviously referring to my Baby Blue and not me Big Pinkie.) That's

nice...

The gardens were fabulous, funded by Yves St Laurent, really relaxing.

Next we headed off on the horse and carriage ride, off the tourist trail.

There is a strike here on the 23rd; a dispute over pensions, food and the cost of electric etc.
Women and men are given a chitty as payment for the work they undertake. The women attend the post office and men the bank, to collect the cash. The queues are long. There is no benefit system here so people rely totally on any work whatsoever in order to live.
Should you decide to holiday here, don't come in October. It's holiday time for the locals and lamby necky slitty. You will pay hugely inflated prices.
Leaving Marrakesh, hop aboard the train. We head west towards the coast and the beautiful resort of El Jadida, an old Portuguese town. This walled town still retains its ramparts, a beautiful sandy beach and a relaxed atmosphere. Any more relaxed and I will be laid out. This is the most perfect place to enjoy a lush lunch, surrounded by the pretty blue and white painted houses. We visit the old courthouse and prison. Our tour guide's father used to be chief of police here and so Mohammed is greatly respected and is known to the world and his wife. It took a while to get around as he was bombarded by people needing his help. Quote of the day. Our guide shows us the old courthouse. The prison is just a hole in the ground where criminals were put years ago when found guilty. No food or water, just left to die. Mr Dipstick asks 'does anyone ever walk out?' Hello, which part of dead don't you understand?
Later, after lunch we head to Casablanca. The town of white houses.

20/09/14 El Jadida.

20/09/14

Travelling down to Casablanca the scenery is flat and barren. Several small communities are dotted here and there. Villagers attending the water trough daily to collect their water required for the day. The animals here look better fed, so I'm guessing there is more work. As you approach Casablanca the skyline is not dissimilar to that of a European city. The satellite dishes are in abundance and litter the skyline. In

amongst the housing and offices the minarets become visible, overshadowed by tower blocks.
The hotel is fabulous. The Hotel Suisse. The view from the balcony is spectacular. I have a sea view and can also see the mosque. I got a bit brave and went out onto the balcony to take photos, then I realised I was six floors up. I had to talk myself down and inch myself back in to the room. I can tell you I was near collapse and sweating profusely.
Casablanca is so different to everywhere else. More 21st century although the internet is crap, hence my lack of communication.
The beers are only 4€ which is better and I'm making up for lost time by spending the evening in the bar. Proud to be last to bed and I utilised our free pass to the disco... oh yeah baby, only ones in there.
They don't like women in the bar and I was refused service, the barman stating I had already had two. Mohammed explained our differing cultures and after my tenth beer I was the topic of conversation. There were others from the coach who were on bottled wine so it weren't just me! The music here is depressing and nearly had me crying in me beer. By the end of the night the Batty Britt got 'em singing, I was in fine voice.
I have had a proposal of marriage from Sheik Ben Yusuf Ahmed-Hussar; yes that was Sheik and not Shrek. Not too happy about the prospect of being wifey 33... so I declined his kind offer. He wanted to marry me 'cos I made him laugh and apparently I have gorgeous eyes. Some would say piss holes in the snow but I'll take his descriptive.
Jason The Facilitator has now taken to wearing an ill-fitting hat with 'POLICE' written on it. He asked me to translate the French words on his rosary beads that he wears around his neck, using me fancy gadget. I took one look at it, instantly I could tell it wasn't French it was Latin. He does his rosary every day; I thought he was talking to himself, which I suppose, technically he is. He has also taken to calling me Cathy. There has only ever been one family that have been allowed to call me that, and they are the Hayward family.
The loos here are vile of viles. Holes in the ground, and they stink. I merely mentioned that they could do with a damn good bleaching. And was asked by Pete the host if that was something else I'd be carrying

with me in my suitcase as I seem to carry everything else!
Viv and Hugh would be a great choice to play Rick and Ilsa in a remake of Casablanca. Viv's life is a one big drama, she'd be a dream for the part.
We are spending the day here, with time to visit the magnificent Hassan II Mosque. Later we head off to Rabat, the Imperial Capital, where we visit the Mausoleum of Mohamed V, Tour Hassan and the Oudayas. Next we are off to Tangier.

Rabat.

Casablanca.

21/09/14

The visit to the mosque was overwhelming and quite emotional. My understanding of the Muslim faith, dress and culture is much more informed. Still can't get my head around the fact that there are millions living in squalor and money seems to be no object when building more and more elaborate style mosques.

The one we visited today is the third largest in the world, and has the tallest minaret. The coach broke down right outside and so we were fortunate enough to hear the Adhan, the Muslim calling to prayer. It went on a bit, in fact it went on and on and on, initially we all thought it was motorbikes revving up. Reminded me of the noise you get on the start line at a motorbike race circuit. Each calling is unique and differs to any other. It's supposed to sound like song.

A mechanic attended the coach and discovered the radiator water hose had broken. We caused utter chaos, people come to the mosque on a Friday to pray and the coach was parked in the Iman's car space. It's an unwritten local understanding that a local person can manage the street parking in a particular area. We couldn't move and they weren't happy. The lads that arrange/extort money, sorry I mean charge for the parking around the roundabout, wanted our water to wash cars; they were really intimidating. They protect your car. Comforting! We needed the water to refill the rad. When Mohammed returned with the mechanic and the part, he dealt with them; getting an apology from one of the main complainants. In Morocco Mohammed is very well known and held in high regard. I have never witnessed such respect before, not like I have here. Something which occurred throughout Morocco and all for

this one guy.
Discovered The Facilitator's religious obsession is something new. He bought the rosary in Madrid on the way down. Explains why he's reading his prayers from scraps of paper.
Aphromighty is all skippity around Boyo Royo at the mo. She's flirting big time. Now, he told everyone his wife couldn't make this trip and had to cancel last minute because her mother was ill. The seating plan for the coach never showed him sitting next to his wife. His story keeps changing and people doubt he is married. There is nothing wrong with having an imaginary friend. After all I've got one, but as you know he always stays at home until we meet up trip end. This type of wife/husband, had-to-cancel-disaster-story is very common and I have now witnessed it quite a few times. I'm not too sure why people go to such lengths. Nothing wrong with being single. Before I met Hugh, and if I'm honest for a very long time, it was just me and me radiator.
Off to the Port of Tangier to take the ferry to Spain, continuing on to Granada for a two night stay. Following dinner we enjoy a late evening guided visit to the Nasrid Palaces, part of the Alhambra Palace complex.

22/09/14
OMG it's all going on. In order to share this story I have had to make Hugh an acquaintance on FB.
Boyo Royo has informed me that The Facilitator is after me. He thinks I fancy him. Reckons I watch him. Well yes I do, because without doubt he is one floor short of the penthouse.
He has a not so fancy little gadget which he is recording me on. Like a camcordery thing. Lots of the other coachcationers have noticed it. They

say he only bought the police hat to impress me!!! While we were in Morocco, Peter the driver was exaggerating the position that I held in my last job to Mohammed. As I have previously explained Mohammed's father was a former chief of police and Peter decided to go one better. Anyway this story gets overheard by Mr Dipstick, his wife Mrs Lost The Plot, and several others. Just prior to going through Moroccan customs Peter warned everyone to put down their correct employment details on the immigration forms. The only person that was allowed to put 'former MI6 employee' was PC Plod. Now, not everyone knows that this is one of many names Peter calls me, along with others such as Dixon of Dock Green, and the most recent Naff. Mr Dipstick, over the past few days, had been imparting the false information that he overheard by eavesdropping to all and sundry. I have continually told him when he questioned me that it was Pete being stupid. Does he believe me? No... He truly thinks my former employment was working for MI6, and states Pete would not have lied; he knew too much detail, and as I have full access to the internet I must be MI6. So Viv is acting out her interpretation of how she believes an MI6 agent would behave.

Anyway back to The Facilitator. At dinner he kept touching my leg and saying 'sorry Cathy'. He's polite, I guess that's one thing. Then I was leaning up against a wall, waiting for the in crowd so we could go into town, and he came up very close to me in front of everyone, blocked me from going anywhere, stared me right in the eyes, gave me a weird smile, winked and walked off. I nearly wet meself. He then comes back and says 'you, me, tapas tomorrow'. OMG BMUS...

The Yorkshire boys on the coach say he will likely take me to the wheel tappers and shunters club. Whatever the bleedin' hell that is.

Eckky Thump.

Exploring the Alhambra Palace Gardens first and then we have the rest of the day to ourselves to explore Granada at leisure which was once a Moorish kingdom.

Granada means Pomegranate. Just in case you wondered!

22/09/14 La Alhambra, Granada.

La Alhambra by day...

22/09/14 La Alhambra, Granada.
Alhambra Park by night...

23/09/14 La Alhambra, Granada.
Don't visit the Alhambra Palace at night especially if you want to take photos. Unless of course you are ghost hunting or want to see it lit up. At night you have to go the long way around and once again it's up hill and down dale, walking on bloody pebbles. UNESCO decided to reinstate the Moorish style onto the footpaths and roads. Fine if you're on bloody horseback. But if you have impediments, get air lifted in. You have to book 3 months in advance apparently but my advice is to do it in the day. Whether you are around after to discuss the delights of the gardens, or the haunting stuff that goes on, is in the lap of the gods and depends what ails you. I will be writing to Irina Bokova at UNESCO upon my return. Idiots!!
The plan was, after the yomp around the gardens, to return to the hotel and rest. Well that wasn't ever gonna happen and it all ended up in a four hour sesh in the bar. With me, allegedly, shouting people's names from the balcony and then hiding. As if!
I managed about two hours kip before the gala night, which was being held in some caves.
Once again we were shown La Alhambra all lit up and route marched along the narrow cobbled UNESCO inspired cobbled effing streets, before being taken to a cavern type cave that needed a damn good bleaching and some electrical work. The dancing and guitar playing was the best I have ever seen and heard and made the hairs on my arms

stand on end. After the show we stayed behind enjoying a few more beers. We got back to the hotel about 0330. Bad idea but great night.
I have developed acne so am not best pleased, especially as I'm meeting Hugh tomorrow. I have made a potion of several of the items I bought in the herb store. They'd better work. I want my man concentrating on me, not me zits.
Quotes of the day once again from Mr Dipstick. 'How long is this two hour display gonna last?'
And over dinner: 'Most of the Scots wanted independence'.
I remarked 'Clearly not!' and got told to 'Shut up. What do you know?'
I replied 'Since Emmeline Pankhurst chained herself to the railings women have earned the right to speak so STFU we ain't all yes women..'
Travelling to Madrid for two night stay.

23/09/14
Hit a wall today, fell asleep on the coach. Picture taken courtesy of Peter. Har, har, har. He entitled it Naff Napping. More like MI6 in disguise...
Fell asleep fully clothed on the hotel room bed. Totally knackered and reliant on room service in the early hours. Pictures courtesy of MI6.

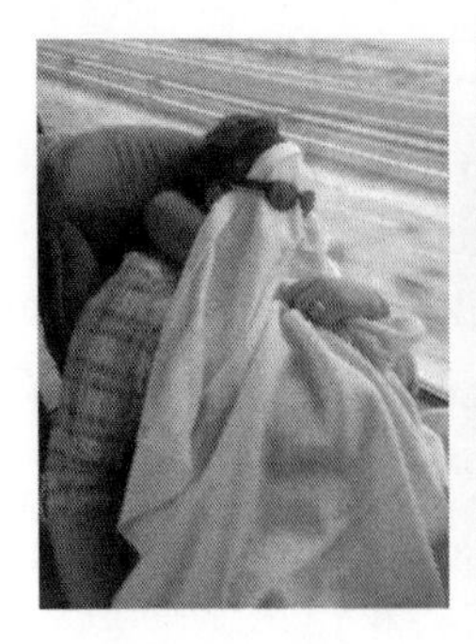 

We explore Madrid today, a truly cosmopolitan city with a wealth of cultural attractions. We visit the famous Salamanca quarter, with its exclusive boutiques and embassies. There is also the Borbones quarter, with its numerous museums, Jardin del Retiro and Parliament House, the Asturius quarter, home to the Royal Palace of Madrid, official residence of the king and queen of Spain. And if that isn't enough to impedimise my impediments there is the New Parliament, 4 towers and Stadium Santiago Bernabeu.
My opinion of Madrid is not good. Could be anywhere. Is a bit spread out and I would suggest using the struggle on and limp off buses to see the distractions. The city is very shaded and overshadowed by Norman Foster's sky scraping towers. Bloody monstrosities.
Definitely a base jumpers dream.
The Facilitator has taken to singing Cathy by Kate Bush every time he sees me. A very out of tune version, but he knows the words. I will not be letting him in at my window. Hugh arrives today. I can't wait...
Decided after visiting the Real Madrid football stadium, not the imitation one, and the palace that I would pay a visit to the bar. Then 40 winks before dinner with PHugh. I need the beauty sleep and time for the homemade concoction to work on me zits.

With Hugh Jardon at NH Parque Avenidas.

24/09/14 Anglet, France.

Aphromighty came back to the hotel in the company of The Facilitator and she was smashed out of her face.

When Hugh and I left for dinner she was snuggled up close to him on the patio.

I am in the room next to her, so am hoping Hugh suggests his hotel. Can't be coping with hearing the bed scrapee noises across the tiled floor all night.

Dinner and an evening with Hugh was just what I needed.

The topic of conversation seemed to be all about the quality of toilet paper for some reason. I have a vivid memory of the tracing paper stuff we used years ago. Jeyes or Izal.

Anyway the evening finished up with me leaving me mark. Hugh left with a smile. I won't see him for a while, hopefully on the Rhine at New Year. Well that's if I survive Pontins with the wild bunch. 😈

Pity the magistrate's court isn't a bit further away from where I live.

May have to play the card...
Today we say Buenos Dias to Spain as we travel through the mountain scenery of the Basque region for an overnight stay in the Ciboure, St Jean de Luz or Biarritz area.

25/09/14 Fresnay-l'Évêque, France.
Just won the quiz on board coach. Naffs Tours a team of 4.
23 out of 41. Difficult questions.

25/09/14 Villejust, France.
Well it all happened, well it might have. Apparently most of the coachcationers stayed awake listening out to hear if Aphromighty and The Facilitator got it on last night. They were the last ones to bed and he was heard by Boyo Royo inviting her back to his room. We were all housed on the same floor. Well I wasn't 'cos I was with Phugh. Anyway, no-one got any sleep. Admittedly a coach load of Japanese came into the mix but nevertheless there was an air of anticipation on floor one. There were a lot of scrapee, scrapee noises heard but no-one can be sure if they came from room 117 or not. Someone asked her at breakfast this morning if she accepted The Facilitators offer but she just giggled. Did she or didn't she, or did he or didn't he?
I only just made it back to the hotel on time. Typical Bennett fashion. Greeted by a coach load of cheers as I entered the hotel foyer having been observed snogging Hugh's face off as we said our au revoirs.
The Facilitator has been feeding me sweets all day. I have been refusing as they rattle me fillings. They are so sweet.
When we arrived at our hotel we were all knackered and so headed straight for our rooms. I discover I have two interlocking doors. Open one. Boyo Royo is stood there. Open the second door and The Facilitator is led on his bed. I run for management who can't see the problem, remarking 'they are both from my coach!' I state 'I don't give a toss I want the doors locked'.
Manager opens door one, Boyo Royo stood there. I open door two, The Facilitator with a towel wrapped around him. Not much left to the imagination I can tell you. It was like a sketch from some comedy. The

manager opening and closing doors, expecting the people to have disappeared. I was helpless. Anyway there are no locks to lock the doors so I have a chair wedged under one handle and my case against the other. If there was ever a duo not to be twinned with, these are the two.

26/09/14 Créteil, France.
I tell you I hardly slept a wink, god only knows what The Facilitator was doing all night. It got to a point where I just screamed through the door 'STFU'. That was at two this very morn. Needless to say I'm grumpy, very bloody grumpy. Me mother always said if I didn't get me full seven hours I was a cross patch. And cross patch I am.
It's alright for The Facilitator, at 0845 he's on the Baileys and coffee.
He's offered to clean my glasses, asked me what he can do when he comes up to Bristol, and if he calls me Cathy once more I will not be held accountable for my actions.
We continue our journey across France to Paris for an overnight stay.
Did a very stupid thing. The Facilitator asked to see my critique/feedback form. It contains my address and telephone number. Have kicked myself so hard my shins are black and blue...
He has asked me so many questions about my life I feel as though I have been interrogated and am totally drained.
There are rats at the Novotel Hotel in Creteil, Paris. Sat there on the patio drinking my €7:20 beer, when rats run past. We are with a Thai girl and her husband and she starts to tell me how she eats rats in Thailand. Also chicken feet and fish heads. Yukhowvile.

26/09/14 Coquelles, France.
We leave our overnight hotel this morning for Calais and the return crossing to Blighty by Euro Train. We have travelled 5424 kilometres in total. This holiday has been fabulous. I have laughed until I cried and have met some lovely people.
It is at this point I have made a decision to go to print with novel 5, **'Terminal to Terminus'.** Hopefully my promotions manager Lucy Lightweight is on it as I write...

I would like to thank Leger holidays for agreeing to carry me on their Silver Service Holidays without insurance and giving me the opportunity to visit as many countries as I have done over the last two years. I have had some wonderful times travelling with Paul, John, Mike, Garry, Peter and Sandra.

Only today Sandra asked me a 'what if' question. In true Blo RJ fashion. 'In the event the inevitable happens how will people find out?' I reply. 'I have a NOK who is aware of my Champions page on FB and my email contacts. Anyone not held on those two mediums are in my phone contacts, they have an asterisk before their name and this is an indication that they need to be informed.' 'Give me your phone' Pete demands. He looks in contacts under P and yes under Pete and Sandra there is an asterisk before their name. Because they matter. In only a way Pete can, he walks away and says 'you will be missed!'

The people, my fellow coachcationers, who provided me with the writing material, unique individuals, some rare. My holidays wouldn't have been the same without you...

I fight my cancer every day and will continue to do so. Hopefully the powers that be will remain on side so I stay well enough to continue my travels and post my stories on FB as normal.

I have only got this far with all the support I have had from my family and friends.

The book has already been dedicated to several people, the reasons not necessary to discuss.

However I must mention three people who are likely reason for me being here today.

Joel Phillips, the person who made me go back to the doctors. I thank you from the bottom of my heart.

Anita Milkins, a very special lady who I carry with me everywhere I go. She knows the reason why, so no explanation required.

Last but not least Hugh, my imaginary friend. Forever love, thanks for being mine. 'My heart holds you just a beat away'.

So FB peeps thx for reading my blogs, I will let you know when the book is available on Amazon and Kindle.

Until the next time...

ABOUT THE AUTHOR

A feisty female with a lot to say for herself, Vivvy Anne Le Fey was born in Bristol in 1958 and started her career as a telesales operator for a large soft drinks company. After thirteen years and the closure of the Keynsham based depot, she took redundancy. Her next career move was working as a temporary staff controller for an employment agency, where she successfully progressed to branch manager.
For the next twenty years Le Fey was in full time employment working shifts as a radio dispatcher for the 1st emergency service, and writing her novels.
Now retired, Le Fey continues her writing and is an enthusiastic traveller; regaling us with tales of her exploits in this, her fourth published book.

Also by Vivvy Anne Le Fey:

Out Of The Closet
Would You Divorce Your Mother?
Just Desserts

Printed in Great Britain
by Amazon.co.uk, Ltd.,
Marston Gate.